**What's a millionaire bachelor to do?
Join the army—with his butler, of course.**

Meet Captain Willard Phule and his company of
misunderstood misfits. Together, they've taken space
by storm—and left a tradition of looniness
and laughter in their wake . . .

Phuling around was never so much fun.

Phule's Errand

Praise for the
New York Times **bestselling**
PHULE'S COMPANY series

"Madcap . . . a welcome send-up of military SF."
—*Publishers Weekly*

continued . . .

PHULE'S ERRAND

ROBERT ASPRIN
WITH **PETER J. HECK**

ACE BOOKS, NEW YORK

THE BERKLEY PUBLISHING GROUP
Published by the Penguin Group
Penguin Group (USA) Inc.
375 Hudson Street, New York, New York 10014, USA
Penguin Group (Canada), 90 Eglinton Avenue East, Suite 700, Toronto, Ontario M4P 2Y3, Canada
(a division of Pearson Penguin Canada Inc.)
Penguin Books Ltd., 80 Strand, London WC2R 0RL, England
Penguin Group Ireland, 25 St. Stephen's Green, Dublin 2, Ireland (a division of Penguin Books Ltd.)
Penguin Group (Australia), 250 Camberwell Road, Camberwell, Victoria 3124, Australia
(a division of Pearson Australia Group Pty. Ltd.)
Penguin Books India Pvt. Ltd., 11 Community Centre, Panchsheel Park, New Delhi—110 017, India
Penguin Group (NZ), Cnr. Airborne and Rosedale Roads, Albany, Auckland 1310, New Zealand
(a division of Pearson New Zealand Ltd.)
Penguin Books (South Africa) (Pty.) Ltd., 24 Sturdee Avenue, Rosebank, Johannesburg 2196,
South Africa

Penguin Books Ltd., Registered Offices: 80 Strand, London WC2R 0RL, England

This is a work of fiction. Names, characters, places, and incidents either are the product of the authors'
imagination or are used fictitiously, and any resemblance to actual persons, living or dead, business
establishments, events, or locales is entirely coincidental. The publisher does not have any control over
and does not assume any responsibility for author or third-party websites or their content.

PHULE'S ERRAND

An Ace Book / published by arrangement with the authors

PRINTING HISTORY
Ace edition / August 2006

Copyright © 2006 by Robert Asprin.
Cover art by Walter Velez.
Cover design by Annette Fiore.

ISBN: 0-441-01423-2

ACE
Ace Books are published by The Berkley Publishing Group,
a division of Penguin Group (USA) Inc.,
375 Hudson Street, New York, New York 10014.
ACE and the "A" design are trademarks belonging to Penguin Group (USA) Inc.

PRINTED IN THE UNITED STATES OF AMERICA

10 9 8 7 6 5 4 3 2 1

1

Journal #760—

My employment with Willard Phule, better known by his nom de guerre of "Captain Jester," has sometimes made me wonder if I have fallen under a legendary curse from Old Earth: "May you live in interesting times." Two additional phrases are less well-known: "May you come to the attention of important people, and may you receive all that you wish for." They apply all too well to my life with Omega Company of the Space Legion.

It was happy hour at the Officers' Club at Rahnsome Base, headquarters of the United Alliance Military Command, and the barrooms were packed. In the luxurious back room reserved for general staff officers, there was scarcely an empty seat to be found. And the noise level was exactly what you would suspect from a group of sophonts who spent a large fraction of their time telling others what to do. Time-honored scuttlebutt around the base asserted that careers could be launched or destroyed right here in this room. To judge from the behavior of the officers present, the majority of them believed it.

The loudest of the blowhards on hand was General Blitzkrieg of the Space Legion. With a highball in one hand and a clear Neo-Havana cigar in the other, he sat in his favorite overstuffed chair by the trophy shelf, brow-beating all who offered to question his preeminence. Normally, there were few who bothered—mainly because the effort was disproportionately greater than any possible reward for success.

Today, Blitzkrieg was holding forth on the utter absurdity of putting gormless civilians in a position of authority over professional military men. Since this was an opinion shared by every sophont in the building (except for the head bartender, who had seen the top brass in its cups far too often to have any faith in its competence), the Legion general was safe from contradiction on this particular subject. For that very reason it was one of his favorites.

"I'll tell you how bad it's gotten," Blitzkrieg rumbled. "Now, if the damned bleeding hearts get their way, the Alliance Council will vet all promotions above the rank of lieutenant colonel. How's *that* for bureaucratic bullshit? Who's better qualified to judge a soldier than his own CO? There's not an officer in the Legion whose work I don't know a hundred times better than some meddling paper pusher or political hack . . ."

That statement was greeted by a nearly unanimous murmur of assent—only nearly unanimous, for once. This time, among the general's listeners was a solidly built man wearing the deep blue uniform of Starfleet. Captain First Class John Arbuthnot shook his head. "That'd be hard to argue with," he growled. "But everybody knows that's not how it works. Talk all you want about the merit system, but the brownnoses always have the minimum-energy course to promotions. It's true in Starfleet, it's true in the Regular Army, and it's damn near official policy in the Legion."

"And what the hell do you know about Legion policy, *Captain*?" growled Blitzkrieg.

Another officer might have backed off at this point. But Captain Arbuthnot had an exemplary record, with meritorious service on a dozen ships, and was widely regarded as one of the most valuable members of the general staff. His one flaw was a stubborn refusal to let nonsense stand unchallenged—no matter who was saying it. That was why, after thirty years in the service, Arbuthnot was stuck at captain first class—a rank equivalent to colonel in the Legion or Regular Army. He'd seen one brownnose after another promoted past him, and he was a long way from being reconciled to it.

So Blitzkrieg's slighting reference to his rank hit close to home. Captain Arbuthnot narrowed his eyes, and said, "Begging the general's pardon, but I'd like to hear him deny that he's given the ablest man in the Legion a dead-end assignment babysitting a company of screwups."

Blitzkrieg's eyes bulged. "Deny it?" he roared. "Deny it? Damn straight I'll deny it, because it's a damned lie." He stood up, looming over the Starfleet captain's chair.

Arbuthnot was unfazed. "I'll overlook the general's last remark," he said, in a voice that would have chilled the blood of anyone sensitive to tone. "He's entitled to his opinion even if all the evidence is against him. But I'm entitled to mine, as well—and whatever the general thinks, I *know* what I know. I'll stand by my original statement." He tossed back his drink, then stood, gave a mock bow, and strode from the room, a smug expression on his face.

"Damned cheek," muttered Blitzkrieg, and he sipped from his own drink. But suddenly it lacked bite—had the ice diluted it that quickly?—and the smoke of his cigar smelled stale. He stared around the room, looking for someone else to argue with. *Nothing like a good fight to get the spirits up.* But the other officers in the circle around him had somehow drifted away, and suddenly he didn't feel like arguing, after all. He stubbed out the cigar, retrieved his hat, and stalked out, still muttering to himself.

The communicator buzzed, and Willard Phule looked up from the screen of his Port-a-Brain computer. "What is it, Mother?" he asked. From the displays, this was a Priority Three call: nothing urgent, but important enough not to defer, either.

"You'll never guess, lover boy," said the comm operator. "There's a ship entering Zenobia orbit just now. It's bringing just what we've all been waiting for."

"That could be a lot of different things, depending on who you're asking," said Phule. Inevitably, he thought of the promotion he'd been assured the Alliance Senate had approved for him, but that had yet to be confirmed by his Legion superiors. Legion tradition mandated a real letter, on actual paper, to confirm promotions. It had occurred to him that General Blitzkrieg might have sent the promotion notice across the parsecs separating Legion Headquarters and Zenobia by some lowest-priority uncrewed freight carrier, chugging its way at sublight speeds from one system to another.

But that way lay insanity . . . he snapped back to the present. "Don't keep me guessing, Mother," he said. "What are we getting?"

He could practically hear the pout as she answered. "All right, big boy, if that's the way you want to be. But just you wait—next time you need something from me, I might not be so sweet about it."

Phule repressed a sigh. "Give me a hint, Mother. Person, place, or thing?"

"Silly boy," came the answer. "Nobody could send us a place."

"Uh, they could send us *to* a place," said Phule. "A new assignment, get it? But I take it that's not what we're getting."

"Right." She waited. Then, after a long silence followed by a resigned sigh, "OK, it's a person."

"A person. Hmmm . . ." Phule tried to think of somebody he'd been waiting for, without success. "Uh, male or female?"

"Female, not that that'll help you much," said Mother, smugly.

Female, thought Phule. *Who could it be? Not likely his mother, or his grandmother. Colonel Battleax had been his strongest supporter among the Legion brass, but she was hardly anybody the company had been waiting for . . .* "Uh . . . Jennie Higgins?" he guessed. The pretty young newspaper who'd put Omega Company in the headlines was a favorite with the troops—and a favorite with Phule himself, now that he thought of her.

"You'd like that, wouldn't you?" teased Mother, who knew of his interest in the reporter. "But you're still way off base. Do you give up?"

"Yeah, I guess so, Mother," said Phule. "Who is it?"

"Headquarters is sending us a medic," said Mother. "How about that?"

"A medic," Phule said. "Now, that's interesting. I wouldn't think a company-sized unit rated a medic. Considering what the brass thinks of us, I'm surprised they let us have an autodoc."

"Considering the company's safety record, I'm surprised they don't station us in an emergency ward," said Mother, dryly. "But there's one more wrinkle you ought to know about, sweetie. Who do you think our new medic is?"

Phule frowned. "Good grief, Mother, how am I supposed to guess *that*? All I know is that it's someone in the Legion, a female, and that she's trained as a medic . . ."

Beeker, who'd been quietly working at his Port-a-Brain computer while Phule spoke to Mother, suddenly sat straight up in his seat, and exclaimed. "By Jove! You can't mean . . . It couldn't possibly be . . ."

Phule stared at him in confusion. "Gee, Beeks, do you know somebody who fits that description? I can't for the life of me come up with any good guesses."

"It's not a guess, sir. It's a near certainty," said Beeker, swiveling his chair round to face his employer. "Perhaps you recall the circumstances of our departure from Lorelei. I came aboard the shuttle with a last-minute refugee . . ."

Phule turned an uncomprehending look on his butler. "A last-minute refugee?" he asked. Then his eyes opened wide. "Laverna?"

"Laverna," said Beeker, nodding slightly.

"You got it, boys," said Mother. "But don't call her that; her Legion name is Nightingale."

"How do you know it's her, then?" said Phule.

"Silly, they sent her personnel file, with a holo," said Mother. "I don't care what name she's using, there's nobody else with that face."

"Nightingale," said Beeker, softly. Hearing the tone in his butler's voice, Phule looked over at Beeker with raised eyebrows. A stranger might not have noticed anything. But to Phule, who'd had the butler in his employ for the better part of a decade, the softness seemed completely alien to Beeker's normal brisk inflections.

"Nightingale," said Beeker again. There was a faraway look in his eyes. That's when Phule should have realized just how much trouble he was in.

In the open parade ground near the center of Zenobia Base, a dozen legionnaires stood chewing the fat. A heavy but muscular woman with first sergeant's stripes on the sleeve of her black jumpsuit emerged from the barracks module and strode over to them. Several of the group glanced in her direction, but otherwise they ignored her approach until she shouted, "All right, squad, fall in. Let's see if you can act like real legionnaires for fifteen minutes."

To Sergeant Brandy's surprise, the training group the

captain had put her in charge of actually obeyed her order. This was unusual. There must be some insidious purpose lurking behind her trainees' stolid expressions. They almost *never* fell in without some kind of argument or delaying tactic. She glared suspiciously—particularly at Mahatma, usually the head conspirator when the squad decided to show her its independence from military discipline. The squad seemed to think she needed some such demonstration two or three times a week . . . if not more often.

Brandy scowled. "I can tell you gripgrops are planning something," she growled. "And unless you've suddenly gotten twice as clever as you think you are, you're planning something really stupid." That was an exaggeration—when pressed, Brandy privately conceded that some of the recruits' stunts revealed a rare twisted creativity—but she didn't want to give them any encouragement. They were doing just fine without her help. And if they'd focus the same kind of creativity toward their actual jobs . . . but in the Omega Mob, that was asking for too much.

A hand was raised: Mahatma's. *No surprise there,* thought Brandy. For a moment, she considered ignoring the little legionnaire . . . but that would just be postponing the inevitable trouble. Best to get it over with. "You have a question, Mahatma?"

"Yes, Sergeant Brandy!" said Mahatma, with a beatific smile on his round, bespectacled face. "We have all heard that Headquarters is sending Omega Company a medic."

"That's the truth, I got it straight from Mother," said someone else in the formation—Slayer, thought Brandy, who had learned to recognize the voices of the legionnaires in her training squad even when they muttered, or when several were speaking at once.

"Yes, we're getting a medic," said Brandy. "It's a step up from the autodoc—a lot more personal treatment."

"But the autodoc is very good," said Mahatma. "I have

used it, and so have most of the company. I don't think anyone has complained that it didn't heal us."

"No, I don't remember any complaints," said Brandy. If past history was any indicator—and Brandy would have given good odds that it was—Mahatma was working his way slowly up to some still-unstated point. Just what the point was probably wouldn't be clear until he got there. There probably wasn't any way to hurry him, but still . . . "What are you getting at, Mahatma?" she asked.

The little legionnaire continued to smile, his round face and round glasses giving the effect of a bright-beaming sun. "If the autodoc does such a good job, there should not be any reason for us to get a medic," he said. Heads around him nodded; Brandy had to give Mahatma points for persuasiveness. That, in fact, was the main problem of having him in her squad. She seemed to spend half her time trying to refute his points.

"Uh, the captain told us that this particular medic had requested assignment to Omega," said Brandy. "So there isn't any reason to go hunting for other reasons," she concluded, realizing even as she said it that it sounded unconvincing even to her.

But to her surprise, Mahatma nodded. "Ah, very well, then," he said. "If that is the entire reason, there is nothing to worry about." And he shut his mouth and stood there. Brandy nearly fell over from the shock. Mahatma had to be planning something really obnoxious if he let her off the hook this easily . . .

Then she shrugged. Whatever it was would come along at its own pace, whether she knew it was coming or not. She looked down at her clipboard and went on to the first item on her agenda for the day. "One announcement," she said. "The captain has assigned buddies for those members of the company not previously paired with someone. The following are now officially paired: Brick and Street; Roadkill and Lace; Mahatma and Thumper . . ." She ignored the exclamations from the troops, and finished the list. Then, not without some trepidation, she asked, "Any questions?"

Thumper's hand went up. The little Lepoid was by a long shot the least likely to cause trouble on any given occasion, so Brandy gave an inward sigh of relief and pointed to him. "Thumper?"

"Sergeant, I don't understand 'buddies,'" said Thumper. "I mean, don't get me wrong, Mahatma—it's not as if I don't think you're a good legionnaire . . ."

"Brandy don't think so, neither," said a voice from the back. The rest of the squad broke out laughing as Thumper tried to recover.

"The idea of buddies is to give everybody in the company somebody to fall back on when there's trouble," said Brandy. "The captain tries to pick somebody you can learn from, too. That's why Sushi and Do-Wop are partners . . ."

"Huh!" said Street, his eyes widening. "Buddies is partners. Now I understand. I always wonder why they two be buddies. Now it all makin' sense. That Sushi, he got a lot to learn . . ."

"The sheer impertinence of that damned SFer," rumbled Blitzkrieg. It was the morning after the Officers' Club encounter, but the incident still rankled. The general had been stomping around the office and haranguing his adjutant, Major Sparrowhawk, for most of the morning. She'd barely had time to glance at her stock portfolio.

"I don't know why you listen to that kind of thing," said Sparrowhawk, who knew which side her bread was buttered on. "It's as plain as the nose on your face—that Starfleet captain's just jealous because the Legion's grabbing the spotlight from his arm of the service."

Blitzkrieg gashed his teeth. "I could deal with that, if it weren't that imbecile Jester and his gang of incompetents who were getting all the publicity," he said. "Jester's idiots have managed to convince the media that they're the best outfit in the Legion. Are those galactic newstapers blind? Or just terminally stupid?"

"It wouldn't surprise me if it's a fair amount of both," said Sparrowhawk. Then an evil smile lit up her face, and her voice dripped acid as she said, "Or, considering that Jennie Higgins and Captain Jester seem to be a very definite item, maybe it's just another case of nasty little hormones at work."

"I wouldn't put it past them," said Blitzkrieg, pacing. "The hell of it is, I've tried half a dozen ways to crush Jester—the despicable little snot—but he keeps bouncing back as if nothing important had happened. Part of it has to be his money—there are plenty of fools who'll suck up to any jackanapes that's got enough money, and Jester qualifies for that, hands down."

"Yes, sir," said Sparrowhawk, who actually had a great deal of respect for money, especially money sitting in one of her own stock accounts. She wished Blitzkrieg would finish his rant so she could pay proper attention to those very accounts, but she knew from bitter experience that it might take all morning for him to run through his list of gripes. She'd have to stay at the desk straight through her lunch break if she wanted to catch up.

"I've just about given up expecting the media to notice what an utter disaster Jester's made of his company," continued Blitzkrieg. "Why, if I didn't have a hundred better things to do, I'd go out to Zenobia myself. If I watch him like a hawk, sooner or later the impertinent pup's going to screw up so badly that not even his money can protect him. And then I can cashier him the way I should've done when he first came up for court-martial, instead of letting those other softheaded short-timers argue me out of it."

Major Sparrowhawk sat upright behind her desk. "Well, sir, why don't you?" she asked brightly.

"Eh? I don't get you," said the general.

"Why don't you just go out to Zenobia and wait for him to screw up?" asked the adjutant. "You said it yourself, he's bound to do it, especially if you're there breathing down his neck with every move. And then you'll be rid of him, and all your troubles will be over."

"Rid of him," said Blitzkrieg, in a dreamlike voice. Then his eyes lit up, and he smacked a fist into his open hand. "*Rid of him. All my troubles will be over* . . . Yes, you're dead right, Major! All I have to do is wait for Jester to screw up, and if I'm right there, the poor little rich boy won't have a chance to cover it up with all his money before I can bust him for it. What a brilliant idea! I'm surprised I didn't think of it myself!"

"Don't worry, you will," muttered Sparrowhawk, who was long accustomed to having her best ideas appropriated by her superior.

But the general was already off and running. "Let's see . . ." he said. "I'll have to find someone to cover for me in the staff meeting. That's no big problem, they never talk about anything important. Colonel Caisson can handle that. And I'll need a substitute in the Scotch foursome on Tuesday afternoons. Caisson won't do—that duck hook of his will have him out of bounds the whole back nine. Can't be anybody too good, though, or they're likely to want to keep him. Hmmm . . ." He wandered through the door into his private office, his mind happily occupied with rearranging the details of his social life.

Major Sparrowhawk gave a deep sigh of relief and turned to her investment portfolio.

2

Journal #764—

Anyone who wishes to reach advanced years will of necessity abandon his fondest dreams and most valued possessions at several points along the way. After a few experiences along these lines, one can even do so without a great deal of regret. But even the most stoical traveler is likely to be shaken out of his complacency when a piece of valuable baggage, long ago given up for lost, shows up unannounced on his doorstep.

Standing back a respectful distance, as specified by safety regulations, the Legion party watched the landing shuttle's approach. The little ship dropped from the sky deceptively slowly, like a flattened rock through some ultradense liquid. Only when it reached the lower atmosphere did its true speed—still a significant fraction of the orbital velocity of its mother ship—become apparent. But even as it fell, it continued to shed velocity, and as it came within a few meters of the ground, it reached a virtual standstill, hovering gently on its jets as it dropped the tiny remaining distance to touch down in a cloud of dust and flying debris—dead center in the ten-meter landing zone defined by four radar beacons.

Even as the noise of the engines fell to silence, the Legion party was closing in. For while safety regulations ordered ground crews to keep their distance, the implacable laws of shuttle economics made it important to unload and return to orbit as quickly as possible. Interstellar freight companies' stock-in-trade was speed; and since any given starship was about as fast as any other at superluminal velocities, time at sublight velocities—especially from orbit to surface and back—was critical. A wasted hour on the ground could make the difference between a timely delivery and a blown schedule.

Moments after the external doors came open, Beeker was standing beside the shuttle. Phule suppressed a grin— the butler had put on a very respectable burst of speed, considering that he was by a wide margin the oldest human on the planet. As the dust settled, a slim figure in a black Legion jumpsuit emerged into the Zenobian air, looked around, eyes adjusting to the light, and then fixed its gaze on Beeker. "You're here!" said a woman's low voice, and the next thing anyone knew, she had thrown herself into the butler's arms.

"Laverna!" said Beeker. "There are people watching!" The butler's voice sounded shocked. But nobody watching had any doubt that he was pleased. And he made no effort to push away the new arrival.

The woman leaned back and looked around at the onlookers, most of whom were doing an excellent job of keeping a straight face. "Screw 'em," she said, with a dry laugh. Then she turned back and looked Beeker in the eye. "Besides, there's no such animule as Laverna anymore— the name is *Nightingale*. Remember that, Beeker."

The tableau was interrupted by a shuttle crewman who

stuck his head out the door. "We've got your luggage, Legionnaire Nightingale, and a sack of personal parcels for the Legion outpost—and then we've gotta get off. You all ready?"

A pair of legionnaires stepped forward to take off the mail and luggage, and then Phule said, "That's it, then. Let's move off so this fellow can get back to orbit!"

"You got it, Captain," said Double-X, who'd taken charge of the mail sack. "Come on, suckers, let's give the shuttle some room, like the captain said." The Legion party quickly complied, and within moments, the shuttle had leapt from the ground and quickly begun its graceful ascent toward the scattered clouds high above the desert floor.

The Legion party stood and watched the takeoff for a moment, then climbed aboard the hovertruck that would take them back to Zenobia Base.

"Well, then, we are partners," said Mahatma, peering at Thumper with a bemused air. The two of them sat at a table in the Legion Club, adjacent to the mess hall in the specially built Modular Base Unit that served as Omega Company's headquarters for its stay on Zenobia. The Lepoid was reputedly the first of his species to join the Space Legion, although a few others had enlisted in Starfleet. Small beings, who bore a striking resemblance to an Old Earth species called "bunnies," they made up in speed and agility what they lacked in brute strength.

It was early afternoon, so only a few of the tables were occupied by off-duty enlisted personnel. The action here would normally begin to pick up a couple of hours later, when the troops gathered for happy hour just before dinner. But for now, Mahatma and Thumper had a corner all to themselves.

"Yeah, I guess so," said Thumper, his gaze cast down at the tabletop. "I guess that means the captain thinks we each have something the other needs. But I can't think of what I might have that you need. You're a veteran legionnaire, and I'm just a rookie ..." The little Lepoid's shoulders slumped, and he looked overwhelmed by the news Brandy had just given them.

"Not quite so," said Mahatma, smiling sheepishly. "I have been in Omega Company less than one standard year, and have seen nothing that resembles combat. I hardly qualify as any kind of veteran, though I do know a fair bit about how this company works."

"Maybe that's what he thinks I can learn from you," said Thumper. "But what does he think you can learn from me?"

"That remains to be seen," said Mahatma. "I will keep my eyes and ears open, and perhaps something resembling useful knowledge will come; perhaps you should do the same. I do not think the captain expects us to work from a printed syllabus."

"I sure hope not," said Thumper, scratching behind one ear. "If he did, he should have given it to us."

"I don't think he wants much more than for us to help each other when we can," said Mahatma, calmly. "That ought to be enough until we decide what else is required."

"OK, I guess that'd be a start," said Thumper. He looked at Mahatma for a moment, then asked, "What do you need help with?"

Mahatma looked at Thumper with wide-open eyes, then broke into helpless laughter.

Thumper sat watching for a moment, steadily growing more perplexed. After a few moments, he said, "OK, what's the joke?"

Mahatma finally recovered his composure enough to say, "Sorry—it's just that this is the first time since I joined the Legion that anyone has really offered to help me without any strings attached or ulterior motives. And, of course, I can't think of anything at all that I need right now. But I think I will, soon enough. Yes, we are going to be fine partners!"

"I'm not sure," said Thumper, drumming his fingers on the tabletop. "I mean, you're always asking questions that nobody can answer. I don't know what good that does anybody. Isn't the idea that we all work together in one team?"

"All one team, yes," said Mahatma, nodding. "But every team has specialists, too. Escrima is the cook; Chocolate Harry looks after supplies; Mother handles communications. And I ask the questions nobody else has thought of yet. Sometimes they are questions that really need answers—and by asking them, I am doing an important service. Other times I do it just to keep people from taking things for granted—even a good sergeant like Brandy needs that, now and then. So that is helping, too."

"I suppose so," said Thumper, skeptically. "I thought you did it just to be a pain in the ass."

"Of course," said Mahatma, with a broad smile. "Being a pain in the ass is very important in the Legion. If this company ever has to face a military emergency, the enemy is going to try very hard to be a pain in the ass—and anywhere else they can. I am working to keep us prepared for that situation."

"Gee, I guess I hadn't thought it through," said Thumper, his ears standing up straight and twitching with excitement. "Maybe I haven't been giving you enough credit, Mahatma. This puts everything in a whole new light."

"It is a humble mission, yet I must confess that I take some pride in it," said Mahatma, lowering his eyes.

"Say, Mahatma," said Thumper, hesitantly. "Not that I'm trying to butt in on your department, or anything, but do you think somebody like me could learn how to do that kind of thing? I'd be willing to study and work hard . . ."

Mahatma sat back in his chair and appeared to ponder the question. The silence grew. At last, Thumper began to wonder if he'd made a mistake in asking for something so important. Just as he was about to back down from his request, Mahatma's face broke out in a beatific smile. "Why yes, my Lepoid partner," he said. "I am sure we can combine our talents to make the company even better prepared for the unexpected."

"Wow, do you really think so?" said Thumper. "You really think I can be a pain in the ass, too?"

"Oh, yes," said Mahatma, nodding wisely. "You are a clever sophont, and you pick things up quickly. I am sure we can find a role worthy of your talents. But first things first. Give me a little time to think about something you can do just to get started, and we will build from there."

"Triff!" said Thumper. He sat back and waited, confident that Mahatma would think up something appropriate.

He was right, of course.

It was already getting hot in the Zenobian desert as Phule and Lieutenant Armstrong set out on their morning run. It had become a pleasant addition to their routine, a chance to see the ever-fascinating scenery of an alien landscape while keeping themselves in the top physical condition that Space Legion regulations specified for officers. Not all Legion officers took those regulations as seriously as Phule, which might explain the Legion's low status among the Alliance military.

But Phule enjoyed the runs, and was actively annoyed when anything prevented him from getting out in the morning. Even so, he knew that running alone in unfamiliar territory would be begging for trouble. Luckily, Armstrong had turned out to be a willing training partner and a useful sounding board when Phule needed to bounce his ideas off someone besides Beeker.

As usual, they'd begun by heading toward the low hills east of the Legion base. Once they reached the rising ground, there were several routes, but the first mile out they invariably took the same level path. It was a good warm-up before they got to the hills and had to decide just how hard they wanted to work today.

They'd gone just over half a mile when a small, black-clad figure emerged from the woods and began to run alongside Phule. "Many salutings, Captain Clown," said Flight Leftenant Qual. The host planet's liaison officer to Omega Company had to take two strides to Phule's one just to maintain the same pace, but Qual did it without apparent strain.

"Hello, Qual," said Phule. "What brings you out this way?" He already knew that something had to be on the Zenobian's mind. Qual was naturally one of the fastest runners on the base, but he rarely exerted himself without good reason. Phule sometimes wondered if that was a trait the Zenobians derived from their reptilelike forebears, who preferred to bask in the sun until either an imminent threat or passing prey spurred them to action.

"A very curious thing that I have observed," said Qual, keeping pace with Phule and Armstrong. His endurance was as good as his speed. "Perhaps you have also seen it?"

Phule automatically cast his mind back over the past few days, trying to think of what Qual might be referring to. At various points in the past, Qual had been utterly fascinated by things that most humans took utterly for granted—like shaving, or the makeup many female legionnaires wore. It was impossible to predict what might catch Qual's attention and sometimes impossible to explain it to his satisfaction. Phule had thought shoes would be trivially obvious, but they apparently weren't—at least, not to Qual.

He thought a few moments—whatever Qual was curious about, it was enough to bring him out into the desert to run instead of just dropping by Phule's office. Finally, he had to admit, "I haven't noticed anything that unusual, Qual. What have you seen?"

"Oho," said Qual, showing his sharp-pointed teeth in a broad grin. "Perhaps it is not curious, after all. I regret to have intercepted your rush."

Armstrong raised a quizzical eyebrow, but by now Phule

had mostly figured out how to interpret Qual's speech despite the sometimes bizarrely phrased remarks that came out of the translating machine. "No problem, Qual," he said, almost unconsciously changing his course to avoid a large rock along the left side of the path. "Glad to have the company. But tell me, just so I know—what do you think is so curious?"

Qual ran a few steps before answering, jumping over the same rock that Phule had dodged around. "I am wondering if Beeker is below the wind," he said.

"Below the . . ." Phule's brow wrinkled as he attempted to work out what Qual meant. "Oh, under the weather. No, not as far as I know. What makes you think so?"

Qual's reptilian grin grew even broader, showing far more teeth than most humans found comfortable. Despite its fierce appearance, the expression meant exactly the same as a human smile—at least, as far as Phule had been able to determine. "He is spending much time with the new medician, which is not to be expected if he is healthy."

Phule's face turned red, but Armstrong broke out laughing. "Well, Captain, it looks as if we've solved one problem and stirred up another," he said. "We make the troops healthier, and poor old Beeker . . ." He left the thought unfinished.

"I'd wondered why he hadn't been hanging around my office quite so much," said Phule. "He and Nightingale were pretty close back on Lorelei, just before we lifted off. I guess I should have expected something like this when she turned out to be the new medic. Well, with any luck, they'll settle back down before long."

Armstrong nodded, then said, "I wonder, though, Captain . . . is this one of General Blitzkrieg's little ploys to make life difficult for Omega Company, or just another coincidence?"

Phule's jaw clenched. "Lieutenant, I wish you hadn't asked that question," he said. He ran on for nearly a hundred yards before adding, "At least, they're both grown-ups. That's supposed to help."

But he didn't sound as if he really believed it.

"I'm worried," said Thumper, in a near whisper. "What if . . . ?" He and Mahatma were standing in the shadows of the observation tower in the center of Zenobia Base, facing toward the Supply depot.

"Do not worry," said Mahatma, patting his new partner on the back. "*What if* is exactly the kind of question you need to be asking, because others have not asked it. The result of your asking will be greater awareness, and that will make Omega Company better able to perform its mission. Is that not what a good legionnaire should be doing?"

"I guess so," said Thumper. "I just remember that, back in Legion Basic, asking the sergeants a question was a quick way to get in trouble."

"This is not Legion Basic," said Mahatma, smiling quietly. "And while Chocolate Harry is undeniably a sergeant, he is not likely to do much more than express himself loudly in very flamboyant language. That is why I am starting you with him; we will work our way up to more challenging interactions. In time you will find that you can even pose questions to Sergeant Escrima without undue anxiety. It is all a matter of the correct attitude."

"OK," said Thumper, still looking a bit dubious. "I'll give it my best shot—wish me luck."

"Luck is an illusion," said Mahatma. "All will be well if you preserve a calm demeanor. Go to it!"

"Yeah," said Thumper. He stepped out of the shadows and walked as nonchalantly as possible toward the Supply depot. *Preserve a calm demeanor . . . preserve a calm demeanor*, he repeated to himself. The mantra must have worked; there was even a trace of a bounce in his stride as he came through the door. "Good morning, Sergeant Chocolate Harry," he said in his politest tone of voice.

"Yo, Thumper," rumbled Harry, looking up from the Biker's Friend catalog he'd been reading. "You need somethin'?"

"Uh, actually, Sergeant, I wanted to ask you a question," said Thumper, self-conscious again. Without Mahatma standing next to him, his demeanor was drifting farther away from calmness with every passing moment.

"Question?" Harry frowned. "This here's the Supply depot, Thumpy—not the freakin' Answer depot. But give it a shot, anyway. Maybe you'll get lucky."

"Luck is an illusion," said Thumper. He felt more confident remembering Mahatma's words.

"Huh? You been talkin' to Qual?" Chocolate Harry's brows knit as he attempted to figure out whether or not Thumper was serious, and whether or not to take it as an insult.

Seeing Harry's confusion, Thumper hastened to ask his question before the Supply sergeant decided he wasn't in the mood to bandy words with nearly raw recruits. "I understand you have a large supply of purple camouflage, Sergeant. Am I right?"

"Sure, got anything you want," said Chocolate Harry, relaxing as he thought he recognized a sucker asking to be fleeced. "Caps, vests, capes, socks, knapsacks—you name it, I got it. How much you need?"

"I don't know," said Thumper. "Uh, that is, I don't know whether I need it or not. How do you know it works?"

Harry scoffed. "Man, everybody in the company knows it works. Time the robots come over the hill lookin' to kick butt, the purple cammy did the job. Ask the captain; ask Brandy; ask anybody—they'll tell you. You want to be safe from robots, you gotta be wearin' the purple."

"I see," said Thumper, his ears perking up. "But do we know that it protects against alien robots, Sergeant? Wouldn't those have different laws?"

"What you mean, different laws?" asked Harry.

"Everybody knows robots can't see purple—they just built that way."

"I'm sorry, Sergeant, I must not have explained my point clearly," said Thumper. "Let me try again. The brains of Alliance robots are all built with Asimov circuits that make them obey the Three Laws. Am I right?"

"Sure," said Harry. "They can't build 'em no other way. And one of the things they build into those circuits is purple-blindness. I can show you that in writin', Thumper, writin' straight from the gov'ment."

"That's very good, Sergeant," said Thumper. "Of course I know the Three Laws—*a robot mustn't harm a sophont, or let a sophont come to harm if it can prevent it*—we learned all that in kiddygarden. And the teachers wouldn't tell us something if it wasn't so. But what happens if we run into robots that weren't made in the Alliance? Wouldn't alien robots have different laws?"

"Alien robots? There ain't no alien robots, on account of there ain't no aliens," said Harry, his voice getting louder. "Everybody's part of the Alliance—all the sophonts in the galaxy. So all the robots is the same."

"But there are new sophonts discovered all the time," said Thumper. "There are two races of them, both living right on this planet, that nobody knew about until the captain discovered them. What if the Zenobians had been building robots before we met them? Wouldn't their laws be different? What about the Nanoids?"

Harry glowered. "Look a-here. Point you're missin' is, they *didn't* build no robots before we met 'em," he said. "So it don't matter, see?"

"But what about the next new race we discover?" asked Thumper, doing his best to preserve a calm demeanor. "Can we be sure they'll build the same laws into their robots? And even if they do, will their robots recognize us as sophonts?"

"Damn it, there ain't no alien robots," growled Chocolate Harry. "If you gonna come around bustin' chops, I just might decide not to sell you any freakin' purple cammy—and then when the renegade robots come bubblin' out of the underbrush with their eyes shootin' sparks and their grasping mechanisms reachin' out for your little furry tail, *you'll* be sorry. You *bet* your ass is gonna be sorry!"

Thumper decided he had time to make one more point. "But if the Three Laws are correct, then the only robots I need to be afraid of are alien robots . . ."

"Take your freakin' alien robots and put 'em where the sun don't shine, bunny!" Harry's voice was a full-throated roar, now. He stood up from his chair, looming over Thumper.

Wisely deciding not to finish his argument, Thumper made a rapid exit, quickly scurrying out the door and back to where Mahatma awaited him.

Mahatma pointed to the Supply depot, from which Harry's voice could still be heard, using language that certainly qualified as flamboyant. He grinned broadly as he said, "Congratulations, Thumper. I believe you have succeeded in being a pain in the ass."

"Mother, have you seen Beeker?" Phule said into the office intercom.

"That depends, sweetie. Do you mean have I seen him today?" said Mother. "Or recently today? Or just have I seen him?"

Phule rolled his eyes. In any other Legion unit, Mother's ongoing impertinence to her commanding officer would've been grounds for a reprimand—possibly some even harder disciplinary measure. But when Phule first came to Omega Company, she'd been a different person. So different that her name among her fellow legionnaires was "Shrinking Violet." Only when he'd put her behind a microphone and let her communicate to the company without showing her face did her assertiveness become apparent. That simple step had turned a cringing liability into one of the company's main assets—and if a bit of smart-mouthed repartee was the price for it, it was one he was willing to pay.

Of course, at times like now, when he was in a hurry, the price seemed a bit stiff.

"Recently today would be good," he said. "And if not recently, just tell me the last time you did see him."

"Oh, let me see . . . it must have been just after eleven hundred hours," she said. "That'd be a little before lunchtime, hon," she added helpfully.

"Eleven hundred . . ." Phule looked at the time readout on his wrist communicator. "That's nearly three hours ago. Where was he when you saw him, Mother?"

"Headed out toward the perimeter," said Mother. She paused a beat, then added, "with Nightingale. They make a really cute couple, don't you think, sweetie?"

Phule sputtered for a few moments, trying to figure out how to fit his mental image of his butler into the same lobe of his brain as the words *cute couple*. After several uncon-vincing tries, he asked the first reasonable question that came to mind. "Which way were they headed, Mother?"

He could almost hear the smirk that accompanied her reply. "Now, dearie, that'd be telling, wouldn't it?"

"Well, er, yes," said Phule, dully. "That's what I was asking you to do, I thought."

"You should think again, silly boy," said Mother. "Or maybe that's your problem. Using your head when it's the totally wrong thing to do. Don't worry, they'll be back, and then you can ask poor old Beekie whatever it was you wanted to ask. I'm sure it can wait until then."

"Poor old Beekie?" said Phule, even more confused than before.

"You heard me the first time, sweetie," said Mother, and she broke the connection before Phule could ask her any-thing else.

• • •

In the hot midday sun at the edge of Zenobia Base, Flight
Leftenant Qual and three members of his team worked to
adjust the *sklern*, their long-range holographic image projector. One of the triumphs of Zenobian technology, the
sklern had already proved its value as a means to spread
terror to an unsuspecting enemy. Now, Qual and his troops
were working on means of using the *sklern* to deceive an
enemy into misallocating forces, defending against nonex-
istent threats, or other tactical and strategic errors growing
out of mistaking illusion for reality.

A short distance away, a pudgy figure in a modified Legion uniform stood watching the Zenobians. Rev's interest
in the saurian natives of this planet had been piqued with
the discovery that, somewhere in the distant past, Zenobia
had been exposed to the charismatic presence of the
King—the guiding figure on whose inspiring career his
church rested its teachings. Some among Omega Company
dismissed the event as a random electronic signal traveling
across the limitless space between Zenobia and Old Earth.
Others . . . well, Rev was one of those others. And he had
long since decided that, when it came to the King, there
was very little that could be called random.

And so he listened to the Zenobians' chatter, hoping
that a stray word might give him a deeper insight into the
meaning of their experience. In his business, a stray word
or gesture could mean worlds upon worlds . . .

"Did you witness Hrap's presentation last twilight?"
one of the Zenobians asked another. Their translators were
always on, so an eavesdropping human could easily follow
their conversations—well, at least more easily than if their
conversation was left untranslated. The idiosyncratic character of the Zenobian language had been one of the oddball
discoveries the members of Omega Company had made in
the year or so its forces had been present on the planet. In
fact, the Zenobian language was quirky enough that Al-

liance military intelligence had developed a strong interest
in its potential as an unbreakable code.

"Hrap is well-known as an open cloaca," said the second Zenobian. "It would be redundant to witness his giving
extended proof thereof."

The first riposted, "I will not contest his cloacahood, but
balanced judgment would consider his favor with the
masses."

"The masses are themselves cloacae," interjected a third
voice. Curiously, as Rev had previously noted, even machine translations of Zenobian voices carried a strong hint
of the individuality of the speakers. Rev would likely have
had trouble telling the three Zenobians apart visually, but
their voices were as distinctive as holos of three different
landscapes.

"Take care not to swerve from your settings," said Qual,
who listened to the previous discussion without comment.
"We approach the activation potential . . ."

"Amplitude settings in perfect alignment," said the
Zenobian who had begun the discussion. Rev thought he
detected a note of condescension in the reply.

"Yo, Rev, you got a minute?" came a voice from the
other direction. Rev turned to see Roadkill, one of the
newer group of legionnaires, standing a short distance
away. Roadkill was an occasional attendee at Rev's services, though he hadn't yet responded to Rev's efforts to
persuade the legionnaires of Omega Company to become
full members of the Church of the King.

Perhaps this was the time, thought Rev. "Why, sure,
son, what can I do for you?"

Roadkill looked down at the ground. "Well, Rev, I been
thinkin'."

Rev nodded benevolently. "That's good, son, that's always good. A feller oughta think about things."

"Uh, yeah," said Roadkill. It wasn't clear whether he really agreed or was trying to be polite. In fact, now that he'd

gotten Rev's attention, Roadkill looked as if he wanted nothing better than to escape. But after squirming and making several false starts while Rev waited with ostentatious patience, he finally blurted out, "It's about the church, Rev."

"Well, that don't surprise me, Roadkill," said Rev. "A lot of the troops like to talk to me about that."

"Well, I've just been wondering . . ."

"Here, son, don't be shy," said Rev. "Whatever it is you want to ask, I'm here to answer it."

"You sure?" asked Roadkill, looking sidewise at Rev. "I mean, I don't want to embarrass nobody . . ."

"Go ahead, spit it out," said Rev. "There's not much a man in my shoes ain't already heard a few times."

"OK, then," said Roadkill. "What I want to know is why the music's so *un*. I mean, the King was some kinda musician, right? So why isn't the church music bein' triffer?"

"Well, son, we gotta go with the talent we have," said Rev, trying his best not to show his dismay. "If you knew some good musicians on the base, I could maybe ask 'em to play once in a while."

"You mean that?" said Roadkill, his eyes lighting up. "Coz me and some of the guys . . ."

"You got a band?" Rev perked up. Attendance had been a bit slack lately; maybe this would be a way to spark interest among the younger legionnaires. "We can talk about you playin' for the King, if you can play somethin' that fits in. You got somethin' I can listen to?"

"Sure," said Roadkill. He reached in the front pocket of his jumpsuit and pulled out a plugin. "Listen to that, and if you like it, we'll talk more."

"Sure, I can't wait to hear it," said Rev. Secretly, he wondered just what kind of music the younger legionnaires were listening to these days. He'd always preferred the classics, himself: Jerry Lee, Gene Vincent, Sheb Wooley, and of course the King. But maybe it was time to open his

ears a bit. That would be just what the King would tell him
to do . . .

He tucked the plugin into his own pocket and promptly
forgot about it.

3

Journal #770—

All work and no play makes Jack a dull boy.

"Neurons, spare, freeze-dried, three cases," said the tall Black woman, bending down to look at the bottom shelf of the medical supply closet.

"Neurons, spare, freeze-dried, three cases—check," said Beeker. He marked the item on the handheld electrotablet he was using to record the information for transfer to the medical supply database that had just been set up. Until just a day ago, Chocolate Harry had been in charge of the base's medical supplies. With an autodoc taking care of the legionnaires of Omega Company, there hadn't been any particular reason to separate the medical materials from the general supplies. But with a live medic on-planet, that was about to change.

Nightingale—formerly known as Laverna—stood up and stretched. "OK," she said, tiredly. "Looks as if we've got almost everything a detached company is going to need. Unless you're planning on some kind of war break-ing out here, I ought to be able to do the job."

"I would have expected that of you," said Beeker, who'd volunteered to help the company's new medic inventory her infirmary's supplies.

"You're a trusting sort, aren't you?" said Nightingale, deadpan. But there was a noticeable edge to her voice.

"Yes, when circumstances justify it," said Beeker, rais-ing an eyebrow. "I trusted you to finish training and come join this company, and so you have. Show me the fault in that."

Nightingale said, "Well-ll . . ." Then she fell silent, with a sidelong glance at the butler.

Beeker elevated his other eyebrow. After waiting a long moment, he said (with an unaccustomed show of impa-tience), "Are you going to continue your remarks, or am I going to be forced to rely on guesswork? I don't pretend to be expert at interpreting silences."

Nightingale shrugged. "If you really want me to point out a fault in your behavior, you might consider that some men would have been glad to come with me instead of waiting for me to come back to them."

"Some men," Beeker repeated, stiffly. "Is that a general comment, or am I to infer someone in particular from it?"

"Infer whatever you like," said Laverna, with a look that might have meant anything.

Beeker was having nothing to do with that gambit. "Ac-tually, I'd like a direct answer," he said, spreading his hands apart, palms up. "Hints and guesses are all very well in their place, mind you, but there comes a point when one needs to know what the other person is really trying to say. If you were expecting me to read your mind, I fear you're in for a disappointment."

Laverna looked at him over one shoulder. "Funny, I thought butlers were good at that kind of thing."

"It's often a professional advantage to give one's master

that impression," said Beeker. "You may have found yourself in a similar position with *your* former employer." He favored her with a small, knowing smile. "Of course, one never reveals that one's employer's unspoken wishes are so transparent that a none-too-bright child could see through them. The master might take it as a reflection on his intelligence."

"Uh-huh," said Laverna. "I've looked down the barrel of *that* gun a few times. All right, I get your point." She took a deep breath, then said, "It seems to me that I'm the one who's made all the adjustments in this relationship. I leave Lorelei, start over in a completely new field, going through Legion Basic—which is every bit as nasty as you'd expect—and then buckle down to a year of advanced medical training. Meanwhile, you get to lounge around luxury resorts, acting as father confessor to Omega Company, with occasional breaks to help your boss juggle his investments. I finally pull some strings to get myself reassigned to your boss's outfit, and what do I find?"

There was a longish silence while Laverna glared at Beeker. At last, the butler shrugged, and said, "We appear to be back where we began. I could venture a guess at what you mean, but it appears highly likely that, unless I were to stumble upon the correct answer at once, it'd be a mark against me. So I'll simply have to take the coward's way out. I'm afraid you're going to have to tell me, my dear."

Laverna wrinkled her nose, opened her mouth, then shut it again. Slowly a broad grin spread over her face. "I happen to know you have some vacation time coming," she said. "Guess where you're taking me?"

Thumper lay back in his bunk, pleased with himself. He had to his credit one definite success at being a pain in the ass. On the negative side, the last couple of times he'd crossed paths with Chocolate Harry, the Supply sergeant had given him a withering look; but Mahatma had explained that being a pain in the ass wasn't going to bring easy popularity with it. It was a duty, and sometimes duties weren't really fun for those who had to perform them.

Thumper could understand that. He'd spent most of Legion Basic being the most unpopular recruit in his unit. But he knew it was more important to work hard and become a good legionnaire than to be popular with the guys. Looking back, he realized that even then, he'd been a pain in the ass. It was good to know that he'd found his niche in the Legion.

But who should he practice on next? He didn't get much chance to interact with the command structure of Omega Company; mostly he dealt with First Sergeant Brandy, who led his training squad. And Mahatma was already making sure that Brandy stayed on her toes. He saw a good deal of Mess Sergeant Escrima; but it was clear that the volatile Escrima wasn't a case for a rank beginner like himself. Even Mahatma tended to tread softly around the volatile mess sergeant. As for the officers, he saw them mostly at a distance; he couldn't really dream up a good excuse for striking up a conversation with Lieutenant Armstrong or Lieutenant Rembrandt—let alone Captain Jester.

As far as his fellow legionnaire recruits, he could see that most of them were having enough trouble without anyone trying to "give them a little eye-opener," as Mahatma liked to describe his endless questioning and probing. Oh, every now and then one of them would get too cocky, and display the need for some instant deflation; but most of the time the entire squad would make it a point to apply the corrective, and if they missed the chance, Brandy was an expert at giving a recruit a quick lesson in the way things worked in the real world of Omega Company. So Thumper's talents probably weren't needed there, either.

Thumper sat up in his bunk; he had a good half hour left on his break. If he was serious about his new mission, he shouldn't just wait for an opportunity to come his way.

Time to go out and find one! He pulled on his Legion boots, custom-made to fit a Lepoid's feet, and bounced out the door into Zenobia Base's spacious parade ground.

As usual, the area was full of activity. To one side, Gears had his head under the hood of a hoverjeep, fine-tuning the engine. To another, several off-duty legionnaires were throwing around a quarble, laughing and joking as it erratically changed course just as one of them thought he'd put himself in position to catch it. In the center of the area, Brandy sat under an open-sided tent, catching up on paperwork. Beyond her, a team with shovels was digging a shallow trench, sweating and griping in the warm desert sun. No obvious opportunities there.

Then Thumper's eyes lit on two figures he'd often seen together: Sushi and Do-Wop. Like himself and Mahatma, they were partners. And like many of the long-term members of the Omega Mob, they had perfected the technique of always seeming to be busy, while doing as little actual work as possible. There, he thought, were two likely customers for his newfound specialty. He smoothed down his whiskers and hopped over to the two legionnaires. "Hello," he said. "You are two experienced legionnaires. May a new recruit ask you a question?"

"Ya just did," said Do-Wop, with a grin.

"That does put everybody in a bind," said Sushi. "If we said *no*, you'd have to take *that* question back, wouldn't you?"

Thumper hadn't been prepared for that kind of response. He could see that being a pain was going to be tougher than he thought. Thinking quickly, he said, "Refusing me the chance to ask one question doesn't automatically mean I can't ask other, different ones. To stop that, you'd have to say I can't ask you any questions at all."

"You're right, kid," said Do-Wop. "Now go away."

"Hang on, partner," said Sushi. "I'd like to find out what the new guy wants—your name's Thumper, right?"

"That's right," said Thumper. "And now you've asked me two questions, both of which I've already answered. If we're going to be fair, you should be willing to answer mine in return."

"Who said we're supposed to be fair?" said Do-Wop. "This is the farkin' Space Legion."

"That's three questions," said Thumper, calmly. Now he was beginning to hit his stride. "I'll answer the last one if you'll answer mine."

That, at last, seemed to have exceeded Do-Wop's ability to parse. He shook his head and rolled his eyes, while saying nothing—at least, nothing articulate.

But before Thumper could relish the taste of victory, Sushi took up the slack. "OK, new guy, it's a deal. You may not ask us any questions. Now, you tell us who said we were supposed to be fair."

Since Thumper hadn't even considered the question as having a real answer, that left him as speechless as Do-Wop. Sushi laughed, and said, "Looks like we're even, Thumper." And with that, he took Do-Wop by the collar and led him off, leaving Thumper to wonder whether he might not need a few more lessons from Mahatma.

"Beeks? Beeks, where are you?" Phule peered around his office, a puzzled expression on his face. He wasn't used to having to look for his butler. It was much more frequently the case that Beeker would appear, unasked for, at exactly the time when his services were most useful.

Fortunately, there was a way to contact the butler even when he was out of earshot. Phule punched the intercom button on his wrist communicator and heard the answering buzz from the unit on the other end. Phule waited for the butler to acknowledge the call; undoubtedly Beeker had just gotten involved in some routine housekeeping task, and time had slipped away from him.

The buzz repeated. Phule stared at the comm unit in annoyance. This was starting to be a nuisance. It was too late in the day to assume that the butler might have removed the wrist comm for a short while to take a shower. (In fact, the comm was designed for all-weather operation, and its manufacturer touted it as capable of withstanding up to six hours of unprotected immersion in twenty fathoms of salt water. Even so, there were times when it was more convenient just to take it off—and this was far from an emergency.)

Phule pushed another button on the comm. "Mother—do you have any idea where Beeker is? I've been trying to raise him, and he doesn't answer."

"Well, honey, if you don't know what he's up to, what makes you think I'm gonna tell?" said the impertinent voice of Comm Central.

"I don't need to know what he's up to, Mother," said Phule, a trifle impatient. "I just need to buzz him. Can you find him for me?"

"Why, sure, sweetie," said Mother. "Let me try a quick trace on his wrist comm . . ." There was a brief pause, presumably while she called up the search programs connected to her console. When her voice came back, it was with a note of puzzlement. "Huh, that's funny. I'm getting a location out in the desert. Wonder what he's doing out there?"

"Desert?" Phule wrinkled his brow. "That doesn't make sense at all. Give me the coordinates, and I'll have somebody run out and check it."

"You got it," said Mother. "I'll send the coordinates to your Port-a-Brain. Later, darlin'." She broke the connection.

A moment later, a series of numbers appeared on Phule's screen. He punched them into his map program; sure enough, they corresponded to a spot some distance from camp. He raised his wrist comm to his mouth again. "Brandy, this is the captain. I want a search party to the following location, soon as they can get there." He read off the numbers.

"Got it, Captain," said the sergeant. "If you don't mind my asking, what's the deal out there?"

"I'm not sure," said Phule. "I've been trying to raise Beeker on his comm, and he doesn't answer. Mother ran a trace, and it comes back with that location. Maybe he's injured . . ."

"Maybe," said Brandy. There was a moment of silence, then she said, "Uh, not to interfere with your plans, Captain, but I have a hunch that maybe you ought to run a trace on Nightingale's comm. Just to see what turns up, y'know?"

Phule's jaw dropped. "Good grief! Why didn't I think of that?" he said, once he'd recovered. "Hang on a moment, Brandy. I'll have Mother check it out—and thanks for the hint!"

Two minutes later he had his answer: Nightingale's wrist comm was in the same location as Beeker's, and both were evidently turned off. Mother snickered as she said, "Hey, Cap baby, doesn't your butler have a private bedroom? You wouldn't think he'd have to go all the way out in the desert for a little privacy with his lady . . ."

Phule's face had turned an especially vivid shade of pink. "I would never have thought of it," he said, glad (not for the first time) that he hadn't ordered full video capabilities for the company's wrist comms. He thought for a moment, then said, "Try them again in—uh, half an hour—no, make it an hour. If they don't answer then, let me know, and I'll decide what to do."

"Yes, sir," said Mother, and closed the connection. Phule didn't even notice her unaccustomed formality. His butler's uncharacteristic absence—and the even more uncharacteristic explanation for it—had driven everything else out of his mind.

It was only after an hour and a half, when he finally sent the search party, that he began to regret not following his first impulses. But by then, it was far too late.

• • •

"So, do you think you can trace them?" Phule said anxiously. Beeker had been his right-hand man for so long that he was having some difficulty even formulating a coherent plan in his absence. But the butler was undeniably off-planet, as the note Phule had just found on his desk made clear.

> *Sir: I have decided to take my vacation, effective at once. I will be traveling with Medic 2nd Class Nightingale—please consider this her formal application for her accumulated leave. Our apologies for giving such short notice, but we were fortunate enough to get reservations for some very desirable events. We shall return in approximately six weeks.—B.*

Now Phule was going to have to do without his butler's help—and that meant drawing on all the resources at his command. Ironic that the first job facing him was figuring out where Beeker had gone . . .

"I have a couple of ideas," said Sushi. "Let me log on and see if what I can find out. Some of it's going to depend on just how hard Beeker and Nightingale are trying to cover their tracks . . ."

"Cover their tracks?" Phule frowned. "Do you mean they might not want to be found?"

"That's not such a weird idea," said Sushi. "I mean, you notice he didn't give you his destination. Look at it from Beeker's point of view. This is the first time I can remember him being away since you took over the company. If you go get him and bring him back to Zenobia, all he's got to look forward to is going back to work again. That's not exactly something to get all enthusiastic about, is it?"

"Perhaps not," said Phule. "But if he wanted some time off, why didn't he just come and ask me? I would have given him his vacation time, either here or off-planet. I'm not that hard to get along with. Why would Beeker just leave?" Phule hadn't ever considered the possibility that Beeker might be far less enthusiastic about returning to his assigned duties than his employer was to have him back.

"Don't ask me, ask him," said Sushi. "You want me to run that trace?"

"Of course. How long do you think it'll take to find out?"

Sushi turned to his view screen and considered. "If we're lucky and they didn't bother to hide their backtrail, I should be able to tell you something right away. If not . . ."

"If not?" asked Phule, leaning forward to peer at Sushi's view screen.

"If not, I can call in some of my family contacts and get you the real dope," said Do-Wop, with a sneer. He'd been sitting in the opposite corner of the room, playing a hand-held martial arts game. "Computers is OK when they work, but there's nothing like the good old grapevine when you wanna find somethin' out."

"Right, your family contacts might be able to tell us whether they bought any pizza and put it on their credit cards," said Sushi. "That's assuming either one of them used their right name, which is what we're trying to figure out to begin with."

"I was with a broad like that, I sure wouldn't give my right name," said Do-Wop. He followed that statement with an appreciative wolf whistle.

"If you were with somebody like her, you'd be likely to get both your arms cut off within fifteen minutes," said Sushi, without looking up from his view screen. "No, make it fifteen *seconds*. She's probably the most dangerous person ever to set foot on this planet, and I think I'm pretty well qualified to make that statement."

"Dangerous? Compared to who?" said Do-Wop. "You wouldn't know dangerous if it bit you in the ass . . ."

"Hang on, here's something that might help us find them," said Sushi. "Hmmm . . . Captain, do you know off the top of your head what model Port-A-Brain you two have?"

"Uh . . . I'll have to look it up," said Phule. "Why, is there some way you can trace it?"

"Not as precisely as I'd like," said Sushi. "But if it's the model I think it is, there's an antitheft feature built in that might let me trace it. It's limited—somebody who spends as much for it as you did doesn't want anybody else always knowing where he is or what he's doing. So the antitheft trace is password-enabled—which means it won't tell us exactly where Beeker is unless he wants us to know. But there's one other trace feature he can't turn off. Every time it goes through interplanetary customs, it records its passage—that's supposedly an antismuggling feature certain reactionary local governments insisted on. And that means we can figure out what world they're on even if Beeker never boots it up."

"Ah, that ain't much use," said Do-Wop. "What if they don't go through customs?"

"What if they never go to a planet?" said Phule. "For now, let's assume we can trace them. If it turns out we can't, we'll figure out what our next step's got to be. Get to work on it, Sushi. Until I tell you otherwise, this is your highest priority. OK?"

"I hear you, Captain," said Sushi, grinning. "Just get me the model number of Beeker's Port-a-Brain, and the serial number, if you have a record of that. I'll find them for you—or Do-Wop can remove my Yakusa tattoos—the hard way."

"I'd better get those numbers for you then," said Phule, standing up and heading toward the door.

"No hurry, Captain," said Do-Wop. "It ain't often I get to see Soosh sweat, and I plan to enjoy it while I got it."

"Yes, but as long as Beeker's gone, I'm the one who'll be sweating," said Phule. "Sorry to cut into your pleasure." He turned and went out the door, walking fast.

• • •

An hour later—an anxious hour, from Phule's point of view, Sushi sauntered in the door of Phule's office. "OK, Captain, here's what I've found," he said. "Beeker's computer went through customs on a planet called Cut 'N' Shoot."

"Cut 'N' Shoot?" Phule frowned. "I never heard of it."

"Neither did I until just a little while ago," said Sushi. "It's a fairly new colony, discovered by explorers from Tejas and mostly settled from there. Main industry right now is mining, but there's some local agriculture and the usual mix of misfits who want a new place to start over."

"Just like the Omega Mob," said Rembrandt, chuckling.

"I would take exception if it weren't mostly true," said Phule. "I wonder what's the quickest way to get there?" He blinked. Beeker had always been the one who arranged travel plans for him. Now he would have to learn to do it himself . . .

"I already had Mother check that out, Captain," said Sushi. "We can get a private shuttle to Lorelei—which is what Beeker and Laverna did—and from there we catch the regular liner to the Tejas sector, where we catch the local. The shuttle can be here on twenty-four-hour notice, so just say when you want it."

"Three days ago," said Phule, wryly. "Remmie, you know the routine—you're the senior lieutenant, so you're acting CO while I'm gone. And I honestly don't know how long that'll be, so you're going to have to be ready for a long haul if that's what it takes."

"We aren't worried about that, Captain," said Lieutenant Rembrandt, smiling bravely. "We can manage, if you really need to be away. But wouldn't it be easier to hire somebody on Cut 'N' Shoot to find them than to go running off yourself? I mean, with your family's connections . . ."

"This is something I have to do in person, Rembrandt," said Phule. "If Beeker runs off without a word, something unusual is going on. I can't trust a stranger with that, not halfway across the Alliance. I've got to be there and talk to him myself. Now, are you sure you can handle the company by yourself?"

Rembrandt nodded. "Armstrong and I have done it before, remember? And if things get really sticky, Brandy and the other noncoms are there to bail us out. Just don't get into anything you can't get out of by yourself."

"Oh, he don't have to worry about that," said Do-Wop. "Me and Soosh are goin' along to get him out of trouble."

"What?" said Phule. "You can't! You're more likely to get me into trouble than out of it. Besides, Sushi's the best computer jockey in the company, and if something goes wrong, Lieutenant Rembrandt is going to need him—and maybe even you—right here."

"Geez, go a little easy on the flattery," said Do-Wop. "You ever stop and think—maybe you *need* to take a sly mofo like me along to Cut 'N' Shoot to show you how to talk nice to the farkin' natives?"

"Right," said Sushi. "And while he's at it, he can take along Tusk-anini to give 'em ballet classes."

"Hey!" protested Do-Wop. "Watch it, Soosh—I thought we was in this together!"

"Well, the final answer is, neither one of you are going," said Phule. "I can travel a lot faster by myself than if I have to keep track of you two. I'd have to check every bar and casino—and maybe a jail or two—before I could leave a town. So you're staying here. It's not as if I can't run my own computer, you know."

"You heard the captain," said Rembrandt, with a warm smile. "I'm sure he can find his way around a frontier world just fine all by himself. Besides which, I'll be needing both of you here. So that's settled."

"OK, Captain," said Sushi, calmly. "So I'm assuming you want the Lorelei shuttle here ASAP—and connections from Lorelei to Tejas and Cut 'N' Shoot. I'll get those right away—shouldn't take more than an hour. Anything else?"

"A little luck wouldn't hurt," said Phule, wryly.

"Here's hoping you don't need it," said Rembrandt. "But if I were you, I'd start packing now. If Sushi *does* get lucky with the shuttle, maybe we can have one earlier than we expect."

"Good idea," said Phule. "Let me know as soon as you know when the shuttle will be here, Sushi."

"Right on, Captain," said Sushi, turning to his console and starting the call to Lorelei shuttle service.

As soon as Phule had left the room, he turned to Do-Wop. "Are you ever going to learn when to keep your mouth shut?" he said. "Now we're going to have to stay out of the captain's sight the whole way to Cut 'N' Shoot."

"Hey, if he bought it, we'd've been riding up in first class with him," said Do-Wop, with a shrug and a grin. "You never try, you never win."

"And when you try something that stupid, you're blowing your chances before you even start to play," said Sushi.

"All right, you guys, cut it out," said Rembrandt. "I'll give you the same advice I gave the captain—get your stuff packed and be ready to go. If you miss the special shuttle, you're going to be a day behind him by the time he gets to Lorelei—and that might be enough for you to miss him altogether. We need somebody to make sure the practical details get taken care of, now that he doesn't have Beeker to look after him. And you're the best I've got—as sad a commentary as that is."

"Don't worry, Remmie, we'll stick to him like glumbions to a cressleback," said Do-Wop. He spun on his heel and swept out, leaving the other two with mouths wide open.

"Glumbions?" said Rembrandt, in a dazed tone of voice. "Cressleback?"

Sushi shrugged. "I'll fill you in if I ever find out," he said. "Which probably won't turn out to be worth the effort . . ."

"I know what you mean," said Rembrandt. "But thanks, anyway."

Phule had just returned to his office when there was a knock on the door behind him. He turned to see Lieutenant Rembrandt standing in the doorway. "Captain, may I speak to you privately, sir?" Rembrandt's voice was—well, not quite urgent, but certainly insistent. So was the look in her eyes.

Phule nodded. "Sure, Lieutenant, come on in." He sat on the edge of his desk and waved a hand. "Have a seat," he said as she stepped inside and closed the door behind her. "What's on your mind?"

"Thank you, sir, I'll stand," the lieutenant said. She stood awkwardly for a moment, then began. "Captain, I didn't want to bring this up in front of everybody else, because I don't want anyone to think I can't handle the company while you're gone. But I really do need to know this: What's so important about Beeker's going away that somebody else can't go to bring him back? Or why don't you ask some of your off-world contacts to find him? It'd be way easier, I'd think."

Phule cleared his throat and said, "Well, Rembrandt, to tell you the truth, I thought I was overdue for a little bit of vacation myself . . ."

"No, sir," said Rembrandt, firmly. "That's a good story, and most of the troops will buy it. But it's not the real reason. I'm going to be running Omega while you're gone, Captain. If I don't know the whole story, I'm likely to say something that everybody can see through—or that has consequences I can't foresee. I need to know the real story. Nobody else needs to know it, but *I* do. And if you don't think so, I respectfully suggest you give this job to somebody else."

Phule nodded. "You're right, Lieutenant. My apologies— I should've been straight with you. The real reason has to do with the Port-a-Brain . . ."

"Surely you're not worried about Beeker stealing it, sir?"

"Oh, that's the last thing old Beeks would do," said Phule. "Even if he decided to give me notice, he'd make it a point of honor to send back the Port-a-Brain—and anything else that belonged to me. No, the problem is a security feature my father had built in when he ordered the twin 'puters for us."

"A security feature?" Rembrandt frowned. "What kind of security feature?"

"Well, of course a Port-a-Brain's got some fairly advanced antitheft and antihacking features as standard equipment," said Phule. "Dad was worried about one of us being abducted along with our 'puter. Somebody might try to kidnap Beeker and use the Port-a-Brain to tap into my stock portfolio, for example—we do have a lot of sensitive data on them."

"So what happens if somebody does snatch one of you?"

"If either of us enters a certain code, they both shut down. It kicks in automatically if the two computers are out of range of one another—which basically covers a normal-sized planetary system—for three standard days. You can turn them back on, but you can't open any programs unless Beeks and I both enter two different passwords within fifteen minutes—and each of us only has our own password."

"OK, I can see how that'd be a pain," said Rembrandt. "You'd have to wait till he gets back to use your computer—unless you can get him to enter the password from wherever he's going . . ."

Phule nodded. "That's not even the worst of it. If we're still out of range and the right codes aren't entered after another five standard days, the Port-a-Brain completely wipes its memory. As far as I know, there's no way to recover it. I'd have to send it back to the factory just to get it restarted."

"Ouch!" Rembrandt made a face. "Well, you've definitely got to email Beeker and set up a time when you can both enter your passwords. I wonder why he didn't take care of this before he left? It's not at all like him to leave you with this kind of problem."

"Well, I have sent an email, of course. But I wish it was that easy," said Phule. He drummed his fingers on the desk and said, "If the 'puters aren't within about sixty light-minutes of each other, it's physically impossible to punch in both passwords within fifteen minutes. Hyperspace asynchronicity, they call it. So now I've got to go chasing after Beeks, in hopes I can stay close enough to keep the security from shutting me down. Luckily, the timing circuits go into stasis during starship travel, to avoid FTL paradoxes. That ought to give me enough time to catch him before the memory wipes. Then I can just ask him to give me his Port-a-Brain until he's ready to return. And then I can come home and let him have his vacation."

"Well, if I were you, I'd start backing up my data," said Rembrandt. "That way, even if you don't catch him quickly enough, you'll lose as little as possible."

"Oh, my data's backed up, all right," said Phule. He stood up and began to pace. "I know enough to do *that*. But there's one more problem—and I'm afraid Beeks doesn't even know about this one. My dad bought a special anti-kidnapping chip. If the computers are outside the sixty-light-minute range for more than five days, a special chip shuts *me* down."

"What?" Rembrandt's eyes opened wide. "You mean . . ."

"Yeah, I do," said Phule. "The chip's implanted in me, and if the computer goes down, it triggers this stasis chip which taps into my central nervous system and throws me into induced super-hibernation. Think of it as like a deep coma, except it's externally controlled. I tried to argue Dad out of it . . ."

"I can see why," said Rembrandt, clearly appalled. "But isn't there an override? What's the point of something that drastic, anyway?"

Phule paced nervously. "If there was an override, kidnappers could make me punch it in, and then what good's the security? There was a case a few years back—the Sojac kidnapping on Arbutus—they bullied a kid into giving up a whole batch of his family's access codes and passwords, then buried him alive in the desert. But you can't threaten someone in stasis. In fact, the super-hibernation field protects the, uh, subject from almost everything. You can apparently even survive hard vacuum for a couple of years. Of course, you can't *do* anything while you're in stasis."

"That's triff, if somebody finds you in time," said Rembrandt. "If they don't?"

"The chip sends out a locator signal," said Phule. He looked around nervously. "I'm not supposed to tell anybody this . . . If kidnappers knew about it, they'd try to dig out the chip before the field kicked in. That's why Dad didn't let me tell Beeker . . ."

Rembrandt shook her head. "Well, Captain, I'm certainly not going to put out the word. But you've convinced me. Now, let's just hope Beeker isn't one of those guys who takes a computer on vacation and never looks at his email."

"Let's hope, indeed," said Phule. "How soon can you get me on that shuttle?"

4

The Space Legion's recruiting posters urge civilians to "join the Legion and see the Universe." The fact is, most of those who join see little more than the hold of a troop ship and the parade ground of a Legion base. My employer had given his legionnaires the chance to see a good bit more than that—including some of the more attractive vacation spots in the Alliance. What he forgot is that, for a man who must be on call at all times, even the most delightful vacation spot eventually begins to look a great deal like a workplace—and workplaces are, by definition, odious.

Normally, anyone traveling to or from Omega Company headquarters on Zenobia stopped over at space station Lorelei. For one thing, Lorelei was a major space liner stop, so travelers could make direct connections to the final destination, at a considerable savings in time. But equally important, Omega Company was majority owner of the Fat

Chance Hotel and Casino, so the traveling legionnaires could spend a night or two in a first-class hotel while awaiting their connections. Not only was that an additional savings, it almost guaranteed that the passengers were in a good mood for the rest of their trip.

For Phule, a visit to the Fat Chance was an additional responsibility. After giving up his share in the ownership to the legionnaires of his company, he felt he owed them a careful look at how the business was going. Sure, he'd put good people in charge; sure, the casino had managed to survive a potential disaster when an outsider won a huge jackpot when all the odds were rigged against it. But it didn't hurt to cast his eye over the books on behalf of his people. And if it meant he was a day late catching up with Beeker—who surely hadn't lingered on the station any longer than absolutely necessary—so be it.

As it turned out, he couldn't have picked a worse time to arrive at the Fat Chance. A drug-resistant flu virus had hit the station, and a quarter of the casino staff—including Tully Bascomb, the casino manager, were suffering through it. Tully had ordered the dealers, waiters, bartenders, and others in public contact positions to take sick leave the minute they showed any symptoms, and that decision had managed to slow the spread of the bug among the Fat Chance employees and customers.

Of course, a shipload of high rollers—lawyers attending the Galactic Bar Convention—arrived at the Fat Chance just as the epidemic was at its peak. None of the estimable barristers (let alone the spouses and other vacation partners accompanying them) seemed to appreciate the pains the casino had taken to keep them from exposure to the virus. All they knew was that they had to wait in line at the hotel desk, and that the service in the restaurants and bars was slower than they liked, and that some of the gaming tables were closed for lack of trained staff to run them. Tully had rushed back from his own convalescence and brought on a fleet of temp workers to deal with the problem. That reduced the lawyers' bitching and moaning to an acceptable level, but it sent Tully into a full-blown relapse.

Phule ended up spending two whole days at the casino, making everything run smoothly so Tully wouldn't have to rush back yet again. A fair amount of his time was spent mingling with the crowd, playing the celebrity for the sake of the guests. By the time he was done, he was almost as exhausted as if he'd had the flu himself—but the casino was running smoothly, and Tully had regained his full strength. And Phule had gotten a look at the books, and could tell Omega Company that its investment was in good shape.

In the meantime, he'd studied up on the planet where Beeker and Nightingale had been reported. They hadn't stayed at the Fat Chance on their way through Lorelei. There would've been too many people who might recognize them, and too many questions, especially since Nightingale's former employers, the Lorelei branch of the Syndicate, had bones to pick with her. But thanks to Sushi's computer work, Phule already knew their immediate destination. An afternoon looking through travel brochures in the casino offices turned up a fair amount of material for Cut 'N' Shoot.

Cut 'N' Shoot had a smaller land area than most inhabited worlds, having a single moderate-sized continent with a few mineral resources, but no industrial prospects worth mentioning. After failing to find off-world customers for its decidedly inferior agricultural products, the governors of Cut 'N' Shoot had brought in outside consultants who (after absorbing a hefty fee) advised them to reposition it as a vacation spot for the galaxy. If Beeker and Nightingale were staying there, they wouldn't have very many places to hide, Phule decided.

The next day, he was on a space liner for Cut 'N' Shoot, determined to bring the chase to an early end.

Journal #783—

Cut 'N' Shoot is widely advertised as "the world of wide-open spaces," a claim that could be as easily made by any number of desolate, uninhabitable planets throughout the Alliance. One assumes that the marketing boffin who contrived the slogan expected it to resonate with some preconceived notion in the minds of the intended audience. In any case, the planet was originally colonized by refugees from Tejas, and the indigenous culture of Cut 'N' Shoot evidently reflects whatever those escapees felt was lacking in their former world.

Perhaps too influenced by the planet's name, I came to Cut 'N' Shoot expecting nothing more than poverty and squalor. To my surprise, the place is a booming success. Tourists from throughout the galaxy come to experience its carefully constructed aura of "the Old West," a mythical time and place in which (to paraphrase the brochures) the land was free and open, men were men, and the only law was right. I leave it to others to judge whether this picture bears any resemblance to historical reality.

My own visit to Cut 'N' Shoot was moderately comfortable and suitably colorful. As for the cuisine, it was for the most part edible, if not especially varied.

Lieutenant Rembrandt was reading over Brandy's draft of a plan for a training exercise using simulated enemies generated by the Zenobian sklern—a highly versatile long-distance holo projector—when her intercom buzzed. She flicked her wrist to turn on the talk switch, and answered, "Yes, Mother, what is it?"

Uncharacteristically, the voice of Comm Central wasted no time getting to the point. "Remmie, we've got trouble."

"We usually do," said Rembrandt. "What flavor is it this time around?"

"Brass," said Mother. "I just got word from one of my spies on Lorelei that General Blitzkrieg has arrived, en route to Zenobia. It's supposed to be a surprise inspection."

"Oh, beautiful," said Rembrandt, meaning exactly the opposite. "How am I going to explain why Captain Jester's not on base? That's the first thing the general's going to ask about, and it's the one thing we don't dare tell him. He'd have the captain up on AWOL charges as fast as he could fill out the paperwork. There's nothing he'd like better."

"You don't have to tell *me* about it, sister," said Mother. "I've seen every message from Headquarters since the captain put me in charge of comms. You don't have to read between the bytes to know that, if Blitzkrieg had his way, Captain Jester would be fighting off the geefle bugs and breaking up rocks in the rottenest military prison in the known galaxy."

"Maybe the captain can get back in time," said Rembrandt, hopefully.

"Not a chance, sweetie," said Mother. "He's already left Lorelei—even if I sent a priority message right now, he couldn't be back in less than two weeks. Meanwhile, the minute Blitzkrieg sees that the captain's off premises, he'll send for one of his brownnosers to run the company for him. Remember that Major Botchup he tried to stick us with?"

Rembrandt made a gagging noise. "Ghu's toenails, who could *forget*? I thought we were going to be stuck with him forever."

"Lucky for us the captain came back," said Mother. "And that robot he had made to run the casino while he was gone kept Botchup from getting too suspicious until he did."

"Sure did," said Rembrandt, chuckling. "We'll be lucky

to get off that easily this time. Any word how soon the general's going to be here?"

"Nothing solid," said Mother. "He could be on the next shuttle out, which would put him here some time tomorrow. More likely, he'll stop and inspect a few of the casinos and the golf courses first. I hear tell the old blowhard spends a lot of time out on the links. Anyhow, my source will tell me when Blitzkrieg ships out. That'll give us just under a day's notice. The captain's in hyperspace, so, it'll be a few days before I can get an intersystem message to him. And depending on where he is when he gets it, it may be as much as a week before he could get back to base."

"I don't think we can justify an intersystem message," said Rembrandt, dubiously. "You know what those things cost? We're supposed to use them for military emergencies only, and even then they better be pretty serious . . ."

"And General Blitzkrieg's not a first-class emergency?" asked Mother. "Hey, sis, play it your way . . . I'm not the one who's going to have to kiss up to him."

"I know, I know," said Rembrandt. She sighed. "If the captain can't get back before the general gets here, there's no point worrying him with messages. Tell the command cadre to meet me in the captain's office in fifteen minutes. Let 'em know what's happening, and tell 'em we've got no more than a couple of days to get ready for the old buzzard. Tell 'em we're going to need every trick in the book. I don't know what we can do to pull the wool over the general's eyes, but we're going to have to do our best. You remember how things were before the captain came . . ."

"Yeah, nobody wants to go back to that," said Mother. Rembrandt could almost hear her shudder over the comm. Then her voice turned bright again, and she added, "Don't worry, though, Remmie. If Omega Company can't outsmart that miserable excuse for a general, we're even dumber than he thinks."

"I hope you're right," said Lieutenant Rembrandt. She cut the connection and stared at the papers on the desk in front of her. After a long moment, she shook her head and sat up straight. *Well, kid, you knew the job was dangerous when you took it,* she thought. *And if you're still crazy enough to want it, you'd better do something about saving it . . .*

"Stranger, yer problems is solved," said the man sitting at the table. His chair was leaned back, and his boots were on the otherwise empty tabletop, giving a good view of his wooly chaps and oversize spurs. His hat was wide-brimmed and tall-crowned, and his moustache drooped nearly to his chin.

"I certainly hope so," said Phule. "I'm Captain Jester, by the way. And you are . . . ?"

"Buck Short," said the man. "Put 'er thar, Cap'n!" He extended a meaty hand for Phule to shake.

"Uh, pleased to meet you," said Phule. "I'm looking for a man . . ."

"Gotcha," said Short, nodding. "Summbitch is good as dead. Jes' tell me what he looks like . . ."

"No, no, I don't want him killed," said Phule. "This fellow used to work for me, and he's run off with a woman . . ."

"Oh, hell, that's different," said Short. He peered at Phule for a moment, then said, "Zit yer woman he's run off with?"

"Hardly," said Phule, somewhat taken aback at the notion. Then he shrugged, and said, "But if she wants to come back with him, that's fine, too."

"*Now* you're talkin'!" said Short. He sat forward and slammed a fist onto the tabletop. "How's about a drink, then? Ol' Ned's got a pert' good line of red-eye here."

"Red-eye? Oh, you mean the whisky," said Phule. "Sure, why not? But what . . ."

Short cut him off. "Hey, Bill!" he shouted. "You heard

the cap'n! Bring over that thar bottle—the good stuff, mind ye, none of yer usual banth sweat—and a couple glasses, too!"

The bartender—a slightly decrepit Andromatic robot with a face Phule recognized as that of a popular Old Earth actor from the days before tri-vee—brought over the bottle and glasses, and favored Phule with the enigmatic line, "This'll put hair on yer chest!" before trundling back behind the bar.

"Ol' Bill always says stuff like that," confided Buck Short. He grabbed the bottle and sloshed some of the contents into the two glasses, then picked one up. "Wal, here's mud in yer eye!"

"Right-o," said Phule, and took a sip. He nearly spit it out—the "red-eye" seemed to be predominantly fusel oil with other less palatable congeners. He sputtered a moment, then managed to ask, "This is the *good* stuff?"

"Best we got," said Short, setting down his empty glass. "Hey, this *is* Cut 'N' Shoot, pardner. You warn't expectin' one of those fizzy drinks with little um-*brel*-lies, was you?"

"I guess not," said Phule, shaking his head to clear it. "By the way, did you say you had a plan for finding my man Beeker?"

Short nodded. "Well, we rents you a hoss, and then I saddles up ol' Dale-8 . . ."

"Day late?" asked Phule, puzzled.

"Dale-8—that's my trusty steed," said Short. "Always liked the name 'Dale'—that's what I calls all my trusty steeds. First seven of 'em done gone plumb busted, but this one's a real peach. Jes' keeps on runnin'—can't hardly wear 'im out."

"I see," said Phule. "But what do we need him for?"

"Why, we gotta go find yer man—and the lady," said Short. "I reckon they's run off to Injun territory . . ."

"Injun territory?"

"Hey, watch it," said the bartender. "Them's folks, too—don't go slurrin' on 'em."

Short gave a derisive snort. "Folks? Hell, Bill, don't go givin' 'em airs—they's lots of 'em robots, same as you."

"Robots? I don't get it," said Phule.

"Well, didn't nobody else much want the job," confided Short. "Ain't too many folks wants to give up a spot in a nice civilized world to live out in a drafty tent without no runnin' water or 'lectricity or even tri-vee, and everybody's hand set against you. Oh, we got some real Injuns, all right—had to have a few jes' to set the right tone. But we couldn't get too many, and had to get robots for the rest, which was hard enough, seein' what prices is nowadays. But I reckon it jes' wouldn't be Cut 'N' Shoot without Injuns."

"If you say so," said Phule, shaking his head. "I guess you're the local expert. So when do you think we can start?"

"Let me have another toot, and we'll hop right to it," said Buck Short. He poured another glass and offered the bottle to Phule, who declined, with a shudder. Short shrugged and drank it down, then put his fingers to his lips and gave a shrill whistle. "Hi-yoh Dale!" he shouted.

A clattering noise came from the front of the building, and Phule turned in time to see a large metallic shape barge through the swinging doors. "Here I am, boss," said the robosteed, in a voice that carried just a hint of a whinny.

"Hey, I thought I told you not to bring that hoss in here," shouted Bill, the bartender. "You gonna mess up my place!"

"Hell, no," said Short. "He's a robot, remember? He ain't gonna crap on yer floor, which is more than you can say for half the reg'lar customers." He leapt into the saddle, then reached a hand down for Phule. "C'mon, Cap'n, we gonna go huntin'!"

Phule took the proffered hand, leapt up behind the cowboy, and in a moment they were out the door and on their way.

The spaceport stagecoach dropped Sushi and Do-Wop off in the middle of a small town, not much more than a crossroads in the dusty landscape. The sun had set beyond the western hills, and a few lights—dim ones, by the standards of most advanced worlds—provided the only illumination on the rustic scene.

Luckily, one of the lights was outside a building that bore a sign with the word HOTEL, and the two legionnaires made a beeline for it. There, on a bench on the plank sidewalk, lounged an old codger smoking an imitation corncob pipe. "Hi, there," said Sushi. "Can you tell me the name of this town?"

"Damfino," said the man, not bothering to remove the pipe from his mouth.

"What, are you stupid?" snapped Do-Wop, who had not enjoyed the stagecoach ride at all. "Don't you even know the name of this dump?"

This time the codger took his pipe out of his mouth. "I said, 'Damfino,' pilgrim," he said.

"Yo, turkey-face," Do-Wop growled. He brushed past Sushi, who was pointing upward and rolling his eyes meaningfully. "Are you tryin' to get smart with me?"

"No, ye gol-durn idjit," said the codger, glaring at Do-Wop. "I've lived here all my life—ask anybody. And Damfino's the name of the town." He pointed to the sign above him, which on closer inspection Do-Wop could read in its entirety: DAMFINO HOTEL.

"I tried to tell you," Sushi said to a sullen Do-Wop, as he opened the door to their hotel room. He plopped down on one of the beds, and said, "Anyhow, now that we're here, we've got to figure out where Beeker's staying, get word to the captain so he can go find him, and then our job will be done."

"Why don't you just hack the Net to find out where he's staying?" asked Do-Wop. "I bet it's there, if you went lookin'."

"Not enough computer power," said Sushi, patiently. "If I had the captain's Port-a-Brain, or the mil-spec equipment I have back on Zenobia, no sweat—I'd probably have it before bedtime. With what I've got here, we might not find out anything useful until the captain and Beeker leave the planet, and their computer registers as it goes out through customs."

Do-Wop nodded. "So you could find the captain if you had the captain's computer, but we don't know where he is, so we can't get it, so we can't find him. Ain't that just the way it always works? Stinker."

"That's about the size of it," said Sushi. "If either the captain or Beeker would disable their computer's security, we might be able to figure out where they are. But that's about as likely as one of them learning to breathe methane."

Do-Wop considered. "Hows about we spread a rumor that the security is really a bug, so they turn it off?"

Sushi shook his head. "Won't work," he said at last. "Even if the captain and Beeker fell for it, they'd get too frustrated trying to get around the safeguards. A Port-a-Brain's security is set so a casual user can't just override it. That's part of what you're paying for."

"Well, I ain't payin' for it, and if I could, there'd be a bunch of other things I could use the money for," said Do-Wop. "But I get your point. These rich guys don't get their hands dirty—they think there's somethin' wrong, they call some rent-a-geek to fix it."

"Which would be fine if I'm the guy they'd call," said Sushi. "But Port-a-Brain probably has a repair shop on any world big enough to have electricity. Which even includes this faux-rustic would-be paradise."

"They hide it pretty good," said Do-Wop, looking around the hotel room. In fact, the designers had made every effort to give the room the appearance of something from before the electronic age. Electrical outlets were concealed behind wooden panels, as was the tri-vee set. The lighting fixture gave off a flickering yellowish illumination that was a fair simulation of a kerosene lantern—although they hadn't taken realism to the point of simulating the smell of kerosene (which few of the guests would have recognized, in any case).

The locals had plenty of modern machinery, although most of it was well hidden in kitchens, back rooms, and other areas where tourists rarely intruded. Robots were configured to resemble mules, oxen, and other "authentic frontier creatures." Cut 'N' Shoot's founders were sensible businessmen, not members of some cult of perverse self-denial. Even the most authenticity-hungry tourists weren't usually ready to leave behind basic conveniences. You might as well have asked them to do without their personal entertainment and communications devices.

Sushi looked around and shrugged. "It doesn't look as if there's much else to do here," he said. He opened his duffel and took out his pocket computer. "I might as well run a search and see if I get lucky. Maybe this planet's smaller than I think."

"Can't be any smaller than I think," said Do-Wop, but Sushi ignored him. He was already at work.

The group in Phule's office was the entire command cadre of Omega Company. Lieutenant Rembrandt presided, sitting behind Phule's desk. To her left sat Lieutenant Armstrong, and to her right Flight Leftenant Qual, the representative of their Zenobian hosts. First Sergeant

Brandy and Supply Sergeant Chocolate Harry sat in two chairs facing the three officers. Unseen, but present via comm, was Mother, who had announced the bad news that was the reason for the emergency meeting.

"All right, people," said Rembrandt. "As we all know, Captain Jester is off-planet and can't get back fast enough to make any difference. The ball's in our court. This can't be the worst thing that's happened to this company. We've dealt with mobsters, monsters, revolutionaries, robots, and enough brass hats to ground a starship. So we ought to be able to deal with a surprise visit from the Legion's commanding general, right?"

"Yeah, oughta be a snap," said Chocolate Harry, the huge Supply sergeant. He spread his hands, with a convincing display of nonchalance. "We doin' our jobs, right? We keepin' Zenobia safe for the Zenobians."

"Demanding your clemency, large one, but Zenobians are doing a great deal toward that end," said Flight Leftenant Qual. He looked like a diminutive dinosaur— perhaps an *allosaurus*—dressed up like a military officer for some costume tri-vee, and his language regularly defied the translator's efforts to make his statements into comprehensible English. But he had a fine military mind, and he was afraid of nothing.

"The sergeant doesn't mean we want to take credit for your efforts, Qual," said Rembrandt. "What he means is that we're doing the job we came for, and that ought to be enough for the general. Which would be true, except that we all know that General Blitzkrieg has a major grudge against this company and especially against our captain."

"That's an understatement," said First Sergeant Brandy. "Fact is, the general's going to be looking for reasons to shove this company right back in the shitcan it was in before Captain Jester came here, and if he can't find any, he'll make some up. Looking at the crazy people we've got here, it's not going to be much of a stretch for him to find 'em. Don't get me wrong, Remmie—I love this company, but we damn sure have to admit we're never gonna win any spit-'n'-polish contests." She gestured at the others in the room. With only two of the five present wearing complete uniforms, her point was obvious.

Rembrandt responded with a wry grin. "We'd have enough trouble filling out the entry forms," she admitted. "Still, we've got a good thing here, and I think we all agree it's worth protecting. The question is, what can we do to keep the general from destroying everything the captain's built up?"

"Be a lot easier if the captain was here," said Chocolate Harry. "Him and Beeker, they can pretty much make their own rules and convince the brass that was the rules all along. Last time we had to do without the both of 'em, all we had to do was get around that jive-ass Major Botchup. And that robot the captain fixed up to mess with the mobsters' heads back on Lorelei did half the work for us."

"Well, give the troops some credit, too," said Rembrandt. "They did plenty of messing with Botchup's head, too. But I don't think we can expect the general to be such an easy mark."

"Why not?" said Brandy, a sudden glint in her eye. "He's the one who sent Botchup here, isn't he? If he was stupid enough to do that, he's likely to fall for just about anything. And knowing my troops, I can guarantee that's exactly what they're going to come up with."

"Yeah, I think we can trust the troops to rise to a challenge," said Rembrandt, dryly. "But what if General Blitzkrieg just happens to bring along somebody smart enough to know when he's being played for a sucker? Colonel Battleax, for example—she's got more than her share of brains."

"Yeah, and that's why he won't bring her," said Brandy, confidently. "He's coming here with one thing in mind, and that's making the captain into a scapegoat. Colonel Battleax plays by the rules, but she's always been willing to give Captain Jester and Omega Company a fair shake—even if it means bending the rules a little. She's the last person the general wants looking over his shoulder when he's trying to screw us over."

"So maybe we've got a chance to keep him off-balance," said Rembrandt. "That still leaves us with one big problem—how long can we keep him from noticing the captain's not here? Especially since he's coming all the way here for the particular pleasure of chewing him out face-to-face . . ."

"I am thinking I have a solution to that," said Flight Leftenant Qual, bouncing out of his seat. "You should severally attend to your own assignments, and I will undertake to provide the general with diversion in that department." The little Zenobian flashed a toothy reptilian grin and, before anyone could ask what he meant, was out the door.

"What the hell's ol' Qual up to?" asked Chocolate Harry, scratching his head.

"I haven't the vaguest idea," said Rembrandt, shrugging.

"Whatever it is, I hope it's good," said Armstrong. "General Blitzkrieg may not have the quickest mind in the Legion, but he's still got stars on his shoulders. If he realizes we're playing games with him, he can make life really lousy for everybody here."

"In that case, we'd better get to work," said Rembrandt. "I think we've all got plenty to do, don't we?"

"No kiddin'," said Chocolate Harry, rolling his eyes. "And when the general gets here, ain't none of it gonna matter." He lifted his ample bulk out of the chair and headed out the door.

"I sure hope he's wrong about that," said Armstrong.

"I don't know whether he is or not," said Rembrandt. "But we've got to act as if he is, don't we?"

There was a resigned murmur of agreement, and the cadre of Omega Company scattered to prepare—as best they could—for General Blitzkrieg.

5

Journal #789—

During the settlement of Cut 'N' Shoot considerable effort went into re-creating the ambience of "the Old West," even down to details not strictly necessary to the functioning of the colony as a vacation spot. Evidently it was felt that tourists—on whom the colony placed much of its hope for income—would expect, upon a visit to the Old West, to encounter Indians, as the aboriginal inhabitants of that legendary territory were designated.

Unfortunately, the historical evidence on these people is rather contradictory. There were evidently three groups to whom the title was applied, and the founders of Cut 'N' Shoot were uncertain just which ones to incorporate into their re-creation. A committee chosen to solve the problem arrived at the Solomonic decision to invite all three groups to participate. And so, East, West, and Wild Indians all arrived and set up villages where tourists could appreciate their exotic lifestyles.

I for one could never understand how the founders could ignore the evidence, plain as the noses on their faces, that the aboriginals of a territory known as the Old West must have been the West Indians. This group, with its quaint traditions of cricket matches, carnival season, and rum-laced drinks, was easily the most exotic we saw during our entire visit.

"Man, you really look stupid," said Do-Wop, pointing at Sushi's furry chaps, fringed vest, and ten-gallon hat.

"Yeah, well, you'll look even stupider trying to ride a robosteed wearing a Legion uniform," said Sushi. "In fact, you look . . ."

"Don't say it," warned Do-Wop, cocking a fist threateningly. He looked mournfully at the bed, where his own Western outfit was laid out. Like Sushi's, it had been provided—supposedly at no extra charge—by the stable that rented them the robosteeds they were going to ride west in search of the captain.

Sushi grinned. "I'll just think it, then. Come on, buckaroo. Get your duds on, and let's go ridin'."

"You ever been on a robosteed before?" asked Do-Wop, picking up the hat. "I don't like the looks of 'em."

"Just another kind of machine," said Sushi. "Think of it as a hovercycle with hair. Chocolate Harry would understand."

"Harry wouldn't wear this crap," said Do-Wop. He looked at himself in the mirror, then flung the hat back on the bed.

"I doubt they make it his size," said Sushi; then he shook his head. "Cancel that—this *is* a tourist world. They've probably got it in all the sizes, patterns, and colors you ever thought of, and a few you wish you hadn't."

"I wish I hadn't thought of coming here," said Do-Wop, rolling his eyes.

"At least this once, it wasn't your dumb idea," said

Sushi. "Blame it on Remmie and Armstrong. Or maybe on the captain, since it was his idea to come after Beeker."

"Yeah," griped Do-Wop. "How come he didn't just call in some of his family connections? I mean, that's what any Italian would do."

"In case you didn't notice, the captain's not Italian," said Sushi. "But I wondered about that, too. Seems like a waste of his time to come looking for Beeker when he could hire a whole team of detectives to do the job for him."

"Well, maybe he just wanted to get away from the base for a while," said Do-Wop, dismissing the question from his mind nearly as quickly as he'd asked it. "The real kicker is why he decided to come to this joint. I can only think of about nine hundred more interesting planets to come to . . ."

"Well, this place was Beeker's choice, not the captain's," said Sushi. "Or maybe it was Nightingale's—who knows? When we catch them, we can ask them why they came here."

"Sure," said Do-Wop. "Tell me again why we gotta wear these stupid outfits to catch 'em."

"These are special riding outfits," Sushi explained. "We're going to wear them so we don't tear up our uniforms riding across the countryside. And we have to ride across the countryside because that's the only way to get around on this planet—unless you just happen to be going someplace you can reach by stagecoach. Or unless you feel like walking the whole way."

"Forget about that walking bit, anyway," said Do-Wop. "I done all the walking I could stomach in Legion Basic, marching here and there and everywhere, as if there wasn't any such thing as hoverjeeps or space liners. What's the deal with those stagecoaches? How do we know there ain't one going where we want to go?"

"We don't, because we don't know where we want to go yet," said Sushi, patiently. "If we have the robosteeds, we can go anywhere, whenever we want to. With the stagecoach, we can only go to other towns on the route, and we have to go on their schedule."

"Stupid freakin' world," said Do-Wop, pulling on the chaps. "Hey, you think Beeker's wearin' these stupid fuzzy pants? That'd be a laugh."

"Who knows?" said Sushi. "The sooner we find him, the sooner you'll find out. And the sooner you finish getting dressed . . ."

"OK, OK, I get the idea," said Do-Wop. He put on his vest and hat and stood back. "How stupid do I look?"

"You don't really want to know," said Sushi, moving to the door. "Come on, the sooner we find Beeker, the sooner you can lose the fuzzy pants."

"Best news I've heard all week," said Do-Wop, following.

Buck Short took Phule down the wooden sidewalk outside the saloon to the local Andromatic livery stable to hire a robot horse for their expedition into Injun territory, as the area outside town was known. Far from being the backwater world Phule had been led to expect, Cut 'N' Shoot appeared to be a hotbed of economic activity. New buildings were going up on all sides, and there was a steady stream of delivery vehicles—Conestoga wagons pulled by teams of reliable roboxen and robohoss-drawn buckboards— coming down the main street from the spaceport and heading down a road out into the country.

Phule nodded, approvingly. "Looks like a lively town here," he said. "Business seems to be booming."

"Yep," said Buck Short. "I been here two years, goin' on three, and the place has jumped up like a hound dog that set down on a cactus. Anybody lookin' to make a little dinero, he ain't got no business tryin' if he can't make it on Cut 'N' Shoot."

"That's the kind of place I like to hear about," said Phule. "Say—if you knew a fellow with a few dollars to put into an up-and-coming business, where do you think he'd get the biggest bang for his buck?"

"I can promise you one hell of a bang if somebody put a couple thou into my personal entertainment fund," said Buck Short, deadpan. Then, seeing Phule shake his head, he shrugged. "Can't blame a feller for tryin', can you? But I reckon the main business hereabouts, after the tourist trade, is gonna be the minin'. It was started out more or less for the frontier atmosphere, but I reckon it's gonna end up being one of the major planetary commodities."

"I'm not sure I'd want to count on that," said Phule. "From what I know about mining, most planets have pretty much the same mineral composition. Most of the time, it's a lot cheaper to mine something locally than to bring it in from off-world. So it's very unusual for a planet to build its economy on mineral exports—not even precious metals or gemstones are likely to be worth the freight charges."

"Well, Cap'n, that's generally the straight-ahead truth," said Short. "But conditions on Cut 'N' Shoot ain't conditions anywhere else, y'know. What we got here is a mother lode of a *u*-nique metal you can't get on no other planet in the sector."

"A rare metal, eh?" said Phule. "That sounds interesting. What exactly is it?"

"Ah, well, maybe I shouldn't say too much more," said Short. "Folks that run the place, they got their trade secrets—and I reckon it might not be too healthy for a feller that stuck his nose in where it don't belong."

Phule shrugged. "That's not the way I see it," he said. "I don't need to know their trade secrets—I just need enough to decide whether I want to buy some of their stock. If they've put together a solid business plan, I'm willing to bet they can pay me a respectable profit on my investment. But I'm not going to give them my money until I know what they're going to do with it."

"Well, I already told you what I'd do with it," said Short, pouting. "I could put on a right good show if somebody give a piece of change to get myself started . . ."

"I'm sure you could," said Phule, with a fixed smile. Then he pointed to the sign facing them. It read, BUDDY'S ROBOT LIVERY STABLE: SALES AND RENTALS. "But isn't this the place we were going to find a horse for me? Let's take care of that—I suspect we'll have plenty of time to talk once we're on the trail."

"You're the boss," said Buck Short, and he fell in behind Phule, who'd already bustled through the door to the livery stable. The door led to a cramped front room decorated with riding tack and bales of hay; behind an antique steel-and-plastic desk sat a man wearing spurred cowboy boots, chaps, and red suspenders; in the pocket of his denim shirt was an antique 'puter of the Palm Pilot variety. A battered Stetson and a wisp of straw between his front teeth completed the picture. Buck Short strolled right up to him, and said, "Howdy, Buddy. My off-world friend here got to rent him a hoss. Reckon you better give him a right tame one—don't believe he's done much ridin' before."

"Oh, I guess I've done my share," said Phule, who'd spent many a long childhood summer at the family's country estates, where riding to hounds was still a traditional pastime. Not even the most curmudgeonly of the family elders ever complained that the hounds and their quarry were all simulated, and most of the horses mechanical . . . tradition was tradition, even if it had to be helped along a bit by modern technology.

The man behind the desk wasn't listening. "City boy, huh?" he muttered, casting a skeptical look at Phule's Legion uniform and rubbing his chin. "I guess we can find *somethin'*," Buddy said at last. "Worse comes to worst, we can recalibrate one of the spare cayuses so this boy won't fall off and hurt himself. If'n we modulate the spirit circuits on these bots far enough down, we can make 'em so gentle they won't wake up a sleepin' baby. Not that we get all that many sleepin' babies askin' to ride, har har."

"Uh, that really won't be necessary," Phule began again.

But Buddy had already picked up his communicator. "Hey, Jake," he said. "Got us a city boy here, needs a hoss he won't fall off of and get a boo-boo. Can y' fix 'im one up? Uh-huh. Yeah, that's fine. All right then, stranger," he said turning back to Phule. "It'll cost you an extra five hundred setup charge. Jake'll have it in just 'bout an hour. Go on down to the tenderfoot bar and have a glass of sasparilly and it'll be ready just about when you're done. And I sure do 'preciate the business."

"Much obliged, Buddy," said Buck Short, with a wink.

"But I didn't . . ." protested Phule.

"Oh, think nothin' of it, stranger," said Buddy. "Any friend of Buck's gets the full A-Number-One treatment, and no mistake. You jes' come on back in an hour's time and Jake'll have you the gentlest robohoss you ever laid eyes on, all ready to go."

His eyes glazed over, Phule allowed Buck to lead him out of the livery stable and down the street.

"What makes you so certain my butler's been captured by the Indians?" Phule asked the weather-beaten cowpoke on the robohorse next to him.

Buck Short spat into the weeds beside the trail. "That's purty much the only plot option hereabouts," he said, soberly. He sported a four-or-five-day growth of beard, a plug of tobacco in one cheek, and crossed eyes that made it hard to tell where he was looking—especially when he was about to spit. He looked more or less at Phule, and said, "Ain't like there's anybody 'cept the Injuns in the capturin' business on Cut 'N' Shoot, 'less'n you done heard somethin' I ain't."

"I see," said Phule, dubiously. "Let me rephrase that, then. What makes you so sure he's been captured at all?"

"I reckon if he had any selection, he'd be back in the saloon, jes' like the rest of the boys," said the cowpoke. "He ain't got a job, he ain't in the saloon—you figger it out, pilgrim."

"In other words, there's nothing else to do in these parts," said Phule. "Why is the planet trying to attract tourists, then?"

"Weren't none of my idea. Alls they do is drive up the prices," Short said, looking either at Phule's left ear or somewhere off behind him. "And the stores is full of fancy-pants city stuff, cappychino 'stead of reg'lar coffee, furrin wines instead of good ol' country rotgut. Don't know what the durn place is comin' to."

"Sorry to hear that," said Phule. "So if Beeker and his lady friend have been captured by the Indians, what do you suggest I do about it?"

"Same as any red-blooded hombre would do," answered Short. "Git on yer horse and go find 'em. Then make 'em sorry they done it."

Phule looked down. "Well, it looks like I already am on my horse," he said.

"Smart feller," said the cowpoke. "I reckon you know what to do next, then."

"Right," said Phule. But almost before the word was out of his mouth, Buck Short had spurred Dale-8 toward the nearby town, and was out of earshot. Lacking any other plan, he sped up his own horse and rode to overtake Short. "Which way are the Indians?" he asked, as he pulled abreast of him.

"How the tarnation am I supposed to know?" said the cowpoke, testily. At least one of his eyes glared at Phule. "Do I look like an Injun to you?"

Phule couldn't quite tell whether he'd grievously insulted Buck, but he hastened to calm the cowpoke down. "Sorry, friend, I didn't mean anything by it," he said. "I just need to find the Indians—and the fellow you think they've kidnapped. Do you know anybody I might ask who would know where they are?"

"Maybe you ought to ask Ol' Ben," said the cowpoke. "He's out on the range, usually. You jes' head west out o' town, and when you get to Brownsville, take that right-hand road. Then look out purt' sharp, and when you see a big cloud o' dust off to the west side, that's sure as shootin' gone to be Ol' Ben's herd. He'll be there with 'em. You tell 'im Jeb sent you."

"All right," said Phule. "Thanks, Jeb."

"Tarnation, *I* ain't Jeb," said the cowpoke, glaring at Phule with an insulted expression. "What's wrong with your memory, pilgrim? I done told you, my name's Buck Short."

"Excuse me?" Phule squinted, puzzled. "Then why do you want me to say Jeb sent me?"

"'Cause that's the *word*," said the cowpoke, with the air of a man explaining the obvious. "Same as if you wants to start a robohorse movin', you got to say *gitty-up*, instead of *let's go* or *move yer arse*. You can't go changing words around and 'spect things to work like they're 'sposed to."

"I see," said Phule. "I head west out of town, take the right-hand road in Brownsville, big cloud of dust—Old Ben's there. I tell him Jeb sent me, and he can tell me the way to the Indians."

"Yer durn tootin'," said Buck Short, with obvious approval, and with that he turned his robosteed and headed on into town, leaving Phule to find his own way to Ol' Ben and the Indians.

Chocolate Harry scowled at the requisition form Lieutenant Armstrong had just handed him, then looked up, and growled, "This is gonna be *really* expensive, y'know? I mean, none of this is standard Legion materiel. I'm gonna have to go to an outside supplier. And you *gotta* be kiddin' about when you want it by . . ."

"The captain's footing the bill, and Lieutenant Rembrandt set the deadline," said Armstrong, stiffly. "If you want to dispute an order from your commanding officers, it'll be your neck on the line. You'd be a lot better off just getting everything ordered, first. Then if you want to waste your breath arguing with the captain, you can do it after he gets back without delaying the project any more. And if he does change his mind, you can send the supplies back afterward—and tell everybody you told them so."

"Uh, right on, Lieutenant," said Chocolate Harry, with a grin. Mentally, he was already calculating which of the supplies he could divert to his own purposes. Was there a way to make some kind of booze out of "fast-setting, low-watering, E-Z-Gro Kentucky bluegrass seed"? If it could be done, he wouldn't bet against one of the Omega Mob figuring out a way . . . Harry grinned and reached for a Supply catalog as Armstrong left the Supply depot, apparently satisfied.

Twenty minutes later, Harry's brow was furrowed, and a string of increasingly foul curses had crossed his lips. Finally he lifted his wrist communicator to his mouth. "Yo, Double-X, get your butt in here."

"Uh, right, C.H.," came the reply. A moment later his clerk ambled in the door. "Whassup?" said Double-X, leaning against the file cabinet.

"What's up is the company's going into the goddamn golf business," growled Harry. "Armstrong brought this list of stuff over, and there's next to none of it we can get from the regular sources, which means I can't get my regular rake-offs. How am I supposed to make a living?"

"What's *supposed* to happen is you get a Legion paycheck," said Double-X, smirking. He quickly dodged behind the file cabinet as Chocolate Harry threw the catalog at his head.

"You ain't so good at this job that I can't get somebody else to do it," bellowed the Supply sergeant. "Now shut up and listen. We got to get the stuff on this list, and I'm putting you on the case."

"Aw right, Sarge," said Double-X, taking the list from Harry's outstretched hand. He glanced down the page, then asked, "Usual deal, right—biggest kickback gets the sale?"

Chocolate Harry paused a moment before answering. "Usually I wouldn't even think twice about it," he said at last. "But this time, no—it's gotta be delivery speed."

Double-X whistled. "Man, this has to be serious. I never knowed you to pass up a little extra pocket money."

Harry shrugged. "Well, you know me. I like my gravy, just like the next guy. But the whole company's under the gun, so just this once, I'm gonna take one for the team. Whoever gets us the stuff the fastest gets the deal, and that's the whole story."

Double-X nodded. "Sure, Sarge." He paused, then asked softly, "Cap'n's in some kind of trouble, ain't he?"

"Man, you didn't hear it from me, OK?" said Harry, looking around the Supply shed that, as usual, was empty except for the two of them. "We got to play it close to the vest, Double-X. The rest of the company is gonna find out soon enough, when they have to put things together. But for now, we're bringing this stuff in on the QT, and it's gotta be smooth. I'm trusting you, 'cause you're the one dude I know can keep things quiet. Got it?"

Double-X's face was serious, now. "Yeah, Sarge, I'm your man. I'll get the stuff so fast you won't have time to wonder where it's comin' from." He took the list and went over to his own desk. Before long, he was fast at work on his console.

"I reckon Ol' Ben's the only one 'round here'd know thet, stranger," said the cowpoke sitting on a wooden bench by the saloon entrance.

"OK, if you say so," said Sushi. "Where do we find Ol' Ben?"

The cowpoke pointed down the street. "That-a-way, out

on the range. Head west out o' town; when you get to Brownsville, take that right-hand road. Then when you see a big cloud o' dust off to the west side, that's Ol' Ben's herd, sure as shootin'. He'll be right there with 'em. You tell 'im Jeb sent you."

"All right," said Sushi. "Thanks, Jeb."

"Tarnation, *I* ain't Jeb," said the cowpoke, exasperation personified.

"I don't get it, man," said Do-Wop, scratching his head. "If you ain't Jeb, why you want us to say Jeb sent us?"

" 'Cause that's the *word*," said the cowpoke. "Same as if you wants to start a robohorse movin', it's *gitty-up*, 'stead of *move yer arse*. You can't 'spect anything to work the way it's 'sposed to if'n you go usin' the wrong words."

"That almost makes sense," said Sushi. "West out of town, right-hand road in Brownsville, big cloud of dust. Jeb sent me."

"That's the ticket, sonny," said the cowpoke, benignly. "Say, you oughta buy a feller a drink when he gives you good advice like thet," he said, turning one of his eyes on Sushi. The other seemed to be aimed somewhere off in the distance.

Sushi began, "I don't know if we've got the—"

"Always time for a drink," said Do-Wop. "Say, what's your name, buddy?"

"Well it ain't Buddy any more'n it's Jeb. It's Buck," said the cowpoke, rising from the bench. "And this here's the best place I know of for a drink. Not that there's very many bad ones."

Recognizing which way the wind was blowing, Sushi went to the bar and returned shortly with a pitcher of beer and three glasses. He set the glasses on the table but didn't pour any beer. "All right," he said, leaning forward on his elbows. "As long as we're in the business of buying information, let's make sure we're getting something worth the price."

"Yo, Soosh, I'm on *your* team," said Do-Wop, making a grab for the pitcher. Sushi batted his hand away.

"Yeah, so you can wait until I'm ready to pour the drinks," said Sushi. "I want to find out what else Buck knows about Old Ben, and about where the captain might have gone—or maybe even Beeker and Nightingale."

Buck Short frowned. "Nightingale? She some kind of singer?"

Sushi looked at Do-Wop and raised an eyebrow. "Funny—I don't remember saying Nightingale was a she. Do you remember me saying that?"

"Hey, I wasn't hardly listen—OOF!" said Do-Wop, as Sushi kicked him under the table. He shot a dirty look at his partner, then belatedly caught the hint. "Uh, no, Soosh—you didn't say nothin' at all about Nightingale bein' a female. Where'd you get that idea, Buck?"

"Well, it's a girly kind o' name, ain't it?" said Buck Short. "'Sides, there was one young lady come through a while back, never did get her name, but she was with a kind of dignified older feller, and wearin' the kind of outfit you said she might be wearin'. So it kind of makes sense she's the one you're talkin' about, don't it, now."

"Maybe it does," said Sushi, directing a doubtful stare at Buck. "But I think you better tell us a little more about this young lady you saw. Where did she and her 'older feller' go? Has anybody else been asking about them?"

"You want me to answer all them questions without a drink? My throat's like to get awful dry . . ." Buck Short put on his most pitiful expression.

"Answer, and you'll get your drink," said Sushi, mildly. "Unless we don't like your answers . . . My friend here can get mighty cross when we don't like answers." He nodded toward Do-Wop, who was scowling fiercely—most likely at the prospect of having to wait for beer, himself. But there was nothing to be gained by letting Buck know that.

It took a few more not-very-subtle threats, but before

long Buck was drinking his beer—and talking up a blue streak. At last, the pitcher was done, and so was the cowpoke. He laid his arms on the table, set his head down on them, and fell almost immediately asleep.

"Well, I guess we've found out what we need to know," said Sushi. "Let's go see what we can do about it."

"Ya sure?" said Do-Wop, looking at the empty pitcher. "If this hayseed wakes up, he might remember some other stuff."

"And cost us a lot more time and bucks," said Sushi. "Let's get on the case while there's still a case to get onto." He grabbed his partner by the arm and out the door they went.

6

Journal #790—

My employer's military career exemplifies one major strategy for success in life: He has never missed an opportunity to build one success into another. Consider the incident on Haskin's Planet, where, entirely by accident, he encountered members of an alien race—a situation loaded with opportunities for horrendous blunders. To my employer's credit, he kept his wits about him, and not only avoided conflict but struck a commercial bargain with the Zenobians, as the aliens called themselves. In addition, he made a friend of the alien commander, Flight Leftenant Qual—who, as it turned out, was destined to become a highly admired hero among his own race.

That might have been a significant accomplishment for most officers; few sophonts are lucky enough to make a first contact with an alien race. But my employer managed to pyramid that initial success into a plum assignment as the commander of the Alliance military mission to Zenobia. A significant posting for a mere captain.

It seems almost irrelevant to note that his superiors believed that they were sending my employer into a position on a backward world from which they sincerely hoped he would never emerge. Little did they think that he would thrive in the post, and that, in the end, they would be coming to Zenobia themselves.

"Listen up, squad, here's Lieutenant Rembrandt to tell us what we've been waiting for," said Brandy, and Thumper was all ears. Everyone in the squad had been trying to guess what kind of exercise the top sergeant had planned for General Blitzkrieg's visit to Zenobia Base. Some of the legionnaires said it was going to be an obstacle course demonstration—that being one of Omega Company's specialties. Others expected some kind of live ammo drill simulating an attack on the camp, or perhaps a march into the desert around the camp, to show off the variety of Zenobian wildlife.

Lieutenant Rembrandt stepped forward, with a nice smile that Thumper thought didn't entirely hide the worry on her face. "Good morning," she said. "I guess you've all heard that we're expecting an inspection by General Blitzkrieg."

"Yeah, and the old wingnut thinks he's gonna surprise us," said a voice from behind Thumper—Street, it sounded like.

"Right," said Rembrandt. "Except we're going to have a few surprises ready for *him*. That's where you guys come in . . ."

"Lieutenant Rembrandt, I have a question," said Mahatma. The squad fell silent. Mahatma's questions were always worth listening to—even though they made the

noncoms and officers nervous. Now that he'd been part-
nered with Mahatma, Thumper had a better idea why. The
little legionnaire was always looking for ways to shake
things up—to keep everyone on their toes, he said. Asking
a question that nobody had a good answer for was a sure
way to do that.

"Go ahead, Mahatma," said Rembrandt, nodding in the
direction of the questioner.

"The captain is away from base, is that not correct?"
said Mahatma.

"Yeah, everybody knows that," said Rembrandt. "But he
hasn't gone far. He's out in the desert, negotiating with the
Namoids. I'll need a party to go out into the desert—Flight
Leftenant Qual will be in command. And I'd like the others
to be Mahatma and Brick and Double-X and Garbo.
You've all been to the area I'm interested in, so you'll
know the ground better than anyone else I could send."

"Oh ho," said Mahatma, stroking his chin and nodding.
The others in the group Rembrandt had named were nodding, too. "I remember that area. It is where we went to
rescue the captain when he was captured."

"That's right," said Rembrandt, a twinkle in her eyes.
"But you have to get out there and back without any wasted
time so he's here when the general arrives. I'd like you to
be ready to leave by sundown tonight; Qual will meet you
at Chocolate Harry's as soon as you're dismissed here, to
pick up your supplies and get your final orders. You'll have
a little time to straighten out anything you need to take care
of before you leave, and then you're out of here. Got it?"

"Yes, Remmie," chorused the group, in near unison.

"Now, the other half of my plan," said Rembrandt.
"Word from Headquarters has it that the general loves to
play golf—which is an Old Earth game involving funny
clubs and little balls and a lot of open ground with holes in
it. I don't know much about the game, but if what I hear is

true, once the general starts playing, he hardly has time for anything else. So we're going to give him a chance to play, to keep him off our backs."

"How we gonna do that?" said Street, scratching his head. "Ain't no golf field here, last time I looked—just lots of desert full of bugoids and funny lizards."

"You're right, Street," said Rembrandt. "We don't have a golf course—yet. But Lieutenant Armstrong's played the game, and he knows what a course is supposed to be like. And from what he says, you can make almost any useless tract of land into a golf course, if you really want to. Harry's also working on getting some clubs sent in. Anyhow, the rest of Brandy's squad are assigned to Armstrong, and you're going to build a golf course. You've got to build it in record time, too, because we want it ready to play on the minute the general gets here. The better the general likes it, the less trouble he's likely to cause the rest of us."

"Do we get to play on the course when it is built?" said Tusk-anini. "Some of the old books I have read mention golf, and I have often wondered how it is played."

"Sure," said Rembrandt, shrugging. "Once the general's gone, it's there for anybody in the company to play on. Which ought to give you even more reason to do a really good job, right? OK, all of you report to Lieutenant Armstrong, outside the Supply depot in fifteen minutes. Any more questions? No? OK, squad dismissed!"

Phule felt as if he'd been bouncing across the prairies of Cut 'N' Shoot on his robosteed for weeks without a rest. In reality, it was just a day and a half since he'd lit out in search of the Indians who had supposedly captured Beeker and Nightingale. Why the Indians would have kidnapped the butler and medic was beyond his ability to understand; but if the other locals with whom he'd had dealings were at all typical, logic didn't have a whole lot to do with how people acted on this planet.

Fortunately, a stretch as a captain in the Space Legion, and commanding officer of Omega Company, had prepared Phule for dealing with illogic in all its glory. He chuckled as he thought of his crew of misfits and rejects, supposedly the dregs of the Legion—until he'd got hold of them and made them into a tight-knit crew that had overcome every obstacle put in their way. The Omega Mob had a distinctly unregulation way of dealing with its challenges; but the Omega way got results, and that was all that mattered to Phule. Now that he faced his own unexpected challenge, the least he could do was to overcome it in the same style and spirit as his own legionnaires.

Which he intended to do as soon as he reached the place Ol' Ben had told him the Indians camped this time of year. He'd have been there long since if he'd been able to take a hoverjeep—but the rulers of Cut 'N' Shoot were fanatics for authenticity, and nothing faster than a robosteed was permitted. He had no doubt that a few hundred credits in the right hands would have uncovered exceptions to that policy. But he'd been in too much of a hurry to catch the runaways to stop and feed the hungry bureaucratic maw— or so he'd thought. Now he was paying for his impatience with saddle sores.

All morning he'd been urging the robosteed westward through a particularly inhospitable landscape—Ol' Ben had referred to it as the "badlands," and Phule could see why. But he had good reason to think he was nearing his destination. When he'd started out, there'd been the merest hint of a column of smoke on the horizon ahead. It had gradually grown thicker, and now the breeze carried a tantalizing aroma of mesquite—and something else. Somebody was cooking, and Phule had an idea that if he could just get his robosteed to move a little faster, he might be there in time for lunch. Whether anybody would offer him anything to eat remained to be seen, but he hadn't gotten as far as he had by being a pessimist.

The robosteed was stoically plodding up a narrow gulch when a tall figure suddenly appeared, holding a hand up palm forward, in the universal halt sign. "You best be stopping dere, mon," said the figure in a resonant alto voice. It was a tall woman in colorful, flowing robes, her long dark hair in a multitude of braids. She did not display any kind of weapon, but both her voice and her presence radiated authority.

"Good morning," said Phule, pulling the robosteed to a halt and raising his own hand in a similar gesture to hers. "I'm looking for two people . . ."

"Maybe you find dem, if dey want you to," said the woman, crossing her arms in front of her. "What makes you think dey be here?"

"Everyone back in town said the Indians took them . . ." Phule began.

"Oh, sure, mon, blame de Indian," said the woman. "What dey know back in town, anyway? Dey think all Indians be the same."

"Well, I'm a stranger here, myself," said Phule. Realizing he hadn't given his name, he added, "I'm Captain Jester, of the Space Legion."

"Captain," said the woman, nodding. "I am glad to know de name. People call me Rita."

Phule nodded back. "A pleasure to meet you, Rita. So, if the folks back in town are wrong about the Indians, maybe you can set me right." He paused, looking the woman up and down. "Uh—you *are* an Indian, aren't you?"

"Oh yes, West Indian," said Rita. She pointed to the north. "You go a little bit dat-a-way, you find de East Indians. And de other way, you find de Red Indians, or de Wild Indians, de tourists like to call dem. Which kind of Indian are you wanting to find, Captain?"

"I don't know which kind," said Phule, now perplexed. "A fellow in town told me the people I'm lookin for were probably captured by the Indians. He didn't tell me there were so many kinds of Indians . . ."

"I told you dey townspeople don't know 'bout Indians," Rita scoffed. "Who dese people you trying to find? Friends of yours?"

"I guess you could call them that," said Phule. "I'm looking for two people, a man and woman traveling together . . ."

Rita cut him off with a laugh. "You know how many tourists fit dat picture? Almost everybody who come here, dey come in couples. You may be de only single man I see dis year, and you say you not a tourist. So how I know dem if I see dem?"

"Hmmm . . ." said Phule, trying to think of a way to distinguish Beeker and Nightingale from other tourist couples. "An older man with a younger woman," he said. "She's maybe thirty, tall and dark-skinned like you. He's shorter and about forty-five—I think. I don't know how they're dressed—the last time I saw them, she was wearing the same kind of uniform I am, and he was in a dark suit. But I doubt they're wearing that on their vacation . . ."

Rita nodded. "Captain, come wit' me." She turned and began to walk back up the trail Phule had been following.

"Wait—where are you taking me?" he said, putting his robosteed into forward mode again.

"We goin' to see de Mon," said Rita, and Phule had nothing to do but to follow her.

Chocolate Harry looked out over the large plot he'd just marked off to the south of Zenobia Base. It was about the most worthless piece of land in the vicinity; good for a practice bombing range, if Omega Company had included any bomber pilots it wanted to turn loose on some simulated targets. Or maybe the plot would've been good enough to con some gullible investor into a land deal, although Harry was fairly sure that no investor who actually laid eyes on the place was likely to buy it. After all, even the Zenobians had no particular use for it—at least, not until they'd ended up leasing it to the Legion as part of Zenobia Base.

Now he'd been ordered to turn it into a golf course. Lieutenant Armstrong had drawn up a set of plans for three golf holes—all they'd have the time to build before General Blitzkrieg arrived on base. It was going to be Harry's job to take that worthless patch of ground and make Armstrong's plan a reality.

Things had come along reasonably well, he had to admit. He'd already turned loose a couple of squads with flamethrowers to get rid of the worst of the gnarly Zenobian desert vegetation. Heavy earthmovers would follow, doing what they could to turn the brutal ravine-crossed terrain into something a sane sophont might want to take an occasional recreational stroll over. With any luck, the brush fires and rumbling machines would have driven off at least the larger local predators by the time he sent the squads back out for pick-and-shovel work.

But to judge by the reports coming back from the construction gangs, it wasn't the large predators that were going to be a problem. The whole area was apparently the prime breeding grounds for some kind of Zenobian critter—Flight Leftenant Qual had identified them as "florbigs," and dismissed them as harmless. Harmless they may have been, and there were even a few of the legionnaires who thought they were "sorta cute," as Brick put it. They also had an unfortunate habit of darting out of the underbrush to steal any small object left unattended for more than a moment. This included hand tools, the workers' lunch, and the occasional article of apparel. And they were fast—most of the time, the workers never got a glimpse of them until they were scurrying away with somebody's sandwich. Harry's first instinct was to send out another flamethrower squad to get rid of the vermin, once and for all.

But Harry made the mistake of asking Lieutenant Rembrandt's permission, which was when he learned of a provision in the treaty that Captain Jester had signed with the Zenobians—a clause inserted on the insistence of the Extraterrestrial Protection Agency, forbidding the Legion to harass any local creature, no matter what the natives thought of the matter. And despite his attempts to prove the contrary, toasting the critters with flamethrowers was definitely a form of harassment. This left Harry with two choices: hire a squad of Zenobians to get rid of the florbigs or put up with them. After a discreet inquiry as to the going rate for local exterminators, he reluctantly chose the latter option.

Then there was some kind of gravitational anomaly in the middle of the tract. Nothing big and dangerous, like a stray white hole, but definitely something that didn't match the gravitational profile of the rest of the plot of land. Harry'd sent a crew out to locate it, but the best they could do was report that it was something like a hundred yards underground, more trouble than it was worth to try to dig up. Besides, its profile on the surface was almost small enough to ignore entirely—an area about twenty feet across that, gravitationally, acted as if it were a sharp pinnacle instead of a flat surface. That would've been almost no problem at all—if it hadn't been smack in the middle of something Armstrong's plan marked as "second fairway." Harry didn't know what a fairway was, but according to the plan he had to get grass to grow on it. That was going to be tricky . . .

Then Harry shrugged. The antigrav anomaly meant that none of the players was ever going to have a ball land in the area. He might as well just leave it alone. It couldn't possibly affect the game—could it?

• • •

Flight Leftenant Qual took a hefty swing and watched the ball fly down the driving range, curving rapidly from left to right. It was remarkable how a hard little sphere, no bigger than a *vlort* egg, could display such unpredictable aerodynamic effects when launched into the air with one of the striking objects—*golf clubs*, the humans called them, although the phrase seemed to have more than one meaning. The rocket scientists could undoubtedly learn something from the performance of the little spheres, although Qual had no idea whether it would be useful. He thought it unlikely to have much value as a weapon unless its accuracy could be improved—a task at which he had been laboring for some time now.

Qual understood that one of the humans' chief leaders, General Blitzkrieg, was on his way to Zenobia to harass the members of Omega Company. Strong-arm seemed to believe that a display of proficiency in launching the golf balls would make the general less harsh toward the local humans. This made some sense if the balls were to be used as weapons, but it seemed that only the officers were being encouraged to launch them. Qual had noticed that in most human military organizations, the officers exposed themselves to danger as little as possible, avoiding the active use of weapons. His good friend Captain Clown seemed to be an exception to that rule, as he was in so many other ways.

Perhaps the balls, like the swords and spears his own race had employed in the distant past, were obsolete weapons used only in symbolic combat. Many human officers seemed to enjoy such symbolic combats—fencing, boxing, driving vehicles at unsafe speeds—so perhaps golf belonged in that category. One of the meanings of "club" did appear to refer to a kind of weapon—although Strong-arm had made it clear to Qual that it was extremely bad form to bash one's opponents' heads with the golf

clubs. Humans were a curious species—but Qual already
knew that.

He removed another ball from the bucket and balanced it
on the conical plastic support called, for some nonobvious
reason, a "tea." It rested there while he addressed it with his
club. (It had taken him a little while to understand that one
did not actually need to inscribe the ball with the name of
the place one intended to send it—though it occurred to him
that perhaps if one did, it might arrive there more reliably.)
He lifted the club—called a "chauffeur," again for reasons
undiscoverable by simple logic—keeping his left elbow
straight, as Strong-arm had instructed him. A swift downward movement of the club and this ball soared off to join
its companion, somewhere in the brush on the right fringe
of the driving range. This was a sort of progress; the last
few shots had ended up in more or less the same place.

Qual was taking the next ball out of the bucket when his
translator spoke to him. "Greetings, Flight Leftenant Qual.
How satisfactory to you is your progress in the practice of
hitting balls with the chauffeur golf club?" Or words to
that effect; Qual had long since learned that the translator's
output was not to be taken as utterly reliable. Much depended on both context and on the actual speaker's choice
of language. He looked up to see the legionnaire known as
Thumper, a nonhuman like himself.

"Greetings, Dull Noisemaker," Qual replied. "My progress remains uncertain; I have only recently managed to
place several consecutive balls in a tight pattern. Unfortunately, that pattern is far to one side of my point of aim."

Thumper made a movement with his head that, when
humans did it, signified understanding or agreement. He
said something which Qual's translator interpreted as,
"That is an awkwardness. I hope it would not be impertinent for someone of limited experience to suggest realign-
ing your point of aim to compensate."

"That is a very rational suggestion," said Qual, putting the golf club over his shoulder. "Of course, it requires consistency of effect, which is what I now strive to attain. With such a realigned aiming point, it would be a misfortune inadvertently to strike a ball so that it flies absolutely straight."

"Agreement," said Thumper. "Consistency is the usual result of assiduous application, so we can hope that principle will apply in this case."

"I appreciate your encouragement," said Qual. "I intend to exert myself to that end." After a pause, he added, "Since this golf is a novel pursuit to my kind, I would appreciate any education you can offer me. I have not made great progress, but after all, this is only my first session. Perhaps you would even be so kind as to serve as my adviser during my attempts to compare golfing skills with the humans."

"Thank you, Flight Leftenant," said Thumper, via Qual's translator. "I would much appreciate the opportunity to assist you in your competition, but golf is hardly my specialty. Also, having fallen into General Blitzkrieg's ill graces through no fault of my own, I have been advised to hold myself as much as possible beyond the periphery of his awareness. I fear I will have to decline the invitation."

Qual thought for a moment, leaning on his driver. "Perhaps not," he said. "As a valued ally of the humans, I have certain privileges, including the choice of my own staff. If I elect to employ the services of one of their legionnaires, it should be seen as an honor to the Alliance, rather than a slight. And"—he paused for a moment—"if I have not guessed wrong, you have insights into human activities I am not likely to get from either a human or from one of my own species."

"The possibility exists," admitted Thumper. "It does appear to have the potential for amusement. But if you do not object, I wish to consider it a little more—and get the advice of a trusted acquaintance—before giving you a final answer."

"Utterly reasonable," said Qual. "And now, if it is not in conflict with your assigned Legion duties, I would appreciate your continued advice on my mode of striking the ball. Please be absolutely candid—it is to my benefit."

"With enthusiasm," the translator said, after Thumper had spoken. "Attempt a number of swings, and I will determine if I can detect anything of use."

"Very well," said Qual, stepping up to address the ball again. "Be alert! Anything might well occur!" He took a powerful swing, and again the ball flew on its way downrange . . .

"What the hell's that up ahead, Soosh?" Do-Wop asked, peering into the darkness that had fallen over the trail. It was clear what he was asking about; some distance away, there was a flickering of light, not quite steady enough to be artificial. They'd been following directions the general storekeeper in town had given them; but it had been dark for some time, and it was anybody's guess if they were still on the trail.

"I think those are fires," said Sushi, in a low voice. "If our map's right, that ought to be the Indian camp they told us about back in town. I think we're on the right track."

"Fires, huh?" said Do-Wop. He pointed to his wrist comm. "You think we oughta call the fire department, then? There must be half a dozen of 'em up there, burning away. Somebody might get hurt . . ."

Sushi shook his head. "Don't bother," he said. "I think they're supposed to be part of the Authentic Western Experience of Cut 'N' Shoot. From what I remember, they used to use open fires all the time on Old Earth, for cooking and light, and to keep wild animals away at night."

"Lousy way to run a planet," said Do-Wop. "Authentic Western Experience or not, I bet the Italians didn't do it that way."

"How do you think they did it?" said Sushi, hunkering down to peer ahead. "Porta-range furnaces? Pocket microwaves?"

"Sure," said Do-Wop, nonchalantly. "We invented everything else any good. Ice cream, pizza, beer . . ."

Sushi rolled his eyes. "Right," he said. "Maybe I'd believe you if I thought you knew enough history to find Italy on a map, which would surprise me no end, considering you can't find the Legion base on a map of Zenobia."

"Hey, I can read a map just as good as you can," said Do-Wop. "Besides, you're just jealous. Italians invented the mob, too, which your guys only got a stoopid-sounding copy of. What's it called, Yazooka? Is 'at some kinda chewin' gum, or what?"

"*Yakusa*," said Sushi. "Which to me, at least, doesn't sound any stupider than *Mafia*, if you want to know the truth."

"Yeah, huh? You call my uncle Nunzio stupid, you gonna find out whether you can walk wit' the fishes . . ."

"I thought it was sleeping with the fishes I was supposed to be worried about," said Sushi. "Y'know, if you're going to try to scare people, you ought to at least try to make a threat that makes sense."

"Ahh, that shows how much you know," said Do-Wop, poking his finger at Sushi's chest. "When I make a farkin' threat . . ."

"You make-um heap big noise," came a deep voice from out of the dark. "Heard you both a long way off, bump and crash like drum roll-um downhill. You lucky no wild animals here look-um for nice rump of paleface for supper."

"Who said that?" said Do-Wop, jumping. He peered out into the dark but could see nothing.

"I think the Indians just found *us*," said Sushi, standing up. "Hello, whoever you are. Can you take us to your leader?"

"What, you think we in some bad movie?" said the deep

voice again. A towering figure glided forward from the shadows, its facial features still obscured by the darkness.

"What's a movie?" asked Do-Wop, moving up alongside Sushi. Almost without thinking about it, he assumed a fighting stance.

"Like a tri-vee, only flat," said Sushi, absentmindedly. He put his weight on the balls of his feet, not in as aggressive a stance as Do-Wop, but still ready to respond if the stranger made a hostile move.

"You paleface boys look like you get ready kick-um ass," said the stranger, amusement in his voice. "Why you don't come smoke-um peace pipe instead? We talk, eat some good food, maybe do some business . . ."

"Food?" said Sushi, suddenly aware of his nearly empty stomach. "Gee, I guess I could use a bite to eat."

"Peace pipe?" said Do-Wop. "Yo, man, *lead the way.*"

7

Journal #793—

A man of fixed habits is thought by many to be unflappable, impossible to upset. As a man whom many would consider to be a prime example of that description, I can tell you frankly that the popular perception is only partly correct.

Granted, a regular routine is one of the best ways to prevent disturbance in one's life. If one knows that the mail arrives at ten o'clock, and that dinner is served at six, such events serve as anchors for the day's activities. Even when the mail is delayed, or when some family member is detained at work until past the dinner hour, one knows that these are aberrations. One adjusts to the variation, secure in the confidence that routine will reassert itself in due course. Indeed, this is one of the appeals of the military life—one of the few, I should add.

But there is an infallible way to disconcert a man of fixed habits, and that this is to deprive him of any routine what-

*soever. The most insidious way to do this is to send him off
on vacation . . .*

Lieutenant Armstrong gritted his teeth, staring out into the
Zenobian desert. There was a plume of dust rapidly ap-
proaching the camp across the arid landscape. General
Blitzkrieg was here. And that meant that, for the foresee-
able future, Omega Company was about to get some long-
deferred experience in the ugly side of life in the Legion.

Well, Armstrong had done his share of brownnosing
and kowtowing to irrational brass; he could undoubtedly
fall back into the routine if he had to. He'd never been
particularly good at it, which is why he'd ended up in
Omega Company instead of in some more desirable posting. That was before Captain Jester had come; back when
Omega Company was the rathole of the Legion, the
catchall for incorrigibles and incompetents no other unit
wanted. Considering that the Space Legion was widely
recognized as the rathole of the Alliance military, that
was saying a lot.

It was well-known that General Blitzkrieg still looked at
Omega Company as a rathole. In fact, he apparently preferred it that way. There had to be someplace so bad it
could be used to threaten anyone who got out of line or
failed to come up to the mark. As far as Armstrong could
figure it out, the general considered Omega Company his
personal property, and soundly resented Captain Jester's
turning it into the best outfit in the Legion.

It rarely occurred to Armstrong to question the wisdom
of a superior officer, let alone that of a general of the Legion. But when it came to Omega Company, he'd seen the
before and after versions with his own eyes and knew
which was better. In his considered opinion, General
Blitzkrieg was full of . . . well, "hot air" was one of the
more genteel expressions that came to Armstrong's mind.

Almost every member of Omega Company had a similarly low opinion of the general. That meant that Lieutenant Armstrong was going to have his hands full preventing the incident that the general had undoubtedly come here intending to provoke. And with the captain off-base—no, worse than that, completely out of reach—it was going to be a major chore to neutralize the general, even with Omega Company's officers babysitting him for the entire length of his visit. Even with the help of the entire command cadre, there was bound to be somebody who snapped. It might be Sergeant Escrima; it might be one of the recent recruits; it might even be the usually phlegmatic Tusk-anini. The problem was that nobody knew exactly who the general was going to go after, or how, and that meant that nobody could completely prepare for it.

But the general's hoverjeep had reached the perimeter of the camp. Now, it was too late for preparations. Anything that wasn't already done wasn't going to get done. Armstrong sighed, then pulled himself upright into his sharpest military posture and strode forward to greet the arriving vehicle.

Now that the dust cloud had begun to settle, Armstrong could see that the general's hoverjeep was a deluxe ultrastretch model, as much a limo as a jeep. Its exterior color was deep Legion black with tinted windows and antennas that, from their size and number, could pick up signals from all over the civilized galaxy. To judge by the size of the hood, it featured an especially powerful engine. On both sides and on the hood, an oversize Legion insignia was painted in gold, surrounded by general's stars. Armstrong had heard some commentator claim that a man's vehicle was an extension of his personality; if that was so, General Blitzkrieg was not a man to trifle with.

The hoverjeep slowed to a stop, settled onto its parking cushions, and the engine noise faded to a low hum. Armstrong stationed himself by the rear door, then nodded to Brandy, who'd brought along her training squad as an

honor guard and reception party. "Ten-HUT!" barked the
first sergeant, and to Armstrong's relief, the legionnaires
responded with almost commendable sharpness as a slim
woman in a major's uniform stepped out of the driver's
seat. She stepped around to the passenger side and opened
the door for a heavyset man—General Blitzkrieg.

Armstrong snapped off his best academy salute and
held it. But instead of returning the salute, the general
glared around the assembled troops and bellowed, "Where
the hell is that idiot Jester? He should have been here to
meet me. There'd better be a damned good explanation, or
I'm going to fry his ass!"

Right that moment, Lieutenant Armstrong knew it was
not going to be one of his better days.

General Blitzkrieg was doing his best to conceal his glee as
Sparrowhawk opened the door to let him emerge from his
hoverjeep. He'd known better than to expect his arrival on
Zenobia to be a total surprise. The damned military
grapevine was far too efficient for a general to travel
halfway across the Alliance without anyone's noticing and
warning his prospective hosts. So by all rights, Captain
Jester should have had at least some advance notice of the
general's impending inspection tour. In any case an honor
guard—if you wanted to dignify a couple dozen legionnaires by that name—had turned out to greet his arrival. So
Jester *did* have advance notice. And by age-old military
custom, Jester himself should have been at the landing site
to greet the arriving brass—putting the best face on the situation, even if he knew his miserable outfit was going to
fall short of the general's standards.

But, to Blitzkrieg's astonishment, Captain Jester was
nowhere to be seen. Such a flagrant failure to kowtow to
the Legion's commanding general was exactly the kind of
opening Blitzkrieg wanted—a lapse so blatant that even
the most ardent of Jester's supporters would have a hard

time explaining it away. Normally he'd have to do some digging to come up with some suitable provocation; he might even have to magnify some molehill of imperfection into a mountain of culpability. But here was a major lapse in military courtesy—if not an outright dereliction of duty—being handed to him on a platinum-plated platter! Blitzkrieg was delighted.

The ranking officer here was a lieutenant, who was at least managing a decent salute. Blitzkrieg hadn't bothered to look up the names of Omega Company's junior officers. The simple fact that they were *here* meant that they were screwups, and that was all he needed to know about them. He hated screwups—they made the Legion look bad, and that made *him* look bad. He wouldn't stand for that.

He stood scowling for a long moment before returning the lieutenant's salute. "As you were, Lieutenant," he grumbled. Then, leaning forward, he hissed, "Where's that idiot Jester? And don't tell me he didn't know I was coming—even *he* isn't that dumb. *Where is he?*"

The lieutenant—Blitzkrieg could now see his name tag, which read ARMSTRONG—had almost imperceptibly relaxed from his rigid stance for a moment, but now was standing at attention again. "General Blitzkrieg, sir!" the lieutenant said. "With Captain Jester's apologies, sir! The captain detailed me to greet you so that he could attend to urgent company business. He . . ."

"Oh, shut the hell up!" barked the general. He waved a hand and stepped past Armstrong, glaring around at the miserable hellhole of a desert world that he'd sent Omega Company to. "If I want any of Jester's bullshit, I can get it directly from the horse's ass." Despite himself, the general chuckled. That was one of his better lines; he'd have to remember it for future use.

"Yes, sir, sir!" said Armstrong, frozen in position.

"That's more like it, *Lieutenant*," said Blitzkrieg. He made the rank sound like an epithet. "Now, I've had all the nonsense I can stomach for one day. Take me to wherever Jester's hiding—on the double!"

"Yes, sir," said Armstrong, again, saluting. "If the general would be so kind as to follow me . . ."

"No need for that, Mr. Armstrong," came a familiar jaunty voice. "Welcome to our humble establishment, General Blitzkrieg—I hope your flight in wasn't too boring."

"Captain!" said Armstrong, whirling around. His voice and his expression conveyed an unmistakable sense of relief.

"Jester!" snarled General Blitzkrieg, his face settling into a long-accustomed frown. If Armstrong was relieved, the effect on the general was the complete opposite. Here at last was the man he'd traveled halfway across the Alliance to wreak his vengeance on—and the very sound of his voice was enough to set Blitzkrieg's blood pressure soaring.

Sure enough, there stood Willard Phule—or, to use his proper Legion name, Captain Jester, grinning as if he'd just seen his best old friend, instead of the commanding general who'd never made much secret of his desire to crush Phule and all he stood for. To Blitzkrieg's utter astonishment, the fellow was out of uniform. Instead of the Legion's standard-issue black jumpsuit, the commander of Omega Company was wearing a summerweight tuxedo, with a sparkling white jacket and an impertinent bow tie with matching cummerbund, in an eye-assaulting pattern of unmilitary colors. In his hand was a half-empty martini glass.

"Glad you could make it," he said, extending his right hand. "How about you join me for a drink while one of the fellows takes your luggage to your quarters?"

General Blitzkrieg's mouth fell open, but not a word emerged. It was with considerable astonishment that he realized that he'd actually taken Captain Jester's hand and begun to shake it. A moment after that, the captain had put a friendly arm around his shoulders and begun to steer him in the direction of the sleekly contoured building that must house the Legion base here on Zenobia. And the whole time, Jester kept up a line of small talk, just as if he was about to plop a contract in front of him and sell him an insurance policy.

Somewhere in the back of Blitzkrieg's mind there rested the thought that he'd come here to ream out Jester like no Legion officer had ever been reamed out in the history of the service.

But he had to admit, right now a drink sounded like just the thing he needed . . . There'd be plenty of time for reaming afterward.

"De Mon" turned out to be a giant dark-skinned man with a shaved head and eyes that seemed to look right through you. Rita ushered Phule into the circle of men, women, and robots sitting around him near a campfire. Like Rita, both sexes in this village dressed in colorful, flowing robes, and wore their hair in long braids. A distinctive odor of smoldering vegetation filled the air. The group broke into excited whispers as Phule came into view but fell silent as de Mon raised his hand.

"Who dis come to see de Mon?" he asked in a penetrating voice—surprisingly, a clear melodic tenor instead of the basso profundo Phule would have expected from someone of his bulk.

Rita had already told Phule to let her do the talking. "Dis be Captain Jester, from de Space Legion," she said. "He lookin' for some frens. Somebody tell he dey be wit' de Indians, so he come looking. I an' I fetch he here."

De Mon turned to Phule. "You frens—what dey look like?"

Phule said, "I wish they were easier to describe. One's an older man, very dignified-looking—he's actually my butler, but I doubt he'd be wearing his usual outfit for a vacation. The other's a woman—younger, maybe thirty? Thin, dark-skinned, short hair, usually very serious. I don't know what she's wearing now, but the last time I saw her, she was in Legion uniform—a black jumpsuit like this one. Needless to say, there'd be a reward for anyone who can help me find them."

Several of de Mon's circle frowned. "What he say?" murmured one of the robots. "He talk so funny . . ."

De Mon glared at his companions until they fell silent, then nodded, and said, "Huh." He fixed Phule with his piercing gaze. Phule looked back, frankly, for a long moment. Apparently satisfied with what he saw, de Mon turned to the others around him. "Anybody see dose people?"

"Sure, dey been to de tourist trap day 'fore yestaday," said one woman, who wore huge golden earrings and at least a dozen bangles on her wrists. "De woman buyin' lots o' books, some jewelry—lots o' pretty stuff. Her mon, he jes look and shake he head."

"Do you know where they went next?" asked Phule. "I'm very anxious to find them."

"Dat your money dey be spendin'?" asked de Mon, with a sly grin. Then he held up a hand and said to the woman who'd spoken before, "You see dem leave?"

"Dey go to de food court," said the woman. "I don't know where dey go after, but dey talkin' bout de roundup. I bet dey done gone dere."

"Dat makes sense," said de Mon, nodding. "All de tourist, dey wants to see de roundup. Dat's why dey run it six time ev'ry year."

"Where would they go to see the roundup?" asked Phule, eagerly. Maybe he was finally making progress. It seemed as if he'd walked or ridden over half the planet to learn this much about his fugitive butler.

"De main place is de Pretty Good Corral in Skilletville—dey bring in de robocows down de streets, whoopin' and hollerin', folk shootin' off de guns. It 'spose to be a stirrin' sight," said de Mon. "You go dere, mos' like you finds dese people you look for."

"Thank you," said Phule. "If someone will tell me how to get there, I'll be greatly in your debt."

"You come t'rough with de reward, dat take care of de debt mighty quick," said de Mon, dryly. "Bes' way to go, you ride east till you past de hills, den swing sout' to de big river . . ."

Half an hour later, Phule was on his way. The weather was clear and warm, and his robosteed made good time along the well-marked trail. He met nobody on the way, although perhaps three or four times he saw the dust cloud raised by some distant rider, and once he spotted a stagecoach on a road parallel to his trail.

As the West Indians had predicted, he was in Skilletville well before dark. And while all the hotels and rooming houses were full of tourists, he applied his Dilithium Express card to the problem and soon had an acceptable, if not really luxurious, room. He dumped his luggage on the bed, splashed some water on his face to wash off the trail dust, and went out looking for Beeker.

Major Sparrowhawk took one long last sip of her coffee— the best she'd ever had in a Legion mess hall, and that included the Staff Officer's mess at Headquarters. And the selection of pastries, and the butter and jam, were of a quality unheard of in most of the restaurants she was in the habit of frequenting. The story that had made the rounds back at Headquarters, about Jester's having brought in a cordon bleu chef to feed Omega Company (and himself, of course), was beginning to seem credible now that she'd had breakfast in their mess.

It was sorely tempting to fill the cup up one more time and have just one more croissant. But no—the general expected her to spy for him, while he went out and socialized

with the officers and enjoyed whatever amenities the base
had to offer. She'd been through the routine dozens of
times over the years since her assignment as Blitzkrieg's
adjutant. Time to do it again. She stood up, carried her
empty tray over to the window where dirty dishes were de-
posited, and turned to head out to the parade ground. If luck
was on her side, somewhere out there she'd find trouble.

"Good morning, Major," said a voice behind her. She
turned automatically to see who'd spoken. It was a youngish
woman with lieutenant's insignia on the shoulders of her
Legion jumpsuit, wearing a broad smile on her face.

Lieutenant Rembrandt, Sparrowhawk recalled. *Nominally second-in-command of Omega Company—to the ex-
tent that means anything at all.* But why was she smiling?
Most of the time, on General Blitzkrieg's inspection tours,
every member of the general's party was considered an enemy . . . with excellent reason. Was Rembrandt so naive
that she didn't that know Sparrowhawk's job entailed finding out whatever dirt she could, to report back to the general? Or did she have some ulterior motive—possibly
orders from her CO to keep an eye on the visiting officers?
It didn't really matter. Quite possibly this fresh-faced junior officer would lead her to exactly the kind of dirt she
was looking for.

"Good morning, Lieutenant," said Sparrowhawk, con-
juring up a smile of her own. "I'm headed for an after-
breakfast walk. Would you have time to join me?" She
made a point of phrasing it in such a way that the lieutenant
could interpret it either as an order or a friendly invitation.

Rembrandt's smile grew even broader. "Why, I'd be
glad to make the time, Major. The very least I can do is
show you where things are so you won't feel lost on this
unfamiliar base."

Right, thought Sparrowhawk. That clinched it; Captain
Jester must have detailed his lieutenant to shepherd the
general's adjutant and steer her away from whatever

Omega Company was trying to hide. Well, Sparrowhawk had gotten the runaround more than once before. In fact, she considered it a useful time-saver. Once she'd figured out what parts of the base Rembrandt was trying to keep her from seeing, she'd have a short list of all the major trouble spots to look at on her own. Better yet, the guided tour would take her to all the really interesting spots in camp, so she could actually enjoy it while she was making her little list. "Lead on, Lieutenant," she said, with a predatory smile. This was going to be far too easy . . .

Rembrandt brightened up. "Oh, great! Captain Jester's done some really neat things here, and I think you'll enjoy seeing them, Major. Although you've probably seen every base in the Alliance . . ." The two of them headed down an outside corridor toward the main exit from the giant prefabricated building that was the central structure of Zenobia Base.

"Oh, I'm not quite *that* ancient," said Sparrowhawk, with a conspiratorial wink. "And why don't we just let our hair down and forget about rank, OK? My Legion name's Sparrowhawk . . . and can I call you Rembrandt?"

"Sure, Maj— Sparrowhawk," said Rembrandt. She smiled and held open a door leading out to the parade ground. *Like a lamb to the slaughter*, thought Sparrowhawk, stepping out into the sunlight.

She didn't stop to reflect that the phrase might equally apply both ways . . .

Skilletville was filled wall to wall with people, apparently about fifty tourists for every local—and a fair number of the locals were "Injun" robots. Among the tourists, most of the men were wearing clearly freshly bought "Western" outfits: broad-brimmed hats, unbuttoned vests, blue jeans, boots with fancy toolwork, and some kind of gun belt. The women's outfits showed more variety, from a feminized version of the hat-jeans-and-boots ensemble to full skirts, parasols, high necklines, and somewhat less practical hats. Most of them looked extremely uncomfortable. On the other hand, Phule's Legion jumpsuit got more than its share of curious glances—which might have made him even more uncomfortable, if he'd been prone to second-guessing himself.

Along all the unpaved streets were rows of tents selling food, crafts, vids, and "collectibles," the latter being junky impulse items so outrageously overpriced that the buyers would probably hold on to them forever in the vain hope of someday getting back what they'd paid. Phule stopped to grab a sandwich and a bottle of the local beer at one stand, and scanned the crowd while he gulped them down. No sign of Beeker or Nightingale. He put his sandwich wrapper and empty bottle into a recycler. Some sort of show was going on near the center of town; he made his way through the thickening crowd toward the sound of music and laughter.

A small wooden stage had been erected in the middle of the street, where a group of musicians—half of them human, the other half robots—were playing banjos, fiddles, and a washboard. A grinning sheriff and a buxom music hall girl performed a lively dance to the music. Phule watched for a moment, then shrugged. Whatever the rest of the crowd saw in the act, it did nothing for him. He went back to searching the crowd for the familiar face of his butler—or the slightly less familiar one of Nightingale. After a few minutes, he realized that he'd just seen another familiar face—one he'd met only a few days ago. He turned his head back, reexamining the crowd . . . Yes, there it was, just on the other side of the stage. Buck Short.

Once again, he began pushing his way through the crowd, this time toward the grizzled cowboy who'd sent him looking for Beeker out in Indian territory. He got several annoyed glances from tourists intent on watching the show, and a couple of elbows came his way, but before long he was right behind his target. "Hello, Buck," he said calmly, putting his hand on the cowboy's shoulder.

Buck spun around surprisingly quickly in the tight-packed crowd. "Why, Cap'n!" he said. "What brings you by Skilletville?"

"Still looking for my butler," said Phule. "The West Indians suggested they might have come here."

"Wa-al, I reckon that could be," said Buck. "Dunno why I didn't think of it myself."

"Yes, I wondered about that myself, once I learned that this is apparently the main tourist destination on the planet," said Phule. He paused, looking directly into Short's eyes. "By any chance did somebody tell you to send me out of the way, so I wouldn't see them?"

"That don't hardly make sense, Cap'n," said Short, his eyes shifting from side to side. "Say, how's about you and me go somewheres, maybe have a drink and figger it out?"

"I'm not buying you any more drinks," said Phule. "But we are definitely going to figure things out." He grabbed the cowboy by the collar and began pulling him along toward the edge of the crowd. The onlookers stared and pointed but did nothing, probably assuming that Buck's squirming was part of the show. Just what they thought Phule, in a custom-tailored modern Space Legion uniform, was doing in a Wild West re-creation show is probably best left unexplored.

Eventually Phule emerged from the crowd, with Buck still in tow. He dragged him over to a horse trough and sat him on the edge. "All right, here's the deal," he said. "I'm going to ask you a few questions, and you're going to give me answers. If I don't think you're giving me the right answers, you get a bath—which maybe isn't a bad idea, after all."

"Hey, pardner, ain't no need to get all hasty," said Buck. SPLASH! Phule ducked him into the trough before he could say any more, held him down for a count of five, then pulled him back up, sputtering. The cowboy finally recovered his breath enough to ask, "What'd you go an' do that fer?"

"To make sure you know I'm serious," said Phule, grinning fiercely. "Have you seen my butler?"

"Wa-al, I can't rightly remem—" *SPLASH!*

"I'll ask the question again," said Phule, pulling him back up—this time after a count of ten. "Have you seen my butler?"

"Yep, I shore have," said Buck. "Him and his lady was here last night, enjoyin' the roundup. Don't duck me agin!"

"I won't, if you tell me where they are now," said Phule.

Buck Short waved a soggy arm in the direction of the Cut 'N' Shoot spaceport. "They went that-a-way," he said. Phule nodded, then let go of his shirt. Buck nearly fell back in the water. But Phule was paying no attention. He was already heading for his robosteed, ready to ride off in pursuit of Beeker.

General Blitzkrieg stepped out onto the parade ground of Omega Base, his best professional scowl on his face. He'd been here less than one standard day, but already he was feeling frustrated. He was used to arriving for "surprise" inspections only to discover that every legionnaire on the planet had known far in advance of his visit, and had prepared for it. He was even used to having the local COs whirl him through a round of wining and dining and VIP receptions in hopes of distracting him from the object of his visit. He couldn't pretend he minded the special treatment one bit; as far as he was concerned, it was one of the more attractive perks of being a commanding general in the Space Legion.

Besides, he could afford to enjoy himself a little on these inspection tours. The local commanders might assume they'd managed to pull the wool over his eyes. Little did they know that while the general was getting the VIP treatment, his adjutant, Major Sparrowhawk, was making note of the real lapses in discipline, preparedness, and security on the bases he visited. Blitzkrieg had to admit that Sparrowhawk had a pretty good head on her shoulders, for a female. Sometimes he didn't know how he'd run the Legion without her.

But somehow he'd failed to realize that Zenobia Base was the sole human outpost on this insufferable lizard-ridden planet. There were no sights to be seen, unless you happened to like swamps and deserts. There weren't any four-star restaurants, unless you counted the mess hall—which, he had to admit, served a pretty decent meal for a Legion base. And, as far as he could tell, the only recreational facilities within a light-year of the place were the casinos of Lorelei Station, where he'd dropped far too much money on his four-day stopover before coming here. He *might* just have to spend this visit actually inspecting the troops . . .

Well, sometimes business had to come before pleasure. He'd come looking for ammunition to finally destroy the career of that damned headline-hunting jackass of a Phule. If he didn't find it, it was nobody's fault but his own. He put on his most intimidating expression and headed toward a group of legionnaires he saw lounging about a short distance away.

"Yo, the brass comin'," said a soft voice. Blitzkrieg had expected that. He'd also expected the legionnaires to fall into a hasty formation and come to attention. Instead, while a few of them glanced his way, they continued to act like unconcerned civilians. His eyebrows rose a notch. Were they that poorly trained, or was this a deliberate affront? He'd soon find out.

"Hey, boss man, what's the bite?" said one of the troops, as he strode up to the legionnaires. "You been all triff?"

Blitzkrieg's eyes bulged out and his jaw fell open. *"Wh-wh-what?"* he sputtered. "Legionnaire, do you know who I am?"

The legionnaire—a tall, thin man with café-au-lait coloration—stepped forward and peered at the general. "Yeah, jes' like I thought—you're the main boss mofo," he said after a long moment's close-up inspection. "They told me you're a gruff and skritty chee, but you look mighty sly to *me*."

"I look what?" said Blitzkrieg. His voice rose an octave. "They told you WHAT?"

"Oh yeah, *that's* sly, all right," said the legionnaire, nodding with evident approval. "Ain't nothin' skritty 'bout *you*, not a hair of it." He stuck out his hand. "Splank it, boss man!"

Blitzkrieg looked around in panic. He knew the Legion took in representatives of every species from every planet in the Alliance. And he knew—better than anyone—that those who couldn't handle the demands of life and work in the Legion ended up in Omega Company, more often than not. But the reality of it was something those abstract understandings had left him unprepared for. The proposition that this fellow in front of him qualified as a fellow sophont was beyond his intellectual grasp.

But before he could make his escape, another apparition in Legion uniform approached him. This one had a shaved head, round glasses, and a beatific smile. "Ah, General Blitzkrieg," it said. "It is with great pleasure that I see you here." He put his hand on the tall legionnaire's shoulder, caught his eyes, and nodded. The tall fellow nodded back and moved away.

"Uh, pleasure, a real pleasure," said the general, glad to be rid of the incomprehensible nuisance, but unsure what this new legionnaire was up to. *Where are the sergeants?*

"I wonder if you could take a moment to inform us on a

few important topics?" said the fellow, still smiling. "It is unusual to be able to learn from a representative of the higher echelons of command."

"Uh, what did you have in mind?" asked Blitzkrieg. He wasn't sure that offering to answer questions was a good idea, but he felt he owed the fellow at least a moment's courtesy in exchange for his having steered away the first man.

"Why, only the most elementary matters," said the smiling man. "Perhaps you would be so kind as to explain the imbalance between merit and reward. For example, this company's previous assignment was on Landoor, a dangerous and demanding environment. But after we achieved our mission there, we did not receive a fine vacation, but transfer to an even more critical mission here on Zenobia. Is this equitable?"

General Blitzkrieg's eyes bulged, then he began looking about for help. *Surely* there was an officer—at very least a sergeant—in charge of this squad, he thought. The round-faced man stood there grinning, with the rest of the squad looking on with evident curiosity. Did they really expect him to answer the question?

With growing consternation, the general realized that they did.

8

Journal #799—

I confess, it is beyond my comprehension what the appeal is of golf. The game was clearly designed by some malignant entity, forcing its devotees to attempt impossible feats with awkward, misshapen implements. And surely the number of heart attacks and fits of apoplexy resulting from the game's manifold frustrations amply belies the presumed benefits of its being played in the healthy out-of-doors.

It hardly surprised me, then, to learn that the game was a favorite of General Blitzkrieg, a man whose entire career seemed to be the apotheosis of cross-purposes.

"See here, Jester, I've had just about enough . . ." General Blitzkrieg got no further than that before his jaw dropped and his eyes bulged out.

"Great, General, we aim to please," said the commanding officer of Omega Company. To Blitzkrieg's utter astonishment, Phule was still out of uniform—except, this time, he had traded in his white dinner jacket for a preposterously bright green golf shirt, blatantly unmatching (largely pink and orange) Madras shorts, and argyle socks that somehow managed to clash with both. A white sun visor and a tasseled pair of blue suede golf shoes completed the ensemble. The captain winked at the general, then said, "I thought I'd go out and hit a few before dinner call. Like to join me? We've got a couple of spare bags of clubs if you haven't brought your own."

"Hit a few? Clubs?" General Blitzkrieg stared in incomprehension. Then his expression changed. "Do you mean to tell me you've got a golf course here?"

"Well, at the moment all I've got is a driving range and three short holes," said Phule, sheepishly. "I'd love to expand to a nine-holer—the terrain here is just ideal, you know. But we're here on sufferance by the Zenobians, and they're likely to raise a stink if we start chopping down all their underbrush. I thought if I could teach a couple of the native officers the game, they'd see the point of the whole thing, but it's slow going."

"Teach them the game?" said Blitzkrieg. His eyes narrowed, calculating.

"Oh yes," said Phule. "Get a bunch of Zenobians out on the links, and it'd do wonders for interspecies relations, and of course it'd be the quickest way to get their support for building a course for my officers. So I've been giving a few of the locals a chance to get out and take some swings. Not that it's been easy, General. You can't imagine how much trouble I've had finding decent half-size clubs for the little beggars—especially since most of them seem to be lefties . . ."

"Captain, Captain—hold on just a minute," said General Blitzkrieg. "I want to get a good look at these three holes you say you've built. And it just so happens, I've got my clubs and spikes along. Tell me where the first tee is, and I'll meet you there in ten minutes."

"Yes, sir!" said Phule. "The course is at the south edge of the base, down where you see the red tents set up. I'll get us a couple of caddies."

Blitzkrieg dashed back to his room. And here he'd been thinking that his visit to Zenobia was going to be all work and no play! It looked as if Jester was good for something after all. Not that setting up a few golf holes was going to get the captain off the hook for all his offenses against Legion tradition, of course. Blitzkrieg was sure he'd find plenty of material to make an open-and-shut case against Jester.

Or, to be exact, Major Sparrowhawk would find it while he was enjoying himself out on the course. If you could call three holes a course . . . well, if they were interesting enough, perhaps they'd keep him distracted from the sordid business of collecting enough rope to hang the fellow. He finished tying on his spikes, grabbed the bag of clubs, and headed back outside.

The red tents, as it turned out, had been set up as an impromptu clubhouse for the little golf course. There Captain Jester waited, leaning on a short iron. Next to him stood a pair of legionnaire recruits who looked more than happy at having been rescued from their morning formation to do some honest work for their superior officers. A canopied hoverjeep sat nearby, with a set of clubs leaning out the back next to a Legion-issue field cooler. Beyond them, General Blitzkrieg could make out a more or less green area with a small red-and-white flag flying from a pole in the middle distance. *About three hundred yards,* he estimated almost without thinking. *Drive, six iron, and maybe a chip—easy five, chance at four.*

"Great, there you are," said Jester, shading his eyes with one hand. "Do you want to hit some practice shots, or shall we have a drink first?"

The general squinted toward the sky. "Looks as if the sun's over the yardarm," he said. He'd never much thought about what a yardarm might be, or how high the sun would have to be to be over one. It seemed as good an excuse as any to have a drink, not that he ever lacked for excuses.

"All right, name your poison," said Jester, pointing toward the cooler. "We'll wet our throats and then see how far the ball's going today. In this dry air, it usually flies pretty well. Rolls a long way after it lands, too."

"Good," said the general, chuckling. "I don't mind a few extra yards, to tell the truth."

"Who does?" said Jester, with a broad grin. "Let's get a drink, and then we can find out how it's playing." He waved toward the waiting cooler, and General Blitzkrieg eagerly stepped forward. This was beginning to look like a worthwhile visit, after all—and he hadn't even started to compile demerits against Omega Company. That would be when the real fun started . . .

Sushi and Do-Wop sat in a circle with a large group of the Red Indians, illuminated by a campfire in the middle. They'd told their story to the chief (the same Indian who'd met them). Then they'd been feasted, they'd been entertained by singers and storytellers, and now the peace pipe was making its way around the circle. At the moment, it was apparently somewhere on the far side of the circle; neither of the two legionnaires had yet sampled it.

Showing unaccustomed patience, Do-Wop nudged Sushi, and said, "Yo, Soosh, what d'ya think of these Indian babes? I think a couple of 'em like me . . ."

"That's just because they don't know you," said Sushi. "Give them five or ten minutes . . ."

"Funny man," said Do-Wop, throwing a mock-angry punch at Sushi. He was about to add something else when a voice behind the two of them said, "Legionnaires come quick—heap bad news!"

"Oh, shit, I just knew it—we're gonna miss our turn on

the pipe," said Do-Wop. "Soosh, how about you go find out what's happening?"

"Both must come," said the messenger, before Sushi could reply. With the strength of robotic muscles, the Red Indian grasped each of them by the arm, pulling them away from the circle around the fire. Reluctant, yet full of curiosity, Sushi followed without objection. True to form, Do-Wop complained bitterly every step of the way.

Their guide took them a short distance to where their robosteeds were hitched. Now, away from the glare of the fire, they could see the chief waiting there for them. Next to him stood another man, who looked as if he'd ridden hard to get there. "What's going on?" asked Sushi. "Is this about the captain?"

"Got it in one," said the new arrival, a lanky copper-skinned man dressed in boots, chaps, a vest, and a hat with three feathers in the brim. "He just left West Indian territory, headed lickety-split toward the spaceport. Word I got is that the guy he's chasing has already booked ship off-planet."

"Oh, great," said Sushi. He looked off into the looming darkness, then turned back to the man with a sigh. "Any report on where they're heading?"

"All the ships off-planet stop on Tejas first," said the chief. He turned and spat off into the field, then said, "Could be anywhere after that. But the ship don't take off till tomorrow noon. You hurry up, you ask-um yourselves."

"Tomorrow noon," said Sushi. "How long's it take to get there?"

The rider looked at the chief, then shrugged. "Depends," he said. "You ride flat out, you can be there by nine-thirty, ten. Longer if you stop for grub, sleep, or trouble. Be another ship on Thursday, no big deal—they all go the same place."

"Hey, that's right," said Do-Wop. "That means that even

if we miss it, we can catch up with 'em on Tejas, no big deal . . ."

Sushi cut him off. "It *is* a big deal. If we wait for the Thursday ship, we're three days behind the captain, maybe further behind Beeker. Even worse if we have to waste time figuring out where he's transferred to after Tejas."

"Aww, come on," said Do-Wop. "It'll make that long ride a lot easier if I get one good hit off that peace pipe."

Sushi wasn't buying any part of it. "There's no way we can do our job if we miss that ship. Chief, our apologies for not staying longer; I hope you understand this is important. If we can, we'll come back and visit you again."

"Not likely," said the chief, with an ironic smile. "But we do understand. Just to prove it, you take this with you." He handed Sushi a small package. "Food for journey—you eat in the saddle and not lose time. Now go ride—and luck ride with you!"

They hopped into the saddle and rode off. It wasn't until morning that Sushi opened the package. There he found tasty meat jerky and chocolate brownies. About an hour after eating, Sushi found himself smiling. He looked over at Do-Wop, who had a silly grin on his face. He winked, and said, "Y'know, partner, I think those people must like you, after all."

Do-Wop nearly fell off his horse laughing.

They made it to the spaceport with plenty of time to spare.

"How long did you say this hole was?" said General Blitzkrieg, squinting down the fairway into the desert sun. He held a driver in one hand, a ball and tee in the other.

"About two-eighty," said Captain Jester, shading his eyes with one hand. "I'd think you could reach the green on this one. There's a bunker on the left, though, so be sure to fade it away from that."

General Blitzkrieg nodded sagely and teed up his ball.

In fact, based on the general's showing on the practice tee, it was long odds against his being able to reach the green with anything less than a howitzer. As for the bunker on the left, Blitzkrieg could safely put it out of mind. The general's tee shots took off with an invariable slice, for which a less stubborn golfer might have tried to compensate by aiming far left in hopes that the wildly curving ball would end up somewhere down the middle of the course. Perversely, the general insisted on lining up every shot as if he were going to deposit the ball in the dead center of the fairway. The unfortunate results of this strategy had not so far deterred the general. He was a hard man to deter.

The general took his stance, wiggled the club head back and forth a few times, glared at the distant flag, and took a mighty swing. The ball leapt off the tee, headed straight down the middle of the fairway, then inevitably began to curve to the right. "Get back, you bastard!" screamed the general, waving his hand as if to direct the errant pellet. "Hit something, damn you!" But as if oblivious of his exalted rank, the ball continued to the right, disappearing at last into the deep brush lining the course on that side.

"Wow, you got all of that one, sir," said Captain Jester, watching the general's ball fly out of sight. "It'd be pin high if you straightened it out. Hey—it's just a practice round. Take another and see if you can put it close."

"Right, just practice," said the general, reaching in the side pocket of his golf bag for another ball. "Got to keep that left elbow straight."

"Sure, we'll get a chance to bend our elbows all we want after the round," said Jester, with a wink. "Hit as many as you like, get the feel of the course. Tomorrow I'll see if I can round up a foursome and we can play for real."

"A foursome?" said the general. "Now you're talking—especially if there's some action on it."

"I think I can undertake to provide that," said Jester. "Worse comes to worst, if our partners don't have the sporting blood, you and I can put a few splazookies on the round. But we can worry about that when it's time to pony up. For now, let's get you some local knowledge. Hit a couple more balls out, and get a look at what kind of lies you've got. Then you can find out how the green's playing . . . and then, you won't be able to excuse getting beat by saying you didn't know the course!"

"Hah!" said Blitzkrieg, gleefully. "We'll see who it is who needs excuses, *Captain*. I'll have you know I regularly shoot in the low eighties, you young pup. Get us a couple of partners who can put the ball down the fairway, and I'll show you a few things about the game."

"That's the spirit," said Jester, twirling a club. "I'll get us a couple of partners, and tomorrow we'll see how this little course stands up to some real golf. I just hope you won't find it disappointing after some of the places you must have played . . ."

"Well, every course is a different challenge," said Blitzkrieg. In point of fact, even the easiest courses were likely to be a challenge well beyond his golfing skills. He'd gerrymandered his average score into the eighties by a policy of taking as many tee shots as he needed to get a decent lie for his approach, bullying his opponents into conceding improbably long putts, and never counting any strokes after either his partner or their opponents sank a putt to win a given hole. When you had enough stars on the shoulders of your uniform, your opponents weren't going to challenge you on the fine points of golf etiquette. And from the way Jester was talking, there was going to be no trouble at all playing his regular game here.

He teed up for his second drive and squinted down the fairway. This time he'd aim a little to the left and try to fade the ball right up to the opening of the green . . .

He gave the ball a mighty whack, and like a missile it took off down the fairway. And even before it reached the peak of its rise, it began its inevitable curve to the right.

Blitzkrieg sighed and pulled another ball out of his pocket. He'd get a decent lie to play if it took him all morning . . .

"Rot'n'art," said Do-Wop, looking up at the departures readout in the Tejas spaceport lounge. "At least this time it's someplace I've heard of before."

"Wow," said Sushi. "I mean, I'm surprised you've heard of someplace outside your own home world."

"You kiddin'? I've heard of lots of places—been to a few of 'em, too. Lorelei, Zenobia, here . . ."

"OK, I get the point," said Sushi. "I guess we need to get ourselves booked to Rot'n'art . . ."

"I guess so," said Do-Wop. "Wonder why ol' Beeks is going there? It sure ain't the place I'd pick for a vacation."

"Yeah, you'd go straight back to Lorelei and blow everything in the slots," said Sushi. "But you're right—Rot'n'art isn't exactly the scenic high point of the galaxy. Some interesting old buildings there, if I remember my history."

"If they haven't all fell down," said Do-Wop. "Our school books had pictures of Old Earth, and you wouldn't believe it. Some of the places—I'm talking 'bout joints where kings and vice presidents and other hot shits lived—were all busted up. You'd think they'd keep 'em in better shape."

"Yeah, we had those same pictures in our books," said Sushi. "They had a few too many wars and other kinds of trouble. But I've never heard of any wars on Rot'n'art, so maybe it's in better shape than Old Earth. I guess we're going to find out."

"Hope they got good beer there, anyhow," said Do-Wop. "Hey, that reminds me—we can't get on the ship for another hour and a half. Let's go get somethin' to drink first."

"Good a plan as any," said Sushi, tiredly. The two legionnaires picked up their duffel bags and headed down the spaceport corridor toward the shops next to the waiting area.

They'd gone just a few steps when Sushi grabbed Do-Wop by the arm and pulled him through a side door into a candy shop. "Quick," he whispered. "Do you see who I see?"

"Where?" said Do-Wop, sticking his head out the door and looking in both directions. "I don't see no . . ."

"Shhh!" said Sushi, urgently. "Down by the vending machines—no, the other way, stupid!"

"Who you callin' stupid, stupid?" said Do-Wop. He looked in the direction his partner had indicated. "Geez—it's Beeker! Yo, Bee . . . *Mpfhh!*" He sputtered as Sushi put a hand over his mouth.

"Quiet! If he sees us, he'll know he's being followed, and then who knows what he'll do?" whispered Sushi. "We might lose him for good!"

"Escutse me, gentlebeinks, ah you lookink f'som can'y?" came a squeaky voice from behind the counter. The two legionnaires turned as one, to see a small grey-furred creature peering at them with enormous sad eyes.

"Uh, yeah, that's what we're lookin' for, candy," said Do-Wop. "Y'got any Green Woofers?"

"Ahh, Greem Wooferts, Aldebaran Cann'y Com'any, ver' gootd, yes," said the little creature. It went over to one of the display cases and reached in the back. "You wan' larch or chumbo sidze bocts?"

While the shopcreature waited on Do-Wop, Sushi stepped over to the doorway and cautiously peered down the corridor again. "I think he's gone," he said.

"Hang on, Soosh, I'm gettin' some Green Woofers," said Do-Wop. He turned back to the shopcreature, and said, "Better make it the jumbo box, I dunno if they'll have 'em on the ship."

"Chumbo, yes, ver' gootd," said the creature, digging out the candy from the display case. "Anatink elts?"

Sushi stuck his head out the doorway again, then abruptly pulled it back and scurried over to Do-Wop. "Damn, I spoke too soon! Here comes Nightingale!"

"Well, she probably isn't coming in here," said Do-Wop, not showing much concern. "Maybe she's not the candy type, y'know? These skinny broads can be weird . . ."

"Even if she doesn't come inside, she might spot us, and then we're totally zickled," said Sushi, suddenly aware that his Legion-issue black jumpsuit stood out like a sore thumb in this spaceport. He turned to the little grey creature. "Is there anyplace we can hide for a few minutes? Someone's coming that we want to surprise . . ."

"Oh, you gon' buy cann'y f' it?" The shopcreature did something with its face that looked like a wink, then pointed to the counter along the back of the store. "You hite ovah derh!"

The two legionnaires scooted behind the counter and crouched down, hoping they'd been quick enough to avoid Nightingale's attention. They suddenly became aware of the sound of footsteps entering the shop; a small human's, to judge from the tempo and apparent weight. Sushi held his breath, hoping that, just this once, Do-Wop would be able to keep his mouth shut.

"Hey'o, missy, you need some cann'y?" said the shopcreature.

"Yes, have you any white chocolate?" The customer's voice was muffled, although it was plainly a human female speaking. Sushi scrunched down lower.

"Ridte disweh," said the little grey sophont, heading directly for the counter where the legionnaires hid. The woman's footsteps followed the shopcreature.

"I want only the finest quality," said the woman. "Nothing commercially processed." Sushi still wasn't sure whether this was Nightingale or not; he had only heard the Omega Mob's medic speak a few times, really close. He wished now that he'd made it a point to listen to her . . .

"Dadt wudbe da Viceroy spetyal ectspo't," said the shopcreature, coming behind the counter where Sushi and Do-Wop cowered. It pulled open a drawer. Sushi held his breath as he heard the shopcreature say, "Disiz ahr ver-abes'."

The woman gasped. "Who is that behind the counter?" she cried. That was the last straw for Sushi and Do-Wop; they bolted from the store, nearly knocking down the shopcreature and his new customer, a petite blonde in an electric blue chiton.

The last thing either of them heard was the shopcreature calling, "Zir! Zir! Yuhaf vergo'in da Wooferts!"

Journal #804:

Rot'n'art is the indisputable "galactic center"—just ask its natives (if you can find any). This despite the planet's location well out on the fringe of the Alliance, which in itself is located a considerable distance from the rather dangerous central regions of our galaxy. As to what Rot'n'art is the center of, the best indication might be found in its nearly universal—and richly deserved—reputation for decadence, corruption, and utter paralysis of every agency.

Unique among the planets of the Alliance, Rot'n'art has been entirely enclosed and roofed over. Seen from space, the planet is an irregular spheroid of metal and synthetics, which extend as much as a mile above the actual surface. It is not at all clear why someone—several generations of someones, to be precise—thought this particular form of development to be worth the effort. I suspect it was the Interplanetary Shippers Guild, who are greatly enriched by Rot'n'art's need to import the vast majority of its food-stuffs, which despite its diminished population the planet can no longer grow for itself.

Rot'n'art's claim on the title of "galactic center" unquestionably holds true if the subject is service robots. Not that robots are at all rare on other worlds—far from it. But on many worlds, they are found only in positions unsuited to human workers: undersea mining, for example, or nuclear reactor maintenance. Because of the positions they are in, the visitor (whose interest in undersea mines or the innards of nuclear reactors is usually nil) rarely sees them.

Not so on Rot'n'art. There, even more than on Cut 'N' Shoot, robots fill the majority of public contact positions. Stop in a restaurant for lunch? A robot takes one's order, brings the food, and collects the payment. For all I know, another is back in the kitchen preparing one's sandwich. Travel to some tourist destination? One robot vends the tickets, another collects them, a third operates the vehicle, and still another directs one to the best places to view the attractions. Robots so dominate the landscape that a first-time visitor is likely to wonder where the people of Rot'n'art have fled.

Phule stepped off the liner to discover an empty, ill-lit corridor, which might have been swept some time in the last month, but not very carefully. There was a row of vending machines on the wall facing him. About half of them appeared to have been vandalized. The door hissed shut behind him, and he was alone. He stopped and looked around, confused; this didn't look anything at all like the entrance to one of the major hubs of the galaxy . . .

"Welcome to Rot'n'art, stranger," said a harsh voice behind him.

Phule whirled quickly, ready for action. But the figure facing him was as unthreatening as he could imagine: a stringy-haired man in a ragged overcoat leaning unsteadily against the doorframe. Hardly the kind of reception he'd expected; but he might as well make the best of it. "Hello. Can you tell me the way to the spaceport office?" asked Phule.

"Spaceport office?" echoed the stranger. "You don't want to go *there*."

"Of course I do," said Phule. "Why would I ask if I didn't?"

With a visible effort, the man stood more upright and took a step forward. "Sheer ignorance, most likely," he said, peering quizzically at Phule. "That's the most common reason, with off-worlders. On the other hand, you might be perverse, or just plain stupid. But I'll give you the benefit of the doubt. Say, could you spare a few credits so a guy could get himself some drugs?" He stuck out his hand, palm up.

Phule bristled. "What, first you insult me, then you ask me for money for drugs? You really must think I am stupid."

The man shrugged and stuck his hand into his trousers pocket. "Well, some people *are*, you know. You can't really tell until you ask. It never hurts, I figure—I just might end up getting some money. And some people might even consider it a commendable sign of an inquiring mind. But tell me, what makes you think you want to go to the spaceport office?"

Phule paused a moment—why should he tell this stranger his business? The fellow had done nothing to inspire confidence. But then again, he had nothing to lose. The sooner he found out how the land lay, the quicker he could decide how to find Beeker. This fellow's information might be as good as anyone's. He looked the man in the eyes, and said, "I'm trying to find somebody who recently came to Rot'n'art, and I thought the spaceport office might have a record of his arrival."

"Not much chance," said the stranger. "There wasn't anybody here making a record of your arrival, was there?"

"Not unless it's you," said Phule, looking at the man again.

The stranger opened his mouth, then shut it again, and looked at Phule with raised eyebrows. Finally he said,

"Say, you aren't so slow after all, are you? Or have you been on Rot'n'art before?"

"First time on-world," said Phule. "Now, friend, it's been instructive talking to you, but I really need to be on my way. I do have to find somebody, and I don't have a lot of time."

"Well, you've come to the right place," said the stranger, putting his hand on Phule's elbow. "Rot'n'art's the galactic center of missing persons. In fact, I do a bit of work in that line myself—maybe I could lend a hand."

"Really?" Phule raised his own eyebrow in return. "For a small fee, I suppose? I have to say, you don't look like the kind of fellow who could be much help."

"Maybe you shouldn't judge people on first sight," said the man. "You spend much time on Rot'n'art, you find out that taking folks at face value can get you in a lot of trouble."

"True enough," said Phule. "But you can get in just as much trouble if you don't pay attention to what's in front of your face. You already tried to beg from me, and told me you'd spend it on drugs. Why should I trust you to help me?"

The man shrugged. "I know Rot'n'art like a native, and you don't," he said. "And I'm for hire. As for the trust, that's part of the standard contract."

Phule smiled. "Ah, *contracts*—now, that's something I understand. What are your terms?"

The man turned and snapped his fingers. A clanking sound came from down the corridor, and after a moment a stenobot appeared, with a printout already emerging from its slot. "Got my boilerplate ready," the man said, with a predatory grin.

"I'm sure you do," said Phule, with a grimace of his own. "Of course, I'll have to see whether I can agree to all your terms. For one thing, I never sign a 'hold harmless' clause . . ."

The negotiations took a little while, but after suitable

modifications, Captain Jester and Perry Sodden—that was the name the man signed to the contract—had agreed to terms. "All right, let's go find your missing man," said Sodden.

9

Journal #811—

Being a tourist is at once a pleasure and a burden. One is liberated from the routines of work and daily business, to be sure. One can arise late, dawdle over breakfast, add a bottle of wine to luncheon, and spend all one's time being unproductive, without anyone thinking ill of it. On the other hand, one feels a certain obligation to "do" the area one is vacationing in. Is there an ancient ruin, a famous battlefield, or a dramatic sunset to be seen? All one's friends will assuredly inquire about it upon one's return, and one will learn that the missed attraction was the high point of everyone else's visit to the world in question. So instead of enjoying a few weeks' leisure, one dutifully exhausts oneself visiting all the various museums, ruins, battlefields, scenic vistas, theaters, stadiums, beaches, cemeteries, jails, and other noted attractions. In the end, one might as well have stayed home and gone to work every day.

• • •

The two men stepped off the star liner into the long, empty corridors of Rot'n'art and looked around. "Wow, some place," said Sushi, looking around at the dilapidated terminal.

"Yeah, the joint gives me the creeps," said Do-Wop. "Just like home . . ."

"I believe you," said Sushi. He looked at the corridor stretching off in both directions. "I don't see any sign of activity. Which way do you think we ought to go?"

Do-Wop looked both ways, then shrugged. "You pick. When we got a whole planet to look for him on, I figure it don't make much difference which way we start out. Just like lookin' for trouble—you wanna find it, it's gonna be there."

"That almost makes sense," admitted Sushi. "OK, it looks a little brighter that way—" He pointed to the left. "Let's go there and see what we find."

They shouldered their duffel bags and made their way along the trash-lined corridor. They dodged around a puddle of dirty water left by a leaking pipe in the ceiling, and rounded a corner to find themselves in front of an old-fashioned self-service newsstand. "Hold on," said Sushi. "I want to check out the news."

"What?" Do-Wop slapped his forehead with the heel of his hand. "These machines are so old, they prob'ly don't even work."

"You're the one who said we had a whole planet to look for him on," said Sushi, stepping up to one of the coin-operated monitors. "And these machines ought to work—I doubt anybody'd leave them here if they weren't bringing in enough to pay the rent on the space. Besides, do you want to spend a couple of weeks hunting all over the planet when a couple minutes research could've told us he's sitting in jail somewhere?"

"Nah—no farkin' way Cap'n Jester's in jail," sneered

Do-Wop. "He'd buy his way out before they got the door half-closed behind him."

"Maybe," said Sushi. "But he might still be in the news. So I'm still going to see if he's gotten himself noticed. You can check out the ball scores, or the numbers, while you're waiting."

Do-Wop scoffed. "What, and pay a couple bucks to log on? I'll just look on your monitor when you're finished playing."

"Yeah, right," said Sushi. He turned and faced his partner, clenched fists resting on his hips. "I'm researching local conditions so we can do our job more efficiently, and you call it *playing*. And then, on my cred, I'm supposed to let you check on how your lamebrain bets came out? Not a chance!"

"Now, boys, it's hardly worth getting upset over," said a quiet voice. "In fact, you can both log on and I'll pay for it," it continued.

At the unexpected words, Sushi stood up and looked around. "All right, who said that?"

For his part, Do-Wop shrugged. "Hey, long as he's springin' for the time, who cares?" he said. Grinning, he walked over to one of the news monitors and began keying in his preferences.

"Wait a second," said Sushi, touching his partner on the shoulder. "It could be some kind of trick . . ."

"Trick? What's a trick?" said the voice. "All I do is offer to give you boys a little free time on the newsnet so you don't spend the next ten minutes ruining my peace and quiet with your arguing, and that starts you off on *another* argument. I'm beginning to wonder if maybe I made a mistake."

"Uh, sorry, we didn't mean to insult you," said Sushi, looking around to see who was talking. "But, excuse me— it might be a bit easier if we could see you . . . I mean, no offense intended, but I like I know who I'm talking to."

"See me? Why, I'm right here in front of you," said the voice. As Sushi and Do-Wop watched, one of the line of antiquated newsreaders rolled forward and stopped, with an audible creak. Its screen flickered for a moment, then a photo of a gently smiling human face appeared. It was the face of an elderly woman, with plenty of crinkly lines around the corners of the mouth and eyes. "Now, does that make you feel better about talking to me?"

"Gee—that looks like my mom!" said Do-Wop, staring.

"Funny you should mention that," said Sushi. "It looks like my mom, too . . ."

"Of course I do," said the newsreader. "I'm designed to project each customer's personal maternal image so they're getting the news from somebody they trust. And whom do you trust more than your mother—hmm?"

"I guess you have a point there," said Sushi. "I'm looking for—my friend and I are looking for—our boss, Captain Jester. Can you tell us whether he's shown up in the local news anytime recently?"

"Checking . . ." said the reader, her screen flickering through a series of graphics too rapid for the unaided eye to scan. After a few moments, the motherly face reappeared, this time with a hint of a worried frown. "I'm sorry, I don't seem to have that name in my local newsfiles—assuming by 'local' you mean this planet, and by 'recent' you mean within the last month. Is that close enough?"

"Yeah, it ought to be," said Sushi. "He should have gotten here before we did—unless the FTL paradoxes are acting up again . . . Well, we'll just have to do our search the old-fashioned way. C'mon, Do-Wop, let's get started."

"Hey! Don't forget—I gotta look up the winning numbers!" Do-Wop said.

"All right, sonny," said the newsreader. "What do you want?"

Do-Wop nodded eagerly, and said, "Gimme the daily

Play-Four and Crazy Six for the last two weeks on Lorelei. I got a feelin' my shuttle's comin' in today!"

"Ooh, I like a boy who isn't afraid to take a risk," said the newsreader, with a convincing simulation of a giggle. "Here you go, then—but remember, bet on your head, not around it!"

"What?" said Sushi, trying to make sense of the newsreader's last words. But neither Do-Wop nor the newsreader was paying him any attention.

"Good morning, General Blitzkrieg," said the robotic Captain Jester. "Allow me to introduce your partner for today—Lieutenant Armstrong."

General Blitzkrieg turned an appraising eye on the clean-cut lieutenant, recognizing the officer who'd greeted him upon landing. "The lieutenant and I have already met," he said. *And if looks mean anything, the fellow ought to be a decent golfer,* he added, silently. Armstrong's erect bearing and trim figure held the promise of a sweet swing and a fair amount of distance. With any luck, the fellow would win his share of holes and in the process help the general shave a few strokes off his own score. He reached out his hand, and said, "Good to see you again, Lieutenant. I hope you're not afraid to put a little hurting on your captain, because when I get on a golf course, I mean business."

"I'll give it my best shot, sir," said Armstrong, timidly shaking the general's proffered hand. "I won't pretend to be the caliber of partner you usually get back at Headquarters . . ."

"Don't put yourself down, man," growled Blitzkrieg, scolding. "I mean to win this match, whether I get any help from you or not. And I can promise you I won't hold it against you if you can help me pick up a hole or two." *And I promise that what little remains of your chance at a respectable Legion career will go straight down the toilet if you let that upstart Jester beat me.*

"I don't think Armstrong will hold you back any, General," said Jester, grinning. "He's a natural, if ever I saw one. Makes me wish I had more time to practice. Oh, and here comes my partner—I was afraid he'd been held up in town, but it looks as if he's ready to go."

General Blitzkrieg glanced at the diminutive figure hauling a half-size golf bag, then did a double take. "What the hell is that?" he exploded, staring at the four-foot-tall dinosaur in a Legion uniform.

Jester chuckled. "General, permit me to introduce Flight Leftenant Qual, our Zenobian liaison. He was the first Zenobian we ever met, and he's taken to Alliance ways as if he was born to 'em. Qual, meet General Blitzkrieg, my commanding officer."

"Ah, the egregious generalissimo!" said Qual brightly. He dropped the golf bag and rushed forward to seize the general's hand in both his, pumping vigorously. "I have followed your career with consternation!"

"Eh?" said Blitzkrieg. "I'm not sure I follow . . ."

"Qual's translator plays some strange tricks," said Jester. "Hard to tell what he means, half the time. Something to do with the Zenobian language, our comm people tell me. They're looking into using it as a new method of encryption. But he's a fine fellow, and nobody loves a round of golf better than he does—though he's apt to try some very strange shots, every so often. Even so, I thought you'd like a chance to meet our native military liaison."

"Well, as long as you're not bringing in a ringer on me," said the general, who'd had exactly that done to him on more than one occasion. The lizard didn't look much like a golfer, but of course, few hustlers ever did.

"Oh, no," said Jester, perhaps a bit too hastily. "No such thing, General. Flight Leftenant Qual started playing just a couple of months ago, and I consider myself lucky to shoot a round much under ninety, these days. That's the downside of running a post like this—way too little time to keep up your golf game."

Blitzkrieg allowed himself a tight-lipped smile; he wasn't about to believe Jester for one moment. He wouldn't put it past Jester to import a professional golfer from Lorelei to give him an edge in the match; he'd "drafted" more than one local pro for the same purpose, himself. And he certainly knew Jester wasn't going to make the effort to put in a golf course on the post and then not make time to play on it himself. He smelled a very definite rat.

But a post commander who had the temerity to show up his commanding general on the links would soon find out that Blitzkrieg had his ways of getting even. Very effective ways they were, too. Few officers ever made *that* mistake a second time. He almost hoped that Jester *was* going to try to pull something fast on him; it'd make it so much more enjoyable to give the grinning jackanapes his comeuppance at the end of the day. For now, he contented himself by saying, "Well, why don't we hit a few practice shots, then get down to business?"

"That is a stupefying proposition," said Qual, flashing a mouthful of fearsome serrated teeth as his caddy—a little long-eared sophont in a Legion jumpsuit—handed him a sawed-off driver. "Let us pound the pellet, O great commanderant! Anterior!" The Zenobian flailed away at the ball, which bounded erratically down the driving range.

Blitzkrieg reached for his own driver. He still wasn't quite sure what to make of the Zenobian's strange language, but there'd be plenty of time to figure out whether or not he was being insulted when the round was over. Until then, he was going to play some golf.

It took Do-Wop and Sushi a while to find the trans station, and when they found it, they had a moment of doubt whether it was what they were looking for.

"Soosh, this place is deserted," said Do-Wop, peering down the ill-lit, dirty platform. Strictly speaking, "deserted" was an exaggeration; there were at least three other people visible: a nervous-looking couple with suitcases at the other end of the platform they were standing on, and a man sleeping on a bench across the way from them.

"It's just the off-hours," said Sushi. He set down his travel bag and stretched his arms. "It's evening, local time—most people are probably home, watching tri-vee or something."

"Yeah, *right*," said Do-Wop, unshouldering his own bag. "Must be somethin' pretty good on tonight, is all I can say. Even back home, there's usually people on the trans any time of day or night. And the spaceport oughta be one of the main stops . . ."

"Maybe we just missed a trans," said Sushi, shrugging. "There could have been two hundred people here, and we'd never know it if they all got on the trans and left just before we came up the stairway."

"And nobody got off? It don't figure," said Do-Wop, suspiciously.

"Off-hours, again," said Sushi. "I bet there aren't any more departures until morning. Most people want to start their travel during daytime hours. Relax, it's nothing sinister."

Do-Wop shook his head. "I dunno, Soosh. This whole planet smells like an abandoned building. Why'd Beeker want to come here, anyhow?"

Sushi shrugged. "I guess you have to know the history. Rot'n'art used to be the capital of the Alliance, the place where all the major decisions were made. The government offices employed billions of people, and they eventually roofed over the whole planet to build housing for them."

"Yeah, I could see that from space," said Do-Wop. He kicked a balled-up food wrapper off the platform and into the trans groove. It hung there in midair, suspended by the antigrav field. "Like one big ball of metal, orbiting out there. Except it's all dented and beat-up—why'd they let that happen?"

"More history," said Sushi. "That all happened after the Alliance grew too big to administer from one single world, even with FTL space travel. Some of the offices moved to other worlds, where it was cheaper and easier to hire local people than to transfer people from Rot'n'art. So a big chunk of the planet was suddenly unemployed."

"Bummer," said Do-Wop. "What'd they do?"

"Put everybody on relief," said Sushi. "Which might've been OK if they'd figured out a way to bring in new jobs for them. But once somebody's used to government work, there aren't a lot of other jobs they're willing to take. Especially not for less money."

"Makes sense to me," said Do-Wop. "Nobody wants to take less money. So everybody left, which explains why there's nobody on the trans . . ."

"Some people left," said Sushi. He stepped forward to the edge of the trans groove and looked down the tunnel, then stepped back and continued, "Most of them stayed, though. I guess they figured the good times and the good jobs would come back. And they ran through their savings, and the job market kept shrinking, and the infrastructure kept getting worse. I can't believe you didn't learn all this in school . . ."

"What school?" said Do-Wop. "Planet I come from, we were lucky to learn how to turn on a tri-vee, if we were lucky enough to have one."

"That figures," said Sushi. "And you must not have had one, or turned it on very often, either, or you'd know that Rot'n'art is still one of the most popular tourist destinations in the galaxy. Most of the slack in the economy got filled with service jobs aimed at the tourist industry."

"That's *gotta* be bogo," said Do-Wop, peering around with an unbelieving look. "I can't believe anybody comes *here* for a vacation."

"Oh, come on," said Sushi. "The Alliance Senate is still here, which means there are plenty of bigwigs on-planet, at least when the Senate's in session. So there're still five-star restaurants and fancy hotels for the senators and their staffs, and the lobbyists and other people who come here for government business. And they attract lots of tourists who want to see the so-called center of the galaxy, which is probably what Beeker's doing here."

"Inspectin' the slums? Ain't my idea of fun," said Do-Wop.

"You still don't get it," said Sushi, his hands on his hips. "As long as the restaurants and museums and public buildings are still good-looking, the rest of the world can fall apart as far as the tourists are concerned. Most of them never even see where the service workers live—just like on Lorelei."

"I guess they don't use the trans, either," said Do-Wop. "In fact, I'm starting to wonder if there *is* any trans this time of night."

Sushi cocked an ear toward the tunnels. "How much you want to bet on that?"

"Nothin'," said Do-Wop. "I can hear as well as you can, sucker." He picked up his luggage just as the trans popped out of the tunnel and glided to a halt at the platform.

"Too bad," said Sushi, grinning. "I was hoping to make enough to pay for supper tonight. Come on, let's not miss this one."

"Not a chance," said Do-Wop. Together the two legionnaires scooted through the open doors onto the waiting trans. After a moment, the doors closed and they were off into the maze of tunnels that served Rot'n'art as a lifeline of communications.

Sushi and Do-Wop must have taken a wrong turn in the winding alleyways of Rot'n'art City—more likely, they'd taken a few wrong turns. Actually, that wasn't very hard; a high percentage of the street signs were missing or defaced, and a higher percentage were unlighted. Even when they could see the name of the street they were on, it was likely as not to change its name without notice at any given intersection. They'd pretty much given up on trying to follow the map they'd gotten at the spaceport. Once they'd gotten out of the trans station, they might as well have been looking at a map of some other planet. With no sky visible, they couldn't even use the stars to get a rough idea of what direction they were going in. In short, no more than twenty minutes after getting off the trans, they were impossibly lost.

They'd finally decided just to find a major street, in hopes of spotting one of the city's landmark buildings and orienting themselves that way. So when they came to still another badly lit intersection, Sushi felt a glimmer of hope when he spotted bright lights a few blocks away along the cross street. "That's got to be a major intersection," he told Do-Wop, tugging on his partner's sleeve and pointing.

"Yeah, or maybe somethin's on fire," said Do-Wop. Having grown up in a blighted urban environment, he was well aware that bright lights weren't always good news.

"Even if it is, there'll be people there," said Sushi. "We can ask directions. Come on!" For some reason, they'd seen almost nobody on the streets. The few they'd seen had either avoided them or, like the ragged man they'd found sleeping on a hot-air vent a few blocks back, had been completely unresponsive to their requests for directions.

As they neared the lights, they became aware of a loud rumbling noise ahead of them. It quickly became clear that there was a large crowd ahead of them. A sporting event? Onlookers at a fire, or some other emergency? In any case, it was people. Sushi quickened his steps, and Do-Wop reluctantly followed.

When they came to the intersection, they were momentarily stopped by a thigh-high ferrocrete barrier. But ahead of them was the first open space they'd seen. They'd come out into some kind of park, or large plaza, one side of which was crowded with citizens. On the other side was a line of emergency vehicles, around which armored police were gathered in a skirmish line.

They'd found people, all right. What they hadn't counted on was finding themselves in the middle of an incipient riot.

For the moment, the center of the crowd's attention was a wiry, wild-haired man standing on an overturned hovercar, exhorting the crowd through some kind of portable amplifier.

"What's the word?" shouted the leader.

"Greebfap!" shouted the crowd. "Greebfap!"

Do-Wop crouched with Sushi behind the barrier. They were perhaps fifty meters from the crowd. Not far away, the riot police were adjusting their gear. "This looks like it's really gonna blow sky-high," said Do-Wop, rubbing his hands together. "Which side you wanna go with?"

"Go with?" said Sushi, horrified. "I want to go as far away from here as I can. If I had any idea which way the nearest trans stop was . . ."

"Ahh, you don't know how to have fun," said Do-Wop, picking up a two-foot length of plastic piping from the ground and smacking it into his other hand like a club. "I think the civilian side's the one to go with." Beyond the barrier the "Greebfap!" chant was building, settling into a rhythm.

"You think it's fun getting your head beaten in, or being knocked down and stomped on? I'll take a rain check," said Sushi. "These cops have got body armor and helmets, in case you didn't notice."

"Yeah, yeah, the cops always have that stuff," said Do-Wop, peering over the barricade. "These guys don't look like much, though. I bet the civvies can take 'em. Come on, Soosh!" He vaulted over the barrier and, crouching low, sprinted toward the milling group of chanters. One of the riot police pointed at him, but they made no effort to stop him.

"Damn!" said Sushi, looking around for a moment. "Guess us Legion guys have got to stick together," he said. He vaulted the barrier and sprinted full speed to join his buddy in the crowd. A cheer went up as he crossed the open space. Behind him he heard a popping sound. "What was that?" he asked as he pulled up next to Do-Wop, who crouched near the edge of the crowd, eyeing the riot police.

"Rubber bullets," said Do-Wop, grinning. "Don't worry, Soosh, they missed ya by a mile. Cops never could hit a moving target."

Sushi's face turned pale. "So why aren't we both moving straight away from here?"

Do-Wop grinned and pointed with his makeshift plastic club. "Too late now, man—here come the cops."

"Greebfap! Greebfap! We want Greebfap!" The chant rose higher as the crowd gathered itself to meet the charge.

"This has got to be totally against Legion regulations," Sushi said, more to himself than to Do-Wop—who probably wouldn't care. In most circumstances, Sushi wouldn't have cared, either. But in most circumstances, a violation of Legion regulations wouldn't get him shot by rubber bullets (or something worse), trampled and clubbed by charging riot police, and thrown into jail for good measure—and that would be *before* the Legion found out what he'd been doing. Then again, if he'd broken a few regulations at some Legion base, he'd at least have a chance to talk his way out of whatever trouble he was in. Somehow, he didn't get the impression that the Rot'n'art police were going to be any more persuadable than Do-Wop, just at the moment.

On the other hand ... there *was* somebody here he might be able to persuade.

He reached over and grabbed a bullhorn from a startled

man who was leading the "Greebfap!" chant, leapt onto an overturned hovertaxi, and began to address the crowd . . .

Phule watched the demonstration from the window of his hotel room, sipping on a glass of imported white wine. Upon arrival on the planet, he'd checked into the Rot'n'art House, where his family had maintained a suite ever since the days when his father made regular trips to close deals with planetary governments, quasi-governmental institutions, wildcat militias, and others with ready cash and a hankering for armaments. He'd already done a quick sweep of the suite for the usual bugging devices—not that Phule had any plans to discuss sensitive business there, but checking was always a good idea, especially on Rot'n'art, the acknowledged galactic center of the espionage game. Now he almost wished he had a bug planted in the plaza below, where tiny figures moved and gestured, but he could hear only the loudest of the group chants. "Greebfap! Greebfap!" What were they protesting, or demanding? He couldn't make heads or tails of it.

Eventually, having decided that the crowd wasn't likely to turn violent, and that there were enough police and robots on hand to handle it if it did, he turned from the window and booted up his Port-a-Brain laptop. The overriding question was how he was going to locate Beeker. He knew the butler was on this planet; the Port-a-Brain had told him that. But where would Beeker have gone, here on this rusty former capital of the Human Alliance? And why hadn't he answered Phule's email?

He called up a guide to local tourist services, trying to guess which attractions would appeal to Beeker (or to Nightingale, although he had much less sense of her taste and interests than of his butler's). There were a few historic buildings that one could tour, none of which struck him as likely to command anyone's interest much beyond half an hour. Slightly more promising were a couple of art museums, although reading between the lines of the guide made it clear that, in an attempt to make up for budget shortfalls, the most interesting artworks had been deaccquisitioned— many to off-planet collectors.

From there it went steadily downhill. With most of the planet having been roofed over in its boom days, there was almost nothing in the way of natural scenery or outdoor activities—at least, from the point of view of anyone who'd been to a real planet recently. And Phule couldn't imagine anyone—certainly not Beeker—wanting to spend his vacation time viewing industrial museums or public works.

So what did that leave? The guide said that the locals were fanatical in their devotion to professional team sports. Something called *haki* was apparently in season right now, and from the publicity holos it looked like a fast-moving, physically demanding game. But if Beeker had any interest in sports, he'd managed to conceal it entirely from his employer.

The performing arts section offered no better clues. There was a large concert hall in town, and tickets for the current attraction—Ruy Lopez and the Bad Bishops— were in heavy demand. Searching further, Phule found a sample of Lopez's music, and endured about seven seconds of it before deciding that Beeker probably wasn't interested in that, either. As for the theater, the stars were complete unknowns (at least to Phule), and the plot summaries of the current offerings ran the gamut from boring to bizarre without ever managing to pique his interest. Granted, his taste differed from the butler's, but as far as Phule could see, the local theater was between golden eras.

For a planet that touted itself as the "Galactic Center of Everything," Rot'n'art was revealing itself to be a surprisingly dull place. Could he be completely mistaken in thinking he knew Beeker's tastes and interests?

Another idea occurred to him. Nightingale might have

been the one who'd suggested coming to Rot'n'art, for reasons of her own. Could she have grown up on Rot'n'art and still have family here? Legion privacy policy meant that there'd be no official record of that, but Phule suspected that Perry Sodden, the investigator he'd hired, could find out easily enough. If she'd grown up locally, or if she had family here, that would give Phule his first useful clue as to why she and Beeker had come here—and maybe tell him where he could catch up to them.

Phule added the note to a list of questions for Sodden. He'd scheduled a meeting with the investigator for the next day. The list was already on its second page. Maybe all these questions would turn out to be superfluous. Maybe Beeker would answer his email. Or maybe Sodden would appear for the meeting with exactly the answers Phule was looking for, and then he could go meet Beeker and convince him to end this silly escapade and return to Zenobia and start doing his job again.

But it didn't hurt to prepare for the possibility that Sodden had had no more luck than Phule. Phule took a sip of his drink, rolled his shoulders to fight the tension in his muscles, and stared at the Port-a-Brain's screen once more.

It was late by the time he turned out the lights.

10

My employer, for all his dedication to the military life, was at bottom a businessman. In that, he resembled his father. He also resembled that gentleman in a firm conviction that his own view of the world was fundamentally accurate, and that others who did not share it were in need of correction. Unlike his father, he was at least willing to let those others find their own way to correction . . .

"That was awesome," said Do-Wop, shaking his head. "I knew you was a con artist, but I never seen you fool that many people at once." The two of them were ensconced in the guest room of a suburban home belonging to one of the ringleaders of the demonstration Sushi had inserted himself into as head agitator. It was early morning, planetary time, and outside the blinds the artificial lights of Rot'n'art were slowly working up to their daytime peak intensity.

Sushi was still exhausted despite a sound night's sleep. Taking over the demonstration had required all his energy, physical and mental, before the crowd had lifted him to its shoulders and carried him away in triumph. "If you ever see me about to try that again, remind me not to," he said. "I kept worrying that the cops would decide to make a charge. I think it was pure luck that they backed down . . ."

"Nah, you had 'em fluffled," said Do-Wop, admiringly. "If I had me some money to invest, I'd have put it in that greebfap you was sellin' the crowd. What is that stuff, anyway?"

"You tell me, and we'll both know," said Sushi. "All I knew is, our best chance to get out of the place without major damage was to throw in with the biggest gang we could find. Thank Ghu it worked."

"Yeah, I couldn't believe it when they all carried you off like some kind of hero," said Do-Wop. "You're a genius, Soosh."

"Thanks, I guess," said Sushi. "Only problem is that my face is going to be all over tri-vee. If Beeker or the captain sees the local news, they're likely to figure out what we're doing here. And if the wrong cop happens to spot me, I could end up in some back room figuring out how to answer hostile questions about greebfap."

Do-Wop scoffed. "No problem, we disguise you, is all. A fake beard and some dark shades oughta do the job . . . or maybe some kinda big hat . . ."

"Yeah, right, I carry that stuff with me all the time. What are you going to do, go out to the local disguise store? I wouldn't be surprised if the cops have your face in their files, too. They had robots taking pictures all during that riot. And unless they're really stupid, they'll be running comparisons with the passport pictures from spaceport arrivals. They probably already know exactly who we are."

"No freakin' way," said Do-Wop. "My passport pic don't look anything like me, and I bet yours don't, either."

"Mine's a lot uglier than I am," agreed Sushi. A tired grin came onto his face. "But yours couldn't possibly be . . ."

Sushi ducked as Do-Wop took a swing at him. "OK, sorry," he said. "Still, we've got this problem of suddenly being way too visible. And we still need to figure out where the captain is, so we can keep him out of trouble—and help him find Beeker, so we can go back to Zenobia."

"Well, one thing we know about the captain—he ain't cheap. Just find out what the best hotel on the planet is— I'll bet you dollars to donuts that's where the captain's staying."

Sushi's mouth fell open. "Partner, you just earned yourself a whole basket of donuts. That's the best idea I've heard all day. And it wasn't even mine."

Do-Wop grinned evilly. "Yeah, well, I'll pass on the donuts. Just remember this the next time you think you can diss your buddy. When they handed out the street smarts, us Italians was standing right by the flagpole. And you can tell that to the Marines."

"Uh, yeah," said Sushi. "So why don't we go downstairs and see if our host will feed us breakfast—and maybe tell us about the local hotels?"

"Now you're comin' up with the good ideas," said Do-Wop. "Lead the way, Soosh." Together they headed out the door; somewhere downstairs they could already hear a coffeemaker bubbling away. It was shaping up as a good morning, after all.

Just before noon, Phule took the dropshaft down to the lobby and entered the hotel bar, where he had agreed to meet Perry Sodden, tracer of missing persons, for business—and lunch. He took a corner booth away from other customers and ordered a pint of Old Rot'n'art IPA, which the locals firmly believed to be the finest beer in the galaxy. Phule knew better, but ordering anything else was practically guaranteed to start an argument with the robot waitress. He didn't need the attention, so he took a sip of the thin, sour-tasting brew and suppressed a shudder. If anything, the home brewery's product was worse than the export version. Just as well; he needed to keep a clear head, anyway, and the taste would discourage him from drinking much of it.

After a few minutes, Sodden slid onto the opposite bench of the booth. "You're in luck," he said, out of one side of his mouth. "I've already got a solid lead on the rascal you're after."

"That's great news, but don't think I'd call old Beeker a rascal," said Phule. "He's just taking a sort of unofficial vacation—with a lady friend."

"Know just what you mean, Captain," said Sodden with a wink. "Say, how about buying a fellow a drink? Talking's thirsty work, you know."

"So I've heard," said Phule, signaling for the waitress. Sodden ordered an Old Rot'n'art, and when the waitbot went to fetch it, Phule said, "Now, what are the chances of catching my man before he takes ship to the next planet? This is the third place I've followed him to, and I'd really like to get him back on the job."

"If I've seen it once, I've seen it a thousand times," said Sodden. "Midlife crisis kind of thing. One minute, your fellow's a sober citizen, and the next he decides it's time to stop and smell the roses, and the next thing you know he's halfway across the galaxy, driving a little red hovertible. Funny how the best roses are always on some other planet. But not to worry, Captain. Soon enough he'll run out of spending cash, and then you're like enough to see him back at your door, his hat in his hand." The beer came, and Sodden paused to take a deep sip.

"I can't imagine Beeks in a hovertible, red or any other color," said Phule, toying with his glass. "And I sure hope I don't have to wait for him to run out of money—the old fellow's as frugal as they come. I think it'd take him quite a while to spend all his savings, even with the lady friend helping him out."

"You'd be surprised," said Sodden. "I used to go with this girl from Varleigh . . ." He shuddered, then knocked back his drink and signaled for another before turning back to Phule. "Anyhow, he's bound to leave a trail an experienced investigator like me can follow. And like I told you, I've got a solid lead. Shouldn't be more than a couple of days before I've got him."

"He could be off-planet and on a ship to who knows where by then," said Phule. "I hope you aren't taking things for granted."

"Not a chance," Sodden said, with a dismissive wave of his hand. "Now, I'll need a bit more of an advance to check out all the angles—I might have to put on a couple of extra people to run everything down. But you can be sure we'll get . . ." The ring of his pocket phone interrupted him. "One moment, Captain. Sorry . . ." He put the earpiece to his ear, listening. "Uh-huh. Really. *Really?* Oh, shit. Hang on, I'll be there." He thumbed the OFF button and shoved the phone back in his pocket.

"What is it?" said Phule, worried.

"Minor problem in the office," said Sodden, getting to his feet. "Now, a couple hundred more for expenses would be a good idea just about now, right?"

"Some straight talk about what's going on with my case would be an even better idea," said Phule, getting to his feet and putting a hand on Sodden's shoulder.

"Uh, well . . ." Sodden rolled his eyes from side to side, like a drowning man searching for help. Suddenly he pointed to something behind Phule, and shouted, "Look! There she goes!"

Phule turned quickly to see a tall Black woman—

Nightingale? or someone else?—vanish through a doorway
leading out of the hotel. He turned back to Sodden—who
said, "Hurry! Maybe we can catch her."

They ran quickly to the door where they'd seen the
woman; but she had already vanished into the crowd on the
sidewalk.

The sign inside Chocolate Harry's Supply depot read,
GOLF POOL—BEST ODDS ON THE PLANET. A smart legionnaire might have pointed out that, since nobody else on the
planet was giving odds on General Blitzkrieg's golf games,
Harry wasn't promising all that much. But since the legionnaire who pointed that out was likely to have it pointed out
that Harry was under no obligation to take bets from anyone, the claim went unchallenged. In fact, Harry had plenty
of takers for his odds—a predictable benefit of running the
only game in town.

Harry wasn't picky; he'd give odds on almost anything
you could find somebody willing to bet on. He was running
a pool on the Zenobians' team sports, which almost none
of the Legionnaires understood (though there were plenty
who claimed to). Bets on the arrival time of the next Supply shuttle were one of his most popular offerings. And if
things were really slow, he could always fall back on orga-
nizing competitions among members of Omega Company,
on which other members were then encouraged to bet.

"Who d'ya want, Roadkill?" said Harry, as one of
Brandy's recruits studied the odds board. "If you're a bettin' man, there's some pretty juicy situations there."

The board currently had the general the favorite at two
to one; Lieutenant Armstrong was at five to two; Captain
Jester was at four to one; and Flight Leftenant Qual was a
rank outsider at ten to one. There were also plenty of side
bets, such as odds on one or more of the players scoring a
hole in one, longest drive of the day on the par five second,
over/under for total putts on the afternoon, number of balls

snatched by florbigs, and so forth. The variety of options was a tribute to Harry's hard work; he'd spent the better part of a weekend researching golf before he had the faintest clue how the game was played, let alone what somebody might want to bet on.

"Why's the general such a big favorite?" said Roadkill, squinting at the odds board. "He don't look like much of a player to me. Way out of shape . . ."

"Ah, but he's got the edge in experience," said Harry, knowingly. "Condition don't mean that much in this game, and there's no defensemen goin' upside your head if you take your eye off 'em. All a dude has to do is hit his best shot and watch it go. How you bettin'?"

Roadkill rubbed his chin. "Twenty gradoojies on the captain," he said, decisively. "And another five on Lieutenant Armstrong for a hole in one."

"OK, got you covered," said Chocolate Harry, smiling. "Who else wants some action?"

"I would like to bet, but first I have a question," said a familiar voice. Harry turned to see Mahatma standing there, an enigmatic smile on his face.

Harry groaned. "Oh, man, I'm not gonna have to explain the whole history of golf to you, am I?" he asked—only half-joking. Every officer and noncom in the company had learned to tread very carefully when Mahatma approached them with one of his questions.

"Not today, Sergeant Harry," said Mahatma. "I found a good history on the Net, although I may have other questions on it later. Today I want to know why the general is permitted to hit several drives for every one his opponents hit, then to choose the best to play."

"Uh, I think that's what they call a handiclap," said Harry, with utter confidence. "That's like a courtesy they extend to the visiting player, so's the local guys don't have an unfair advantage."

"That makes some sense," said Mahatma. Harry

breathed a deep sigh—prematurely, as he soon learned. "But tell me, Sergeant Harry—this is a new course, so our local players have not played it any more than the general has, have they?"

"I guess that's right, Mahatma," said Chocolate Harry, doing his best to appear unruffled. "But of course, Qual's a native, and the captain and lieutenant have both had a good long while to get acclimated to these here desert conditions, which the general, being from off-world, hasn't done. So they'd still have that local edge. Can't beat that local edge."

"The general seems to be beating it very consistently," said Mahatma, brightly.

"So *bet* on his ass," grumbled Harry, finally losing his patience. "I ain't got all day to talk, y'know. And if you ain't bettin', go mess wit' somebody else's head."

"Why, that is a wonderful suggestion, Sergeant Chocolate Harry," said Mahatma. "I believe I will do just that." And he turned on his heel, leaving C.H. to wonder just which of his two suggestions Mahatma was going to follow.

"Look here," said Phule. He was in the spaceport departure lounge, his luggage already checked, and a first-class one-way ticket to Hix's World in his hand. "I've been on Rot'n'art for nearly a week. I came here to find my butler and his girlfriend, and that was all I really cared about. And now I found out they're gone to Hix's World . . ."

"Bad luck," said Sodden, firmly. "If we'd just been a little bit quicker following up that one lead—you'll remember I was urging you to do just that . . ." He slapped his hand against the molded symwood arm of the waiting-room bench in evident frustration.

"No point in might-have-beens now," said Phule, with a shrug. "You've done the best you could for me, and I don't hold it against you that my butler moved too fast for us to catch him. I've just got to go to the next place and try to catch him there."

"Well, that's mighty big of you, Captain," said Sodden. He stood up and stuck out his hand. Phule shook it. "If you ever come back this way and need somebody in my line of work, just give a yell and I'm your man," said the detective.

"Well, there is one last thing I'd like to figure out," said Phule, holding on to Sodden's hand. "The longer I've been here, the more I've realized that this whole planet is obsessed with something I don't understand at all."

"Really?" said Sodden. He rubbed his chin with the free hand, a contemplative look on his face. "I can't for the life of me figure out what you mean, Captain."

"Greebfap," Phule barked.

"Hey, no point in getting fritzy about it, Captain," said Sodden, pulling away his hand and stepping backward. The bench kept him from retreating farther. "Just tell me what you're talking about, and I'll let you in on it."

"I'm talking about greebfap," snarled Phule, stepping forward and grabbing Sodden's lapel. "People are rioting in the streets, about to bring down the planetary government, all because of greebfap. Greebfap! Greebfap! Sodden, you're going to tell me what greebfap is before I leave this planet!"

A mechanical voice from the speaker interposed itself between his question and whatever Sodden might have been about to say. "Sagittarius Arm Special now ready for preboarding," it said. "Stops at Leibnitz, Hix's World, New Baltimore, and Glimber. First-class passengers, those who need assistance in boarding, and sophont groups with immature family members, please come to the gate for preboarding." A wheeled methane enclosure trundled noisily forward, its inhabitants dimly visible through the portholes. In a pocket Velcroed to the outside a set of tickets to Glimber was visible.

"There's your ship," said Sodden, pointing in the general direction of the gate. "Better get on board . . ."

"I heard the announcement," growled Phule. "I still have half an hour before they dog the doors shut. And that's all the time I need to make you tell me what greebfap is all about."

"Willard Phule! Or should I say, *Captain* Jester! What a surprise to see you!" came a chirpy voice from just behind him. Surprised, Phule turned his head, a look of half recognition already on his face. Almost involuntarily, his grip on Sodden's shirt loosened.

"Mrs. Biffwycke-Snerty," said Phule, recognizing one of his mother's comrades-in-arms from the charity gala circuit. "What a surprise . . ."

"Equally, I'm sure," said the woman. "I take it you're here on Legion duty, helping put down those *dreadful* rioters. It's *such* a reassurance to know that the *right* kind of people are doing their part to keep the galaxy a *safe* place to travel."

"Yes, ma'am," said Phule, as noncommittally as he could manage. "I hope you haven't been inconvenienced . . ."

"Fortunately, only slightly," said Mrs. Biffwycke-Snerty, putting on her most courageous expression. "My hoverlimo was *forced* to take an alternate route out to the spaceport to avoid the rioters. I saw some of the most *appalling* neighborhoods—one would think there'd be a better class of groundskeepers on *this* world, of all worlds. But my business here is finished, thank Ghu. It'll be such a relief to get home to poor Biffy; the silly boy never knows what to *do* with himself when I'm away."

"Yes, ma'am," said Phule again. He'd learned long since that it was the safest thing one could say to women of a certain social class. "Please give Mr. Biffwycke my regards."

"Thank you, Wilfred—I mean, *Captain*," Mrs. Biffwycke-Snerty beamed. "I certainly will, and please give your dear mama mine." She leaned forward and kissed the air a couple of inches from his cheek, then turned and went her way.

And of course, when Phule turned to look for Perry Sodden, there was nothing at all to be seen of the detective.

Chocolate Harry carefully avoided mentioning to any of the bettors in his golf pool that both Lieutenant Armstrong and the "Captain Jester" robot were playing to let General Blitzkrieg win. (Nobody was quite sure what Flight Left-enant Qual was playing for.) Harry expected the members of Omega Company to back their own officers, whether from loyalty or because of apparently favorable odds. And in fact, to date there was almost nobody betting on the general—which had allowed Harry to pocket a substantial profit at the end of every single day of the pool.

Harry had also made every effort to involve the anxious bettors in the action taking place out on the golf course. As much as General Blitzkrieg might have appreciated the idea of an audience raptly following his every stroke on the course, he (and his adjutant, Major Sparrowhawk) would have been quick to seize on any evidence that the legion-naires of Omega Company weren't hard at work. Luckily, Harry remembered that one of Phule's early purchases for the company was a set of state-of-the-art spy gear, with miniature video cameras and microphones. That allowed one of the caddies, suitably wired, to relay a running com-mentary back to an oversize tri-vee player in the Supply shack. Today it was Thumper, caddying for Flight Left-enant Qual, providing the play-by-play.

Considering how new the game was to everyone except Armstrong and the general, it had caught on amazingly. On any given day, every off-duty legionnaire on the post was likely to be crowded into the Supply shack. Of course there was a fully stocked bar right next to the odds board. Just as in his poker games, Harry figured that keeping the cus-tomers nicely marinated was good for business. Besides, it was a surefire way to even out the cash flow, even when he had to pay off an unexpected long shot—such as the time Flight Leftenant Qual managed to hook a tee shot smack into the middle of the gravitational anomaly on the second fairway, which kicked it straight down the course even faster than it had arrived, a good hundred-fifty yards past the pin. Of course the ball ended up well out in the brush, and when Thumper finally found his ball, Qual needed four more shots just to get it on the green. But the Zenobian handily won that day's long driving pool, at thirty-to-one odds.

The one thing Harry hadn't quite counted on came knocking on the door to Supply one afternoon, just as the golfers had teed up for their seventh hole. For once Blitzkrieg appeared to have figured out what it took to keep his shots in the center of the fairway. For his part, Flight Leftenant Qual was having uncanny luck with his putter, regularly sinking the ball from ten or more meters out. So the match was more competitive than usual, and as a consequence the bets were even heavier than usual. Harry had just begun to anticipate a killing when Double-X came hurrying over to him. "Sarge, we got trouble."

"Trouble?" growled Chocolate Harry. "What kind of trouble?" In answer, Double-X nodded toward the entrance to the Supply depot. There, to Harry's horror, stood Major Sparrowhawk, clipboard in hand and a determined expression on her face. "Shit," said Harry, in a low but sincere voice. "Guess I better take care of this. Be ready to close things down if I give the signal."

"Right on, Sarge," said Double-X. He glanced nervously first at the woman at the entrance, then at the small but enthusiastic group of bettors crowded around the tri-vee display. After a moment, he turned back, and asked, "Uh, what's the signal?" But by then, Chocolate Harry had already moved to intercept Major Sparrowhawk.

Chocolate Harry had long since perfected a number of

techniques for covering his tracks. When bluster and misdirection failed, he could usually fall back on misunderstanding and flat denial. And when all else failed, feigned ignorance was almost always good enough to get him through a crisis. From the look on the major's face, he was likely to need his entire repertoire today. "Hey, Major, good to see you," he began, in what he hoped was a convincingly hearty tone. "Need some supplies today?"

"Cut the crap, Sergeant," said Major Sparrowhawk. "You're making book on the general's golf game, which is against all regulations. And if I couldn't find a few dozen other violations of the Uniform Space Legion Code just by walking around in here for a few minutes, I'm a Centauran tree slug."

"Maybe you could," said Harry. "What're you gonna do if you do find 'em? Assign me to Omega Company?"

"Very funny," said Sparrowhawk. "If you don't think I can make unpleasant things happen, try me. A general's adjutant can give you way more trouble than most field officers. But think about this, Sergeant—if I was just looking for a way to bust you, I wouldn't be giving you even this much warning. You'd never know what hit you until it was way too late."

"Maybe," said Harry again, somewhat less cockily. Then, his curiosity aroused, he asked, "So what's the deal, then? You got a proposition for me, Major?"

Sparrowhawk looked around the Supply shack. Up front, the off-duty bettors were crowded around the screen, waiting to see the foursome hit their tee shots. Double-X was staring at Harry with obvious anxiety. "Too many people in here," she said, after a moment. "Let's go somewhere quiet to talk."

"OK," said Harry. He looked around. "Your place or mine?"

"Watch it," said Sparrowhawk, with an expression that had been known to make senior officers cringe. Then, after a moment, she said, "I know exactly the place. I'll meet you in the captain's office in ten minutes."

"The—what?" said Chocolate Harry.

"Captain Jester's not there," said Sparrowhawk, waving at the tri-vee screen. "He's playing golf. So's my boss, and so is Lieutenant Armstrong. And I happen to know that Lieutenant Rembrandt's down in Comm Central. So who are you worried about, Sergeant—more than me, that is?"

"OK," said Harry, nodding slowly. "Ten minutes."

"See you there," said Major Sparrowhawk. Then she turned on her heels and left the Supply shed, leaving Chocolate Harry scratching his head in bewilderment.

11

Journal #822—

A visit to Hix's World appears, at first glance, to be a step into the deepest past. Yet nowhere else are you likely to find a society so completely dependent on an intimately inter-connected, highly technological, spacegoing galactic community—and oblivious to that very dependence. Hix's World appears to have been founded on the premise that one can eat one's cake and still have it to admire. That, at least, is the only way I can interpret the notion of a bucolic existence that somehow manages to avoid such bucolic inconveniences as labor, famine, pestilence, and general misery.

Perhaps the most remarkable feature of Hix's World is the belief of many of its citizens that their way of life embod-ies the deepest spiritual values of modern civilization. From the point of view of a thoroughgoing pragmatist such as myself, such a belief appears as paradoxical as the in-habitants' belief that they have freed themselves from de-

pendence on the technological infrastructure of the Alliance as a whole.

As far as I can tell, this belief is an utter delusion.

The customs inspectors at Hix's World gave Phule's luggage an unusually thorough going-over. Having spent part of the voyage reading up on the planet's culture and customs, he was neither surprised nor unprepared. After replacing a couple of toiletry items with "Hix's-safe" equivalents at the shipboard store, he received the inspectors' thumbs-up and went on his way after only forty minutes. His immediate destination was a boardinghouse that catered to off-world clients, a likely place for Beeker and Nightingale to be staying—and a good place to stay, himself.

He arrived at La Retraite Rustique to find the sitting room full of tourists dressed in casual but expensive outfits, waiting to be called for the evening meal. The well-dressed young woman behind the desk shot an exasperated look in his direction, wrinkling her nose at his Legion jumpsuit. "May I assist you?" she asked, in a tone of voice that made it clear she hoped she couldn't.

"Quite likely," said Phule, setting down his bag. "First of all, I'm interested in a room."

"Impossible," said the woman, throwing up her hands. "We have been fully booked since the beginning of Waarmth." Hix's World had adopted its own eccentric calendar, featuring supposedly natural names for the time units equivalent to months.

"Ah, good for you," said Phule, smiling broadly. "I'm glad to know that such a fine establishment is so popular—but I'm sure you can find an open room for one of the old regulars." Phule himself had never been there, but his mother had taken vacations on Hix's World several times while he was growing up—which was how he knew of the place.

"Regular or irregular, it is simply impossible," said the woman, with an air of finality. "There's not even a closet to be had. The entire district is full for the Floribunda Fete."

Phule kept a broad smile on his face as his hand went into his pocket and returned with a small rectangular object which he placed on the counter just in front of the woman. She dropped her gaze to inspect it; when she looked up, with a gasp, her eyes were open wide. "A Dilithium Express card!" she whispered.

"Yes," said Phule. "Do you think that's good for a closet?"

"I think we can arrange something," she said. "At your service, Mr.—uh . . ." She tried to make out the name on the card.

"Captain Jester will do," said Phule. "Now—about that room . . ."

"Madame will be delighted to have you here, Captain!" she said. The young woman clapped her hands, and a man appeared from a door behind the desk. His tastefully rustic attire did not in the least disguise the fact that he was the bellman. "Andrew! Show the Captain to the Olympic Suite!"

The Olympic Suite was several degrees more elegant than any closet Phule had ever seen. Phule tipped Andrew, closed the door behind the bellman, and poured himself a cold glass of mineral water from the suite's refreshment center. He sat down at the suite's communications center, which was tastefully hidden inside a faux-Victorian rolltop desk. He'd learned from his mistakes on Cut 'N' Shoot and Rot'n'art. No more dashing about on a wild *gryff* chase, or worse yet depending on locals whose entire stake in the success of his search consisted of a generous paycheck— an overly generous one, considering the lack of results on Rot'n'art. This time, he was going to use his own very ample resources to track down Beeker and Nightingale.

He synchronized his Port-a-Brain with the hotel's web hookup, and began an automatic scan for Beeker's machine, a virtual twin of his own. If Beeker's computer had been connected to the planetary network anytime in the last two weeks, Phule's machine would be able to detect it. Better yet, if the machine was currently in use, he should be able to locate it instantly. If that happened, he intended to charter a private jumpcraft to the exact location—with any luck, in plenty of time to catch his errant butler. Of course, if Beeker had turned on his computer, he should have seen Phule's email. Had he not turned it on? Or had he seen the message and decided, for some reason, not to answer it?

Much to his relief, the Port-a-Brain was still functional; the special security systems hadn't taken over. So Beeker must be in range. He started his custom search engine, and, while it ran, went to look out the suite's picture windows, which overlooked a stretch of countryside that could have been somewhere in Provence, several centuries earlier. In fact, it *was* a careful reproduction of a stretch of ancient Provençal countryside, brought about by the most unintrusive and organic methods available, of course. If an occasional bush was the wrong species or color, that was a small price to pay for a program of minimalist terraforming.

As he cast his gaze over the pleasant contours of the rolling hills, covered with Old Earthlike greenery, Phule could hear the Port-a-Brain gently whirring in the background. It was a very soothing sound, telling him that one of the most powerful artificial brains in the known galaxy was working to solve his problem. In the middle distance he saw something moving; just what, he couldn't quite determine. Probably some creature imported from human worlds; the settlers hadn't so much expelled the indigenous flora and fauna from the terraformed sections as gently persuaded them to take their business elsewhere. Even so, a few species had stubbornly resisted the program—part of the charm of the place, Hix's World old-timers would tell you.

Then, all of a sudden, his eyes went into sharp focus and

he forgot entirely about the whirring of the Port-a-Brain. There, crossing the faux-Provençal landscape, was none other than Nightingale!

The owner of La Retraite Rustique sat in her office, looking over architects' renderings of the new addtion she planned for her hotel. She hated trying to extrapolate from the drawings to the actual structures they purported to represent. "Damn lying pictures," she muttered. "Why can't they show you what it's really going to look like?" The answer was obvious, of course—if the drawings looked like the finished product, the customer was a lot less likely to pay for the work.

There was a knock on the door. "Come in," she growled, not really annoyed at the interruption as much as generally disgruntled. She'd once owned the most fashionable and lucrative resort hotel and casino on Lorelei. Now she was trying to start over on a new world—and finding it a lot more work than she had any appetite for.

Robert, the concierge, entered. "Good news, Madame," he said. "We've just rented the Olympic Suite, at double the regular rate. Some Space Legion officer with a Dilithium Express card . . ."

"Space Legion officer? Dilithium Express?" Maxine Pruett sat bolt upright in her seat. "It can't be . . . what's this man's name?"

"Captain Jester," said the concierge. "Of course, all Legion names are pseudonyms . . ."

"Pseudonym, hell—I know Jester," said Maxine. "For your information, his real name's Willard Phule. The little son of a bitch nearly ran me out of business on Lorelei—or did you miss that particular episode?" Maxine had plenty of reason to remember it, since it had broken the mob's control of the casino business on Lorelei. Combined with the defection of Laverna, her most trusted assistant, it had also toppled her from her perch at the top of the Lorelei syndicate—which was ultimately why she'd moved her operation to Hix's World.

"I must confess I hadn't remembered the man's name," said Robert, warily. "Would you like me to find some pretext to deny him the room? It should be simple enough—I can always claim that some high official of the planet needs the space."

Maxine frowned and lit a cigarette. "No, that would just move him someplace else. Let's keep him here where I can keep track of him. What I want to know, though, is what's he doing here? He has to know it's my place—why else would he be here?"

"He apparently claimed a family connection," said Robert. "That's not impossible—but not very likely, either. I'll tell the waitresses and bartenders to see if they can find out the real reason from him."

"Tell 'em there's a bonus if they get what I want," said Maxine, pounding a fist into her other palm. "He's got to be here to interfere with my plans for the casino. How the hell did he find out? Bastard!"

"We'll learn whatever we can, Madame," said Robert. "I can probably have his suite searched while he's out, as well. Are there any other instructions?"

"Yeah, search the suite," said Maxine, nodding. "But be careful—I don't want him to know he's being spied on, and he's probably got better security systems than most banks. We don't want to make him suspicious. Find out where he's going when he leaves the hotel, and who he sees. And let me know if anyone comes asking for him—especially anybody else in a Legion uniform."

"I'll tell the staff," said Robert. "Anything else?"

An evil grin came to Maxine Pruett's face. "Yeah. I'd like to set a trap or two for him. Here's my idea . . ."

It took Phule something less than five minutes to get from the Olympic Suite to the gardens he'd been viewing from the window, where he'd seen Nightingale—or her twin sister. By the time he got there, the woman was nowhere to be seen, of course. But short of jumping out of a third-story window, there was no more direct way he could have gotten to the gardens.

He stared around in frustration, trying to figure out which way she could have gone. There were three paths leading away from the clearing where he'd spotted her, all of which turned corners quickly enough that he couldn't see very far down them. He picked the path that seemed closest to the direction she'd been going when he saw her. Fifty paces down the path he came to a clearing, with three more forks leading away. There was no sign that anyone had come this way recently. Making a snap decision, he took the middle fork. Fifty paces farther, there was another clearing, again with three paths . . .

Phule stopped and scratched his head. Running blindly after her—without even knowing which way she'd gone—was a waste of time and energy. For one thing, he was likely to make enough noise to warn anyone worried about avoiding pursuit. On the plus side, he now knew that Nightingale and Beeker were in the near vicinity. Perhaps they were even staying at the same hotel! He was likely to get much quicker results by asking the right questions. He turned and headed back to the hotel; *time to use my head instead of my feet, he told himself.*

His first stop was the front desk, where he pushed the call button for the manager. As he waited, the gentle sounds of ancient folk music drifted out from the dining area: a harp, a flute, and some kind of soft percussion instrument. Phule wasn't sure whether the sounds were live or recorded, although given the Hix's World passion for rustic authenticity, live was a fair bet.

After a moment, the desk clerk appeared. This time the woman's face broke into an eager-to-please smile, a predictable effect of his having flashed his Dilithium Express card at check-in. "Yes, sir, how can I assist you?" she chirped.

"I just saw an old family friend's wife out the back window," Phule said, in a casual tone of voice. "But she was gone by the time I got out there to look for her. I had no idea she and her husband were visiting Hix's World, or I'd have looked them up to ask them out for dinner. Could you tell me which room Mr. Beeker is staying in?"

"Beeker, Beeker," said the woman, knitting her brows. "Are you certain he's staying with us? I don't recall the name . . ."

"Older fellow, tends to dress a bit conservatively," said Phule. "His wife's a younger woman . . ." Phule gave as complete a description of the fugitives as he could, right up to what Nightingale had been wearing when he saw her out the window. But by the time he finished, the manager was shaking her head.

"That doesn't sound like anyone who's staying with us," she said. "Our gardens *are* open to the public. She could have come in from the streets, or anywhere."

"I guess that's possible," said Phule, rubbing his chin. "Is there someplace else they might be staying? Someplace close enough that one of them might be walking in your gardens?"

"Our gardens are a widely known attraction," said the woman, spreading her hands apart as if in welcome. "They so regularly won top prizes in the Floribunda Fete that the former owners withdrew them permanently to give others a chance . . . But as for where this person might be staying nearby . . . Well, there are several private homes that take in tourists. Your friends might be at any of them."

Phule nodded. "Fine, can you give me a list?"

"It's not something we usually track," said the woman. "Any list would be out of date rather quickly. Besides, your friends could well be staying with someone whom they know socially, rather than one of the boardinghouses."

"That's a chance I'll have to take," said Phule, leaning his elbow on the counter. "Just tell me any that you do know, and I'll see if Beeker's staying with them. If not, I'll just have to catch up with the old rascal back home and tell him he missed a free dinner on Hix's World."

"Best of luck finding him, sir," said the woman. "And if you do turn up Mr. Beeker and his wife, I think you'll find our dining room a very pleasant place to entertain them."

"Thanks—I'll remember that," said Phule. "Now—you were going to give me a list of places?"

The woman smiled and gave him the list. A few moments later Phule was placing the first of his calls . . .

The sign on the wall behind the hotel desk read, NO DIS- CLAVERY. Sushi stared at it, trying to figure out whether it was a misspelling of some more familiar word, but nothing seemed to fit. He shrugged; if he didn't know what it was, he decided he wasn't likely to be doing it. He reached out and touched the bell on the desk.

After a delay just long enough to be annoying, a sour-faced woman appeared at the desk. "What 'n the world you want, stranger?" she sniffed.

"Do you have a room for two?" asked Sushi. "We're probably going to be here at least two nights, maybe more if business is good."

"*Probably* and *maybe* don't pay the rent, mister," said the woman. "How many nights do you *want*?"

"I'll take two," said Sushi. "Can we extend that if we find out we need it longer?"

"Maybe," said the woman, with a shrug. "This here's a busy town, and there's more people than rooms sometimes. You want to hold it longer, you give me up-front money. Nobody makes a better offer, you get to keep the room."

"Any refund if somebody makes a better offer?"

"You sure do ask a lot of questions, stranger," said the woman. "We don't take kindly to Nosy Neds hereabouts."

"Two nights, then," said Sushi, firmly. "And my name's not Ned."

"You know, there's a law 'gainst giving wrong names to hotels," said the woman, with a suspicious stare.

"That's triff, lady, but maybe you noticed we didn't give you no names, yet," said Do-Wop. He squinted at the sign behind the counter. "Does that sign mean you've run out of disclavery? I got pretty good connections—I bet I could get you a batch, real cheap."

"Disclavery's against the law on *this* planet!" said the woman, giving Do-Wop the kind of look reserved for admitted criminals. She stepped back from the counter a pace.

"Well, that won't matter with my connections . . . OOF!" Do-Wop doubled over and began to make strangling noises. Probably the elbow Sushi had jammed into his solar plexus had something to do with his sudden distraction.

Seizing the opening, Sushi stepped forward, flashing his brightest smile. "No need to worry about that," he assured the landlady. He fished out his wallet and continued, "My friend's a real joker, but he doesn't mean anybody harm, not one bit. We really do respect the laws of all the worlds we visit, and that certainly includes Hix's World. Now, how much do we owe you for that room?"

The landlady favored Sushi with a suspicious glare, but the money in his hands seemed to settle the issue. "Ninety-two," she said. After a moment she amended herself: "Ninety-two *apiece*, and no rowdy stuff." She sketched a nod in the direction of the NO DISCLAVERY sign.

"Fine," said Sushi. "Here's for two nights."

"Number six, in back," said the woman, jerking her thumb in that direction. "You c'n carry yer own bags."

"I guess we can," said Sushi. "Come on, buddy, let's stow the bags, and then we can get down to business." He reached down and picked up his duffel bag, and motioned to Do-Wop to do the same."

"Yeah, yeah," said Do-Wop, who'd more or less recovered his breath. "I can't wait to find the captain so's I can go back to goofin' off."

"Remember, you two," said the woman behind the desk. "I find out you're up to any kind o' mischief—and I p'rtic'rly mean disclavery—I'm callin' the sheriff!"

"Great freakin' place you found us, Soosh," muttered Do-Wop, as he shouldered open the door to the outside. Perhaps fortunately, the woman behind the desk didn't seem to hear him.

Chocolate Harry boldly strolled into the captain's office as if he had every legitimate reason in the world to be there. In fact, he knew nobody was likely to question him. That was just as well, because inside, he was all but quivering in his oversize boots. Like many men who exploit loopholes and ambiguities in the rules, he had a secret fear of being caught—and while he was damned good at lawyering his way out of a situation, he always worried that he might someday meet his match. Captain Jester had given him considerable leeway. But at the moment, the captain wasn't here to protect him. And that could mean big trouble.

"Well, right on time, Sergeant," said Major Sparrowhawk, who'd taken the liberty of sitting in the captain's desk chair. "Pull up a chair—no point being uncomfortable while we're talking business."

"Business?" Chocolate Harry's expression was guarded. "'Scuse me, Major, but I didn't know we had any business to talk about."

"Well, Sergeant, I'm about to fill you in on it," said Sparrowhawk. "Sit down; the chair's not wired."

"OK, I'm sitting," said Harry. He turned the chair around so the back was between him and the general's adjutant, as if to give him some protection in case she started throwing things at him. "What's the scam?"

"Good choice of wording," said Sparrowhawk, dryly.

"You've probably noticed that General B is getting really involved in his golf game here."

"Hard to miss that," said Harry. "In fact, considering how many of the guys are getting into the daily pools, I'd say it's become the main attraction. What about it?"

Sparrowhawk crossed her arms and looked Harry directly in the eye. "What if I told you that, in spite of the wonderful attractions and thrilling people here on Zenobia Base, I'm a city girl at heart? In fact, suppose I said I'm getting utterly bored out here and want to get back home?"

"What, and give up Escrima's cookin'?" said Harry with an evil grin.

"I'd even give up that, good as it is," said Sparrowhawk, with a look that left no doubt she meant it. "To put it bluntly, I need to come up with a way to make the general stop whacking around that stupid little ball."

"And then?" said Harry. "S'pose he decides to start busting Captain Jester's chops, which everybody knows is why he came to Zenobia Base to begin with. That don't do nothin' for me."

"I know this might come as a surprise to you, Sergeant, but it doesn't do a damned thing for me, either," said Sparrowhawk. "As I said, I just want to get back to Rahnsome Base and my own home and friends. I hope this isn't a serious blow to you."

"I'm tough enough to take it, Major," said Chocolate Harry. "It'll put a hole in my bottom line, but I can take it." He shrugged and looked back at Sparrowhawk. "But you didn't haul me in here to talk about that—or did you?"

"My, you're slow," said Sparrowhawk. "Getting the general off this godforsaken base and back to Legion Headquarters is exactly what I'm trying to do. And the whole reason he's still here is that stupid game. Bad enough he putzes around with it in his office. Outdoors? In those silly shorts? Puh-leez! About the only good side of things is that he hasn't asked me to cabby for him."

"I think it's called *caddy*, Major," said Harry.

"Whatever it's called, I'm glad I'm not doing it," said Sparrowhawk. "Now—it has occurred to me that you can put a stop to the game if you're so inclined. And I mean to see that you are so inclined."

"Say *what*?" Harry's voice went up an octave, and his frown betrayed utter bewilderment. "How you think I can stop the game?"

"What's the one thing they can't play without?"

Harry rubbed his chin. "You got me, Major. Grass? Clubs? Those flags that show 'em were the holes are? Whisky?"

"Balls," said Major Sparrowhawk.

"Hey, no need to get nasty," said Chocolate Harry, drawing himself up to his full height, which was impressive even in a sitting position. "I'm tryin' to give you a straight answer . . ."

"Balls," repeated the major. "Those little white balls they keep hitting around the park. They can't play the game if they run out of those, can they?"

"I guess not," said Harry. "Only thing is, there's plenty of 'em. The captain had me order up three gross of Titleists when we were settin' up the golf course, and the supplier threw in six dozen PoDos for a bonus . . ."

"They're all going to disappear," said Sparrowhawk, grimly. "All of them. I don't care how you do it—I don't need to *know* how you do it, as long as it's done. I don't want a single golf ball to be on this base by this time tomorrow."

"I could do that," said Harry. "It'll be a little chancy, but I can do it." He leaned forward. "What's in it for me?"

"Getting the general off your back isn't enough?" Sparrowhawk sat back in the chair, an expression of disbelief on her face.

"It ain't my skanky ass he's after, pardon my French," said Chocolate Harry. "What's the worst gonna happen to me? Kicked out of the Legion? Transferred to another unit? He can't throw me into a combat unit, 'cause there ain't no wars to begin with."

"How about military prison?" said Sparrowhawk. "You've run up a rather spectacular record of corruption . . ."

"Which is different from the rest of the Legion how?" said Harry, with the demeanor of an utterly reasonable man. "Alls I say is, you take care of me, I take care of you. Here's what I got in mind . . ."

They talked for another hour, but at the end they had an agreement.

It was a beautiful morning. The air was clear and pristine; the temperature on the warmer side of moderate; and the sounds of birds (or something with very birdlike vocal equipment) wafted upon the gentle breeze.

Do-Wop stepped out onto the immaculately kept lawn in front of the hotel and sneezed loudly—twice. "Jeez, this dump makes me itch all over," he said, wiping his nose on the sleeve of his uniform. "Can't they do somethin' 'bout the air?"

"I think they already took care of that," said Sushi. "Or didn't you read the Mandatory Visitor and Immigration Notices they handed out on the shuttle down?"

"Who had time for that?" said Do-Wop. "I had twelve replays on the padouki console, best run in years."

"Well, good for you. But all those replays kept you from finding out that because of the environmental regulations, the air here is the healthiest in the galaxy," said Sushi, shrugging. "Or so the Hixians claim. Maybe you're just allergic to uncontaminated air . . ."

Do-Wop interrupted him with another sneeze. "If this is healthy, gimme some industrial fumes," he growled. "Where we goin' today, anyhow?"

"The captain's staying in a little place a couple of miles away," said Sushi, pointing in the general direction. "He must think Beeker's somewhere in the neighborhood, so we have to work on the same assumption . . ."

"Why?" interrupted Do-Wop. "What if the captain's wrong, and Beeker's halfway around the planet?"

Sushi rolled his eyes. "If he's wrong, we've got the whole planet to search—and no idea where to start. If he's right, we've at least got a plan. Which way do you want to play it?"

"Depends," said Do-Wop, wiping his nose on his sleeve again. "Is there somewheres else we could go look, where maybe the air's a bit unhealthier?"

"Gee, great attitude from a guy who's met Barky, the Environmental Dog," said Sushi. "If you'd read the Notices, you'd have found out that the whole planet is a pollution-free zone, which means there isn't going to be a whole lot of difference in the air wherever you go. So the best thing for you is probably to work your butt off trying to help the captain find Beeker, so we can get off this planet and back to Zenobia before your nose falls off."

"That'd be a great idea except for the part about work," said Do-Wop. "It don't look like I've got a whole lot of other choices, though. So how are we gonna find ol' Beeker?"

"Good question, considering we already haven't managed to find him on two other worlds," said Sushi. "I guess the best place to start is to ask ourselves where we'd be on this planet if we were Beeker?"

"I already know that," said Do-Wop. "I'd be on some other planet, where there's some life. This place is way too laid-back for any city boy."

"If that's the way you feel, you ought to be even more anxious to get the job done and head for home," said Sushi. "Come on, there's supposed to be a row of touristy shops in the center of town. Let's take a stroll down there and see if we spot our guy—or our Nightingale."

"Aw right, aw right," said Do-Wop. "I can't feature Beeker doin' touristy stuff, though. You think the dude even owns a T-shirt?"

"For all I know, he's got a hundred of 'em," said Sushi, as the two legionnaires started off toward town at a leisurely pace. "Who knows what he wears underneath that starched shirt of his?"

Do-Wop frowned, then answered, "For all I know, it's purple antirobot cammy."

Having exhausted the subject of Beeker's wardrobe, Do-Wop and Sushi trudged along, staring at the pathway leading into town. Like most paths they'd seen on Hix's World, it was paved with native flagstones, carefully chosen to harmonize with the scenery. It rarely held to an absolutely straight line, preferring gentle curves that followed the natural contours of the local terrain. A split-rail fence paralleled it on one side. It was thoroughly lovely, in a self-righteously rustic way.

Around the curve just ahead of them, there came a woman riding a bicycle. She saw the two pedestrians, and reached out to squeeze the bulb of an old-fashioned air horn mounted to the handlebars. Sushi and Do-Wop looked up and automatically moved to the side to let her by. It was only after she was past them and rolling around the next curve in the path that Sushi turned around and stared after her. "Hey, did you see that? That was Nightingale!"

"No shit?" said Do-Wop, wheeling around. "Hey, let's go get her!"

But she had more than enough of a head start to outrun them both.

12

Journal #829—

After the rust and incipient riot of Rot 'n 'art, Hix's World came as a breath of fresh air. Quite literally—air quality standards were written directly into the Settlers' Bill of Rights—in effect, the planetary constitution—by the members of the first colonization. Any device or organism known to emit any of 253 listed noxious gases or any of 728 listed noxious particles in atmospheric suspension was subject to confiscation without appeal. Noise regulations were equally stringent; certain musical instruments were officially contraband, unless accompanied by a certificate of performance proficiency from a recognized institution of musical education. Any performer not so certified was subject to expulsion from the planet.

What was remarkable about Hix's World wasn't the existence of the regulations—after all, any competent lawyer can probably think of dozens of equally stringent legal provisions around the Alliance. Nor was the total ruthless-

ness with which they were enforced especially odd; again, almost every society has at some time pursued a "zero tolerance" policy regarding some practice it frowns upon. No, what set Hix's World apart was the lack of dissent from the standards its original settlers had imposed upon the populace. Some ten generations after the settlement, the only changes in the environmental standards of Hix's World have been their extension to irritants unknown at the time of founding.

Surprisingly, the result of all this thicket of regulation is one of the most tranquil worlds on which I have ever set foot.

"All right, we know she's here," said Sushi. "So Beeker has to be here, too." He and Do-Wop sat on the low stone wall to one side of the footpath on which they'd been going into town when Nightingale—or someone who looked a great deal like her—rode past them on a bicycle. They'd dashed off in pursuit of her, but she'd had far too long a head start for them to catch her—though they'd certainly tried. And, whether she simply didn't hear them or deliberately ignored them, their attempts to get the cyclist to stop had failed.

Do-Wop scowled. "Maybe you're right, Soosh. But the way she was riding that thing, there's no tellin' where she's going. Could be miles from here."

"Could be," said Sushi. "But she was coming from Crumpton, which either means she's staying there—and will be back, probably later today. Or it could be she's staying someplace else close by and was headed there. In which case we've got a larger area to search . . ."

"I bet she's still in town," said Do-Wop, pointing in the direction in which Nightingale had gone. "Too early in the day for her to ride in, go shopping, and be done already."

Sushi shook his head. "It's after ten o'clock, you

know—*you* may like to sleep all morning, but not everybody else does. She could've gotten up early . . ."

Do-Wop cut him short. "Ahhh, you think you know everything, but you don't know how women shop," he scoffed. "Woman goes shoppin' for soap, she's gotta look at every bar of soap in three different stores. Not just look at it—she's gotta smell it, and heft it, and look at the color, and read the label, and compare the price, and talk to five, six other people about what kinda soap they like, and then go back to all the other stores again to look at *their* soap. Me, I'd grab the cheapest soap in the store and go home and wash my hands before she even figured out how much it cost."

"Hmmm, maybe you're right," said Sushi. "I didn't see her carrying anything, so she probably hadn't been shopping. Which means instead of following her, we should just wait for her to come back."

"Good thinkin'," said Do-Wop, standing up. "I say we both go find a good spot and hang out there and see if she comes past."

"All right, that makes as much sense as anything," said Sushi, rising to join his partner. "But we'd better keep our eyes and ears open while we're walking, just in case she comes back this way."

"Nothin' to worry about, Soosh," said Do-Wop, with a grin. "I'm all eyes."

"Yeah, well keep 'em open—I'd hate to miss her," said Sushi. After a moment he said, "I wonder what she's doing going out without Beeker. I hope they're still together—if they're not, we're totally wasting our time."

"Aw, man, Beeker might be old, but he ain't stupid."

"That's what I'm worried about," said Sushi. "Why isn't he out riding with her? What if she had some kind of accident?"

"Yeah, them two-wheel thingies look dangerous as hell to me," said Do-Wop.

"Bicycling's supposed to be good exercise," said Sushi, with a shrug. "It's fun, too—I used to ride one at summer camp, out on Earpsalot. But there could be other reasons Beeker's not with her this morning. Maybe he had some shopping of his own to do . . ."

"No way Beeker's gonna spend all morning on that. I bet there's somethin' fishy goin' on . . ."

"What is it with you, anyway?" said Sushi. He stopped walking and turned to point a finger at his partner. "Two minutes ago you were saying Beeker wasn't out with Nightingale because he didn't want to ride a bicycle, now you say there's something fishy because he isn't. Don't you listen to yourself? Or do you just like to contradict people for the sake of argument?"

"What the hell you talkin' about? I never contradict no-body," said Do-Wop, his hands on his hips.

"You do it all the time," said Sushi. "Especially me, and I'm getting tired of it."

"Oh, yeah?" said Do-Wop. "Listen up, wise guy . . ."

They were still arguing hotly when Nightingale gently honked her horn and zipped past them on her bicycle, headed back to Crumpton.

Lieutenant Armstrong took a deep breath. Everything was going according to plan—so far, at least. Barring some dis-aster, General Blitzkrieg would be happily occupied during his stay, out of the company's hair, and blissfully unaware that Captain Jester was off-planet. The essence of the plan was for Blitzkrieg to win—ideally, by a narrow enough margin to keep the general from walking off with a signif-icant bundle of Omega Company's cash. Just to be on the safe side, Armstrong had instructed the caddies to make certain the general always had a good lie, and that the flor-bigs left his ball alone, and that his drink was never empty.

To Armstrong's great relief, the general had taken to Omega Company's new golf course like a Zenobian Realtor to virgin swampland. And the Andromatic robot duplicate of Captain Jester—originally built to impersonate Phule in his capacity as owner of the Fat Chance Casino—evidently had the general completely fooled. The robot was custom-built to escort rich customers around a gambling resort. So the robot "Phule" came from the factory programmed to play a respectable golf game—automatically modulating its game to play just a couple of strokes worse than the opponent.

Flight Leftenant Qual had been briefed on the plan, of course. Armstrong wasn't entirely sure just how much Qual understood, or whether the Zenobian was sufficiently in command of his game to play his part without mishaps. The little Zenobian's style was completely unorthodox, with both feet usually coming off the ground when he swung. Qual got excellent distance off the tee with his cut-down clubs, but his shots seemed to have a near-magnetic attraction to the deep rough and the bunkers. That should have resulted in a horrible score; but despite spending most of his time in the hazards, Qual had pulled off some near miracles with his short irons and putter, and shot a very respectable thirty-nine on the first nine. Armstrong had had to sink a couple of fifteen-foot putts to keep Qual and the robot from taking the lead. He did his best not to think of what the general's mood might be if he'd missed them . . .

But after nine holes, the score was just where it ought to be: The general and Armstrong were one up against Qual and the robot. General Blitzkrieg had hit something over a hundred balls, but by incredibly selective scorekeeping, had managed to put only forty-two strokes down on his scorecard. It was his custom to hit as many as four drives— "Just getting a feel for the course," he'd say—then play whichever ball happened to lie best. "This is the one I hit first, right?" If an approach shot went astray, he'd take another mulligan or two. What was most astonishing to Armstrong was that Blitzkrieg appeared to have no notion whatsoever that his score for the front nine was in any way questionable.

In any case, General Blitzkrieg was in the lead, and in a good mood. The florbigs had left his ball entirely alone, he'd had a long cool G&T after the front nine, and now he was gleefully rehashing every good shot he'd made—some of them completely imaginary, but not even Qual was clueless enough to challenge him on that point.

Armstrong had won the last hole with a par four; the other three players had holed out in five, with Qual and the robot "Captain Jester" both missing tough six-footers. True to form, General Blitzkrieg had picked up his thirty-foot uphill putt once Armstrong's ball was in the hole, saying "that one's a gimme, now." In any case, Armstrong had the honors, and responded by thumping a number two wood straight down the middle, with a clean shot at the fat of the green. "Great golf shot," said Captain Jester, with a broad grin. It was uncanny how much the robot resembled its prototype, right down to the nuances of behavior; it was exactly the way the real captain would have responded.

Qual and the general followed, and for once both somehow managed to keep the ball in the fairway, though short of Armstrong's drive. Now the robot was up, waggling a driving iron at the teed ball. "Let's see if I can put this one past you, Armstrong," it said, shading its eyes to peer down the fairway.

The general said, "Ten dollars says you can't." He'd made three or four similar side bets, and lost all but one of them, but if he had any memory of his losses, it didn't deter him. Maybe it was his way of putting pressure on an opponent.

"Like taking candy from a baby," said the robot. "You're on, General—watch this!" It took a long backswing, then brought the club head down on the ball with frightening velocity. The ball streaked off down the center of the course, seemingly inches off the ground.

Whether by sheer blind luck, or as a cleverly disguised
way to let the general win another hole, the robot's drive
was aimed directly at a low, flat rock perhaps forty yards
down the course. If it had hit at almost any random angle, it
would have bounced off in some unpredictable direction—
most likely, into the deep rough. But, as luck would have it,
the ball hit square on almost the only face of the rock per-
pendicular to its line of flight, and before anyone could say
a word, it had rebounded directly back to the tee and struck
the robot square in the forehead with a sickening *thunk*. As
three horrified golfers, and four openmouthed caddies,
looked on, the robot crumpled to the ground—seemingly
lifeless.

Phule had spent a good fraction of the morning learning
that, if Hix's World had a private detective agency, it was
extremely private. Secret might be a better description—at
least, there were none listed on the Net, nor in the business
directory, nor in the phone books. And Carlotta, the receptionist who'd greeted him upon arrival, showed no sign of
comprehending what he was looking for when he asked her
advice. He was beginning to wonder if anybody on Hix's
World did anything that required investigation, improbable
as that seemed.

In fact, it didn't make sense at all. There was certainly a
government here, and Phule had even seen evidence of a
police force, although not one that would have impressed
visitors from a built-up world like Rot'n'art or New Baltimore. And he had no doubt that people here were swin-
dling their business partners and cheating on their spouses
just as frequently as on any other world he'd been to. But
he couldn't for the life of him figure out how they found out
what was going on—unless everybody did their own private investigations. Which is what it looked as if he was
going to have to do if he was going to find Nightingale—
and ultimately, Beeker.

So: back to square one. He knew they were here, and in fact they couldn't be far away. If he visited the nearby hotels and rooming houses, he had a good chance of either spotting them or getting a desk clerk or waiter to recognize them by description. It would be labor-intensive, but it was fairly straightforward.

Alternately, he could start visiting places they were likely to go, hoping to intercept them there. That also required time, but a bit less legwork. He could pick a museum gallery or a park bench and wait—if he picked the right one. It'd be just his luck to spend hours inspecting the crowds someplace they'd already checked off their list. What kind of attraction would Beeker be drawn to? He realized he had no better idea than he'd had on Rot'n'art.

Well, one thing they had to do was eat. And even if their hotel had a four-star restaurant, they'd likely want to sample the others in the neighborhood, if only for a change of scenery—or to avoid a special trip back in the midst of a day of sightseeing. That was the ticket! He'd pick a popular lunch spot near tourist spots, and lie in wait for them there. The Directory of Local Attractions provided by the hotel gave him the names of several likely spots; he chose one, got directions there, and headed out.

Encore Silver Plate was a little cafe and wine bar with outdoor tables, half a block from the main shopping street in the largest nearby town, New Yarmouth. The walls were hung with works of local artists, all priced for sale, and none to Phule's taste. But the place was obviously popular—nearly full, in fact—and the colorful sign in front was large enough to catch the eye of any jaded shopper looking for a place to take a lunch break. Best of all, the outside tables gave a clear view along the street in both directions, as well as of the foot traffic on High Street.

Phule ordered a large coffee and settled himself at a table near the curb, with a local newsprint he'd picked up on the way into town. A look around at the clientele suggested that the place was frequented equally by locals and off-worlders here to see the Floribunda Fete.

The tourists sat in small groups, ostentatiously dressed in expensive walking or cycling outfits, noisily comparing notes on maps and guidebooks, or off-world newsprints. The locals—most of them wearing casual outfits that wouldn't have raised an eyebrow on any of the settled worlds of the Alliance—also kept to themselves, swapping hilarious gossip about their neighbors or playing some local card game—which looked to be an improbable cross between cribbage and tonk. They paid no attention to the tourists, who returned the favor.

Phule wasn't especially interested in either group, except for a particular pair of tourists. He'd already determined that neither Beeker nor Nightingale were in the cafe or on the nearby streets. He took a sip of his coffee, opened the newsprint, and sat back in a position where he could see along the street in both directions without lowering the paper or otherwise making it obvious he was looking for someone. He figured that even if someone noticed him scanning the crowd, they were most likely to assume he was—like at least two other men in the cafe—a bored tourist awaiting his wife's return from a shopping expedition.

An hour passed; Phule bought a second coffee and some kind of sweet pastry, overtipping the girl behind the counter—if he had to sit at his table a long time, he didn't want her to get too annoyed at him, maybe even decide he looked suspicious and call the authorities on him. He'd already lost interest in the newsprint. But he'd made up his mind to stay here till after lunchtime, then move on to someplace else and take up the vigil there—unless he got a break first.

After another hour, he was beginning to regret the two coffees, good as they were. There was a restroom inside the cafe, of course. But to use it was to risk missing Beeker or Nightingale, should they by chance pick that very moment to pass by. He sat there a while longer, crossing and un-crossing his legs as he wondered what professional detectives did in this situation. Finally, after convincing himself that the odds of missing his quarry were so slim as to be negligible, he gave in to the inevitable and went inside.

Naturally, he'd been gone mere seconds before Beeker and Nightingale strolled slowly past the cafe, stopping to read the menu and peer inside before moving on down the street. But by the time Phule was back outside, they'd turned the corner. He never knew how close he'd come to finding them.

Worse yet, he never finished reading his newsprint. If he'd gotten as far as the sports section, he could have seen a headline reading: "Rot'n'art Edges NB in Alliance Cup." In smaller type, just below, it read, "Greebfap Beams in Shot at Beeper to Ice OT Win."

"Why do you want to go to the captain's hotel?" asked Sushi. "Rembrandt ordered us not to let the captain know we're here trying to help him. Or did you forget that?"

Do-Wop shrugged. "I didn't forget nothin'," he said. "Thing is, we've seen Nightingale twice, already. So we know she—and Ol' Beeky—has gotta be close. But the captain, he don't know that. So we're gonna leave him a 'nonymous tip sayin' the people he's lookin' for are right here under his nose."

"Well, that makes sense," said Sushi. He found a piece of paper and jotted down a brief message. He folded it, wrote on the outside "To Capt. Jester," and stuck it in the pocket of his jumpsuit. "OK, let's go," he said.

They walked over to the local bike shop, where they rented a tandem model, the cheapest alternative for two traveling together. True to form, Do-Wop was initially reluctant to trust himself to the "two-wheeled thingie."

"Aww, come on," said Sushi. "Little girls can ride these things. What's the big brave legionnaire afraid of?"

"Fallin' off and breakin' my neck," said Do-Wop, eyeing it warily. But after a little more joking, Sushi persuaded him to give it a try. Sure enough, he picked up the knack in short time, and admitted that it came close to being fun. That was likely to change the first time he took a fall, but Sushi coached him in the basics and soon he was satisfied that his buddy was ready to roll.

With that settled, they hopped on the rented tandem and set off for Phule's hotel. Not surprisingly, La Retraite Rustique was in a considerably fancier neighborhood than their own modest digs. Several of the neighboring properties appeared to be large country estates, perhaps in the same family since the time of the Founding. So when the two of them pulled their well-used tandem up to its front door, the doorman appeared ready to direct them to the delivery entrance.

His attitude didn't improve when Do-Wop tossed him a small coin and said, "Yo, bud, make sure nobody messes wit' da ride."

"I am certain it will be perfectly safe while *you* are gone," said the doorman, with just the faintest emphasis. His left eyebrow lifted a fraction of an inch.

"Great, I knew I could trust ya," said Do-Wop, as he followed Sushi through the door. The doorman gave the door a baleful look, then turned to the coin he'd caught in midair. After a moment, he shrugged and pocketed it. After all, it'd buy him a coffee or a nut bar, no matter where it came from.

Inside the lobby, Sushi and Do-Wop stopped and looked around for a moment. For all its pretense at rustic simplicity, La Retraite fairly reeked of money. The hardwood floorboards were nearly a foot wide, with tight, clearly delineated grain that indicated old-growth timber to a practiced eye. The art on the walls was all original, and while the artists' names weren't familiar to the two legionnaires, Sushi suspected (rightly) that they would be to any visiting connoisseur. Even the lighting was of a discreet tone that gave a suggestion of candlelight without the trouble of wax drips or smoke.

Their admiration was broken by a deep voice. "May I be of help, gentlemen?" The tone somehow made it clear that the final word was included as a matter of courtesy, with the speaker carefully reserving his personal opinion as to its relevance.

"Sure," said Do-Wop—coming here was his idea, so he felt entitled to take the lead. "We're lookin' for Captain Jester, Space Legion. This is where he's stayin', right?"

"Offhand, I couldn't say," said Robert, the concierge—for that was who had greeted them. "Perhaps you could tell why you want to know."

"Just so happens, we got a 'nonymous message for him," Do-Wop said out of the side of his mouth.

"Really," said the concierge, with a hint of a smirk. "And what makes you think we would convey anonymous messages to our guests—assuming this captain is in fact one of our guests?"

"What, are you playin' the dumbs with me?" said Do-Wop, putting his hands on his hips. "Yo, I can play the dumbs, too."

"Relax, buddy," said Sushi, putting a hand on Do-Wop's shoulder. He turned to the concierge. "My friend here didn't quite make himself clear. We need to get a note to the captain, and there's a little something to make sure it gets to him." He offered the message, along with a folded bill. "If he asks, you didn't see who brought it, OK?"

"I'm afraid it's not OK," said Robert, looking down his nose at the note and the bill. "I don't see what legitimate business one of our guests could have with the likes of you two."

"Whaddaya mean?" growled Do-Wop, making a fist. "Y'know, this honker's startin' to rack me off . . ."

Sushi grabbed his partner's arm. "Easy, buddy. The guy

thinks we're not fancy enough for his place. We'll get our
message to the captain some other way. Come on."

"OK," said Do-Wop, glaring. "I guess we better get
outta here before I stink up the rich people's air." He turned
on his heel and walked away so rapidly that Sushi had to
hurry to keep up.

According to the literature in Phule's hotel, travelers
came from light-years away to enjoy the annual Floribunda Fete on Hix's World. And, to judge from the variety of costumes and accents Phule saw and heard around
him in the hotel dining room and in the nearby town, that
was no exaggeration.

Unfortunately, what he'd seen of the festival didn't im-
press him. Maybe it just wasn't a guy thing—most of the
male tourists he saw seemed as little interested in the abun-
dant flowers as he was. Just as likely, he was too focused on
trying to find Beeker and the Port-a-Brain to have much attention left over for the colorful blossoms that decorated
every home and business he passed. Some of the ones he
noticed were sort of pretty, but he wouldn't have come
halfway across the galaxy to enjoy them. Probably he
wouldn't even have crossed the street.

On the other hand, it did seem that Beeker must have
come here for the festival—as he'd discovered, the planet
was booked solid for weeks in advance. As far as Phule
could tell, his butler had never shown any particular interest in flowers. Of course, as he'd already discovered, he
knew far less of Beeker's tastes than he'd realized. Maybe
it was Nightingale who'd convinced him to come, though
that seemed out of character, too—or maybe he just didn't
know her all that well. Obviously, *somebody* had made advance reservations for the couple, well before Nightingale
had joined Omega Company. He stared out the window at
the gardens where he'd seen Nightingale two days earlier,
trying to figure it out. How could he know so little about

people he'd lived with for months—in Beeker's case, for years?

He realized that beating his head against these puzzles was beginning to give him a headache. What he needed was a walk in the fresh air. He slipped on a light jacket— the evening air could be brisk, even in Floribunda season—and headed downstairs to the gardens. But no sooner had he entered the lobby than he was waylaid by Carlotta, the receptionist at Retraite Rustique.

"Captain Jester," she said, wide-eyed. "I must warn you—you are being followed by two very suspicious men!"

"Really?" he said. "What do they look like?"

She glanced over her shoulder. "I have not seen them myself, but they approached Robert, the concierge—he was immediately put on his guard, and sent them away without telling them anything. But you must be aware at all times—you may be in danger!"

"A Legion officer is used to danger, ma'am," Phule assured her. "But I think I'll have a word with your concierge in any case. No point walking into something blindfolded, if you can get advance knowledge. And thank you for the warning."

Robert looked so competent, distinguished, and professionally discreet that Phule easily could have believed he'd been selected for his role by Galactic Central Casting. The concierge nodded politely as Phule approached him. "Yes, sir?" he said, with an inflection suggesting that he was awaiting orders.

"Your receptionist tells me a couple of fellows were asking about me," said Phule. "She says they were suspicious characters, so I thought I should follow it up, just so I don't get caught off guard. What can you tell me about them?"

"Not a great deal, I'm afraid, sir," said Robert. "They were rather young, I'd guess in their early twenties. They were dressed all in black—that seems to be much the fashion at that age—and they asked if you were staying here. I sent them right away, of course."

"Asked for me by name, I assume," said Phule.

"Exactly, sir," said Robert. "Name, rank, and branch of service—*Captain Jester of the Space Legion,* they said. Well, I didn't like the look of them at all. Not that I'd have given them information even if I thought they were princes. That's not what Madame employs me for, if you know what I mean."

"And I'm glad to hear it," said Phule. "Can you tell me any more what they looked like?" Phule had no idea who might have some reason to be looking for him. He'd settled accounts with the Intergalactic Revenue Service sufficiently to get them off his back for several years to come. He didn't think the Lorelei Mob wanted anything more to do with him, after he'd shown them what kind of muscle the Legion could bring to bear on its targets. And while he'd probably left some ruffled feathers behind, he hadn't made any real enemies on his visits to Cut 'N' Shoot or Rot'n'art.

"Well, as I said, they were young and dressed in black," said Robert. "Both males—I don't think I said that. One of them was probably of Earth Asian ancestry; the other was big-city trash of some sort, to judge from his accent."

"Hmmm . . ." Phule pondered. "Thank you; I'll have to keep an eye out for them."

Outside in the garden, he mulled over what the concierge had told him. The description he'd been given could fit dozens of people, including several members of his own Legion company—Do-Wop and Sushi, in particular. Of course, it was unlikely that the two of them were on Hix's World. The expense alone would have prevented it. In any case, if the concierge was describing them accurately, the black-clad youngsters would be fairly obvious here on Hix's World, with its crowds of casually—but expensively dressed tourists and ecologically correct locals. But if the two really meant him trouble, he'd have to be on the lookout. Just what he needed—something else to worry about.

13

Journal #840—

A person fond of an orderly existence will find much to admire about life on a military base. (Given the rarity of chances to admire the military, one probably ought to appreciate the few that do present themselves.)

As soon as Phule had left, the concierge walked briskly across the lobby to the owner's private office. He knocked, waited an instant, then opened the door. At her desk, Madame looked up at him, annoyance turning to expectation as she recognized him. "Well, Robert. How did Jester react to our little ploy?"

"He seemed to take it at face value," said Robert, easing into a chair without awaiting his boss's invitation. "He managed to act as if he had no idea what those legionnaires were up to. We know better, of course, but he was quite convincing."

"He's a damn good actor," agreed Maxine Pruett—

Phule's old rival from the Lorelei casino wars. "Do you think he knows I'm planning to turn this joint into a new casino?"

Robert shrugged. "Why would he show up here if he didn't suspect it? The only other possibility is coincidence—which is too far-fetched to believe."

Maxine wrinkled her nose. "I see your point. The question is, what are we going to do?"

"Realistically?" Robert drummed his fingers on the arm of his chair, then said, "I see only two ways to play it: Plow ahead and hope no one catches on before we're home, or get out before everything collapses around us."

Maxine nodded. "What do you recommend?" She raised a quizzical eyebrow.

Robert chuckled. "Is this an intelligence test? If we pull the plug now, I'm personally going to lose a lot of money, and so are you. My instinct is to stick it out. On the other hand, if we're caught . . ."

"Hix's World throws the law books at us," said Maxine, not letting the pause drag out too long. "High risk for high profit, or bug out now and lose it all—and no guarantees with either choice. But my gut instinct is the same as yours. That gives us another problem . . ."

"Whether to eliminate Jester before he ruins our entire plan," said Robert, nodding. "Luckily, those two flunkies of his aren't going to pose any threat to us."

"Don't be so sure," said Maxine. "I've run up against the Space Legion before . . ."

"Forget them," said Robert, waving a hand. "The Legion is a laughingstock, even in military circles. And that's saying a mouthful, if you have any idea of the level of incompetence and corruption in the Alliance military as a whole."

"You haven't had them shooting cannons over your head," said Maxine. "I have—and that makes me want to think twice before I call in the rough boys to deal with Jester."

Robert leaned over the desk. "All right, then. We wait and see how he responds to my hint that someone's after him. I'm hoping it'll scare him off—or at least slow him down enough to let us finish our business before anything else threatens us. If he doesn't scare off—well, we'll have to see what kind of trouble we're in at that point."

"That's my Robert—I can always depend on you to argue for the plan with the least risk," said Maxine.

"And it's gotten me a long, nearly trouble-free life," said Robert. "But least risk isn't no risk. If circumstances dictate, I'm ready to take steps against Jester. If that doesn't work, I have a bag packed, ready to go—and if the fellows with badges and handcuffs are close enough behind me, I'm content to leave without it. I advise you to make similar preparations."

"You'd think it was a crime to try to make a profit," said Maxine, dryly. "The damn Settlers' Bill of Rights wasn't supposed to kill off business, was it?"

"I'm sure it wasn't," said Robert. "I'm equally sure that the party now in power has consistently interpreted it so that our little enterprise can be seen that way. A good attorney could probably convince an appeals court otherwise. But there'd be a lot of expense and other unpleasantness before we reached that point. I'd just as soon grab my profit and get out before anybody comes around asking questions."

"Good point," said Maxine. "All right, we wait and see. But be sharp—I don't want any surprises. If Jester starts snooping into something we don't want him to know about, I want you to tell me instantly."

"Not a problem," said Robert. "Believe me, I have as much to lose as anyone. Do you need me for anything more, Madame?"

"Right now, no," she said. "Remember—keep your eyes on Jester!"

"There is *definitely* somethin' weird goin' on back there," said Do-Wop, as he and Sushi walked down the path from La Retraite Rustique.

"Really," said Sushi, stopping and putting his hands on his hips. "I am, like, completely blown away by your powers of observation."

"Yeah, well, I guess not everybody would notice it," said Do-Wop. He looked back over his shoulder, as if to ensure nobody was watching them. "You sorta hafta know what you're lookin' at."

"That would never have occurred to me," said Sushi, scaling unprecedented heights of sarcasm. "What exactly made you suspicious? Perhaps I can learn something from you."

Do-Wop grinned. "Well, yeah, that's why they made us partners, ain't it? Thing is, that *consigliere* . . ."

"You mean the *concierge*?"

"Hey, you say it in your language, I say it in mine," said Do-Wop. Together they strolled casually over to the rack where they'd parked the tandem bike they'd come on. "Anyways, I seen that sucker before, in another hotel. And guess where?"

"We've been in a few hotels together," said Sushi, trying to think back to the various places Phule had quartered Omega Company since taking command. "I can't say I remember him from any of them, though."

"Well, here's a hint," Do-Wop said, mounting the tandem bike behind Sushi. "It was back on Lorelei—that help any?"

"Not exactly," said Sushi. "I stuck my nose into a lot of places there, dropped a few bucks . . . *Wait a minute.* Was it by any chance one of the mob-owned hotels?"

"Got it in one," said Do-Wop. "Course, that covers pretty near *all* the hotels on Lorelei."

"Huh," said Sushi. "That's very interesting, even if it could be just a coincidence. The guy's entitled to get a job in the same line of work he's been in—and you can't just assume that everybody working for a gangster is crooked, themselves . . ."

"Nope, but it's where the smart money's gonna be. And you know what else I'm thinkin'?"

Sushi grunted, starting to pedal the bike. "Maybe. Do you mean it hits you as a little bit fishy that the mob boss's old secretary—now known as Nightingale—is running around the same planet as this guy?"

"Naah, I was thinkin' I'd like a sandwich . . ." Do-Wop put his feet down, bringing the bike to a halt. Sushi just managed to keep from flying headfirst over the handlebars. "Wait a minute, do you really think that?" said Do-Wop. "But she's part of the Omega Mob, now. She wouldn't sell out the captain, would she?"

"She sold out her old boss—or seemed to," said Sushi. "And her old boss is likely to be holding a really serious grudge against the captain. What if running away with Beeker was just a way to get herself some credibility, so she could spy on the captain? What if she's brought Beeker—and the captain—here so the mob can get another shot at them?"

"Geez, Soosh, that's a really scary idea," said Do-Wop. "You think the captain's in trouble?"

"I think maybe we're all in trouble," said Sushi. He turned around on the bicycle seat and grinned. "Not that that's anything new, is it? Come on, let's see if we can figure out what our next move's going to be and make it before the bad guys realize that they're in even worse trouble than we are!"

"Oh my God, the captain's dead!" shouted Brick, who'd been caddying for General Blitzkrieg. She dropped the general's golf bag and rushed over to the prostrate robot simulacrum of Phule, which lay apparently lifeless on the ground. Armstrong was already there, kneeling to feel the robot's wrist in search of a pulse. *Does an Andromatic robot have a pulse?* he wondered, idly. Then he decided it didn't matter; checking the pulse was what he'd have done if the robot had been the real captain, and for the moment, at least, he figured it was best to keep up the pretense that this was the real Captain Jester.

Meanwhile, General Blitzkrieg had rushed over to his golf bag, and was examining it for grass stains. For his part, Flight Leftenant Qual stood watching with lively curiosity, perhaps taking mental notes on human behavior for the Zenobian intelligence service.

"Captain! Speak to me!" said Armstrong.

There was a long and disconcerting silence from the robot. Armstrong had a sudden flash of terror, realizing that there might well be no one in Omega Company capable of repairing the robot if some component had been jarred loose when the golf ball struck it. They could hardly send it back to the factory—not with the general on base. As much as Blitzkrieg appeared to be enjoying the golf, he was beyond any doubt still ready to jump on any excuse to break up the Omega Mob and drum the captain out of the Legion—or at least, to send him someplace where he would never again have the opportunity to use his unique talents to overthrow military discipline.

Armstrong was ready to order the caddies to load the robot onto a golf cart and take it—where? Omega Company's new medic Nightingale had gone off-planet, taking along Beeker, and the captain had followed them, which was why they were in this fix to begin with. All of a sudden, the robot opened its eyes and said, "Hell of a way to wake a fellow up. What can I do for you?"

Uh-oh, thought Armstrong. That wasn't an encouraging response. "You just got beaned by a golf ball, Captain," he explained, hoping to reorient the robot. "Do you feel all right?"

"I think so," said the robot. "Let me try to get up." Somewhat shakily, with Armstrong and Brick each holding on to one arm, the robot rose to its feet. "There, I think I'm fine—at least, there's nothing wrong a good drink won't fix. Who's tending bar?"

"Uh—I guess I am, Captain," said Brick. Timidly she added, "How about a cold drink of water until you figure out whether anything's wrong?"

"Legionnaire, are you presuming to tell your CO he's had enough to drink?" growled General Blitzkrieg.

"Uh, no sir, General Blitzkrieg, sir," said Brick. It was undoubtedly the most "sirs" she'd gotten into one sentence since joining the Legion. Omega Company didn't encourage ostentatious military etiquette.

"Not to worry, General," said the robot, grinning broadly. "Let's just play out the hole—as long as I can hit the ball straight, I guess I'm all right."

"If you insist, Captain," said Armstrong. "Uh, you're away."

"That's right, Lieutenant," said the robot Captain Jester. He stepped up to the ball, which had rebounded off his forehead and ended up perhaps six feet in front of the tee. "And that reminds me, General—I owe you ten dollars. Want to make it double or nothing I can't outdrive Armstrong from where I lie?"

"You're on!" said the general, sensing an easy win. Without a tee under the ball, it would be even harder for Jester to get the kind of distance he needed to best Armstrong's tee shot. "I like a man who's not afraid to put his money on the line!" In fact, the latter statement was true only if the fellow putting his money on the line then proceeded to lose it to the general. But for the moment, Blitzkrieg felt a glow of appreciation for his gallant if foolhardy opponent.

"All right, then," said the robot, stepping up to the ball and waggling the driving iron. "Now I'll show you how the goddamn game's supposed to be played!"

There was something really wrong with that remark, thought Armstrong. But before he could place it, the robot had taken a mighty swing. The bystanders heard the distinctive *ping* of a ball caught precisely in the sweet spot of the club head. It took off straight as a laser beam down the middle of the fairway. When it finally came to rest, it was in the center of the green—some seventy yards past Armstrong's tee shot.

"Wow, some shot," said Brick. "Ain't nothin' wrong with *you*, Captain."

"A fine shot indeed," said the general. "However, he does lie *two*. If our short game's up to scratch, we've still got a fair chance to win the hole, eh, Lieutenant Armstrong?"

"I don't plan to concede the hole, General," said Armstrong, remembering whose partner he was supposed to be. He grabbed a short iron from his bag and the foursome set off down the course.

Armstrong was still trying to figure out what had bothered him when they got to the green and it became obvious to everyone—except perhaps the general—that something had gone seriously haywire.

Phule's instincts all told him something was wrong—very wrong. He found an empty bench in the garden of La Retraite Rustique, sat down, and began trying to piece together what was bothering him.

First of all, he knew that Beeker and Nightingale were on the planet, probably even in the close neighborhood. He even had a pretty good idea what they were here for—unlike Cut 'N' Shoot, where he hadn't learned about the main tourist attraction until the last day of his visit. He still didn't have any idea what had possessed them to spend any of their vacation days on Rot'n'art, one of the least interesting places he'd ever visited.

Here, at least, the Floribunda Festival was clearly the magnet drawing tourists from around the galaxy, although he couldn't quite picture Beeker getting excited about flowers. Maybe Nightingale was the flower fancier. It didn't seem like her, but how well did he know her, anyway?

But even knowing why they'd come to Hix's World, he hadn't managed to find them—not counting the one glimpse he'd gotten of Nightingale from his hotel window. Was it just bad luck, or was something else going on?

That brought him to the question of who'd been asking about him in the hotel. One way to figure out who was following him might be to let them catch up . . . but then, they might just turn out to be somebody he really was much better off not letting catch him. It was silly to pretend that he didn't have enemies. He could think of several people who thought they had some reason or another to stick their noses into his business—some of them even had pretty legitimate reasons, if you granted their particular point of view.

Most likely, the people looking for him were just local newspapers who'd learned he was on-planet and wanted an interview. Not that he was going to give one and reveal his location to various people who would use the information for their advantage. General Blitzkrieg, for one, would consider Phule's being away from his company's base nothing short of a capital offense. Or whoever was currently in charge of the Lorelei crime syndicate might see this as an opportunity to eliminate their main competitor in the casino business. At least, Phule's hotel had turned away the mysterious visitors . . . if only for the time being.

Phule stood up and stretched his muscles. In the absence of any real danger signs, his best bet was to go about his business, keeping an eye open for any suspicious characters in the vicinity. Considering that he was already keeping an eye open for Beeker, and one open for Nightingale, that was going to be a strain on his eyesight. But he'd cope. He always had.

Suspicious characters or not, it was important to keep his priorities straight. His main business was still finding Beeker, and that meant figuring out where the butler was likely to be the next day or so—after that, the Floribunda

Festival was over, and most of the tourists would be leaving Hix's World. Beeker and Nightingale would probably be among them. Chasing them to still another backwater planet was not Phule's idea of fun, but neither was going into an induced catatonic state, which was what would probably happen if he gave up the chase. If he could just get Beeker's Port-a-Brain, the entire problem would be solved. He could return to Zenobia, the butler and medic could continue to enjoy their vacation, and that would be that.

He reached in his pocket and brought out the Festival schedule he'd gotten in his tourist information packet at the spaceport. This afternoon's big attraction was a "floral ballet," whatever that was, in the Festival Pavilion. A map showed the Pavilion at the edge of town, not far from La Retraite Rustique. He didn't know for certain that Beeker would be there, but if the butler had come all this way for the Floribunda Festival, it was just a good bet he—or Nightingale—would want to see the floral ballet, as well.

Phule double-checked the map, returned it to his pocket, and set off in the direction of the Pavilion. It was a long shot, but at the moment it was still the best shot he had.

Do-Wop and Sushi sat on the ground, in the shade of a hedge a short distance from the entrance to La Retraite Rustique. Their bicycle was propped up next to them. The day had turned hot, and they both felt a certain dissatisfaction that their mission remained unfinished. Even Do-Wop, a firm believer that "If at first you don't succeed, it's a good time to quit," was trying to find alternative strategies.

"What we need to do is sneak back in the joint," said Do-Wop. "Then we can figure out what room the captain's in and put a message under the door."

Sushi shrugged. "It could work," he said. "That concierge, Robert, could cause a lot of trouble, though. How do we know when he's going to be away without sticking our faces in?"

"Uglypuss Robert has to eat some time," said Do-Wop. "My cousin Louise, she useta be a waitress, told me the staff always eats before they start serving the customers. I bet that's when this guy eats, too—before the dining room opens for lunch."

Sushi checked the time. "If you're right, that'd be in maybe half an hour. But there'll be somebody covering for him—you can bet he's going to warn them about us. What are we going to do about that?"

Do-Wop grinned and pointed a finger at Sushi. "We go in disguise!" he said.

Sushi rolled his eyes. "Yeah, sure. It'd be really triff if we had a whole kit full of different costumes, and fake beards, and all the other stuff. Except we don't. Tell me when you come up with a real idea."

"No, Soosh, this'll work," said Do-Wop. "Like, if we sneak in the employees' entrance while everybody's eatin', we can pop into the locker room and snag ourselves some hotel uniforms—janitor's coveralls or maybe a bellhop jacket. Then we just zip right into the main part of the hotel without anybody battin' an eyeball. You got the right uniform, you can go anyplace you want."

"How do you know they have a locker room?" said Sushi. "This isn't that big a place, you know . . ."

"If that happens, we go straight to Plan B," said Do-Wop, nonchalantly.

"Which is?"

"Run like hell and try to think of somethin' else," said Do-Wop, with a wink. "C'mon, Soosh, have a little faith in your buddy."

"I guess I don't have any better ideas," said Sushi. "Besides which, if this goes sour, I can outrun you. When the bad guys catch you, they'll probably forget about me." He stood up. "We might as well go try it."

They left the rented bike behind a privet hedge bordering the back garden of La Retraite Rustique, then worked their way through the gardens, dodging behind trees and other bits of greenery just as they'd been taught in basic training—Brandy would've been proud of them. She'd have been even prouder if there'd been anybody in the gardens for them to hide from.

The two legionnaires stopped outside the back door, which bore a sign reading SERVICE ENTRANCE. They exchanged a glance, as if to ask whether they were still going through with it. Then Do-Wop shrugged, pushed the door open, and they went inside.

They were in a hallway with a pair of swinging doors in front of them, and closed doors to either side saying MEN and WOMEN. From directly ahead came the low buzz of talk and the clatter of utensils—the kitchen, most likely. Do-Wop poked Sushi to get his attention, pointed to the door marked MEN, and they quickly slipped through it. As anticipated, they found themselves in a locker room, with showers and toilet facilities visible through an opening at the far end. For the moment, at least, no one else was in the area.

"OK, look for somethin' we can use as a disguise," said Do-Wop. "Long as it covers up the Legion uniform, it oughta work."

"What makes you so sure?" said Sushi. "Don't you think the bosses know who works here and who doesn't?"

"Sure, when they stop and think about it," said Do-Wop. "But most of the time, they're not payin' attention, doin' something else, y'know. If you act like you know what you're doin' and where you're goin', you can walk right past 'em and they don't even notice. There's always new guys on the job. My cousin Rufo useta pull this trick all the time when he was stealin' stuff." He walked over to some shelves, where jackets, aprons, and other items of employee apparel were laid out. "Maybe one of these will fit," he said, tossing a jacket at Sushi. It was lavender with gold trim.

"What happened to your cousin Rufo?" said Sushi, slipping the jacket over his uniform. It was a loose fit, but close enough to pass.

"He got nailed," said Do-Wop, putting on a jacket of his own. "Shit happens, y'know."

"Just what I wanted to hear," said Sushi, rolling his eyes. "Guess there's nothing to do but give it a try, though. Let's go . . ."

Wearing uniforms taken from the employee locker room, the two legionnaires stepped into the hallway. For the moment, at least, they were alone. But there were clearly people in the kitchen, where the sound of conversation and food preparation was audible. Unfortunately, the path into the rest of the hotel led through the kitchen.

Leaning against the wall on one side were a push broom and a dustpan. Do-Wop picked them up and handed them to Sushi, with a wink, then brandished a roll of paper towels he'd taken from the locker room. "Just like the Legion," he said. "Look like you're workin', and they leave you alone."

Sushi pointed the broom handle toward the swinging doors into the next room, as if to say, "After you." Do-Wop shrugged, then strode forward as if he had every right in the world to be where he was. After a moment, Sushi followed.

The kitchen was small but well lit, and full of wonderful odors—definitely in a league with Mess Sergeant Escrima's back at Zenobia Base, Sushi thought. The three men busy with food preparation had their backs to the two legionnaires, who moved past quietly. At the other end of the kitchen, several employees sat at two long tables, eating and talking. None of them spared more than a glance at Sushi and Do-Wop, as the two walked briskly through the room, doing their best to appear that they were on the way to some job. This was going almost too smoothly, Sushi thought to himself.

Then a door opened in front of them, and Sushi's heart leapt into his throat as the concierge came into the kitchen, walking directly toward them, a scowl on his face. But Do-Wop dodged back against the wall to let him pass, and a frightened Sushi followed his lead. To his enormous relief, Robert strode past them with no sign of recognition. Without saying a word, Do-Wop continued out the doors.

Sushi was right on his partner's heels. "Wow, I thought we were dead there," he whispered. They had emerged into the hotel dining room—at the moment unoccupied except for the two of them.

"Ahh, nothin' to it," said Do-Wop, out of the side of his mouth. "Just remember, act like we're just doin' a job and nobody's gonna look at us twice. Come on, let's see if we can find out what room the captain's in."

Do-Wop led the way through the dining room and out into the lobby, where a handful of guests sat reading or conversing. The guests ignored the two legionnaires, who strode over to the desk. There, Sushi glanced at the guest register while Do-Wop leaned on his broom. For whatever reason, Sushi's partner found it impossible to read upside down, a skill that came easily to Sushi. "Three-thirteen," he said softly.

"Upstairs, then," said Do-Wop. "Let's go get it."

They started up the stairs—Hix's World had apparently legislated gravshafts and elevators out of existence, along with almost every other really convenient modern device. At the second-floor landing, Sushi was slightly ahead, but as he looked around the corner to see which way to go, he ducked back quickly and whispered hoarsely, "The captain! He just came out of his room—quick, up the stairs so he doesn't see us!"

They scuttled up to the fourth floor, hoping that Phule

was headed in the opposite direction. Pausing to listen, they heard the captain's footsteps heading downward, and heaved a sigh of relief. Their disguises might be good enough to fool the hotel staff, but they certainly weren't going to get through a face-to-face encounter with the captain without being recognized. And Lieutenant Rembrandt had ordered them to keep the captain from learning that she'd sent them to look after him. Not that they were especially afraid of disobeying Remmie—but if the captain knew they were here, he might come up with ideas of his own how to put them to work. And that might be a lot less fun than what they were doing.

Then their luck ran out. Just as the sound of the captain's footsteps faded out into the lobby, a raspy female voice behind them growled, "If you two clowns are through goofing off, I've got some work for you. Or maybe you want to find jobs somewhere else?"

Half-recognizing the voice, they turned around slowly, and saw before them the scowling face of Maxine Pruett. "Well?" she said out of the corner of her mouth. "You working or not?"

Sushi and Do-Wop followed Maxine down a hallway and through a door marked DANGER—UNPREDICTABLE QUANTUM FLUX. As they entered, a light came on, and the two legionnaires could see a stack of packing crates. Sushi's first thought was that he'd walked into a warehouse full of ultracomputers—but that made no sense. The amount of processing and storage capacity even one of these crates might hold would satisfy the needs of most planetary governments. So it must be something else.

Maxine interrupted his train of speculation. "You boys are gonna restack everything in this room so these crates are at the back, where nobody can see 'em without moving a bunch of other stuff. And you're gonna do it without taking anything out of the room and without making enough noise to attract attention. You got it?"

"Man, that's gonna take all day," said Do-Wop.

"So, you're gettin' paid for all day," said Maxine, frowning. "Or would you rather punch out and go find jobs that don't hurt your pretty little hands?"

"We've got it covered, boss," said Sushi, before Do-Wop could say anything else. "Shall we report to you when we're finished?"

"No, just tell Robert you're done, and then go finish your regular jobs. Oh, one more thing—you don't talk about what you've done here. Understand?"

"Yes, ma'am," said Sushi, and Do-Wop joined in a half beat behind him. Maxine nodded, then turned and left them to their devices.

"Man, this rots," said Do-Wop. "By the time we're finished with this, it'll be way too late to get our message to the captain."

"Never mind that," said Sushi. "Did you see who that was? That's Maxine Pruett, the mob boss from Lorelei. "What's she doing here?"

"Makin' us hump boxes, it looks like to me." Do-Wop scowled at the pile of crates. He looked up and said, "It is pretty weird to find her here, though. What d'ya think we oughta do about it?"

"Fear not, I have a brilliant plan," said Sushi, grinning. "Help me with this crate."

"Some plan," said Do-Wop. "I throw my back out, it's your fault, y'know."

"Don't sweat it," said Sushi. "You ought to know me better than to think any plan of mine involves real work. What we're going to do is open this crate up and see what's in it. Then we're going to sneak out, put our message under the captain's door, and get out of this dump before the boss lady or anybody else figures out what's happened. You with me?"

"All except the part about opening the crate," said Do-Wop. "Why we gonna waste time with that?"

Sushi grinned. "Because, anything Maxine Pruett wants to hide, I figure it's to our advantage to know about. Come on, it can't take more than a couple of minutes. You see anything we could use to pry one of these boards off?"

Do-Wop dug into his pockets and produced a laser cutter, and in a few more moments they had the crate open and the packing strewn around the floor. There in front of them sat a familiar item: a quantum slot machine, just like the ones they'd guarded in the Fat Chance Casino back on Lorelei. Do-Wop whistled. "I'm feeling lucky," he said. "Got a quarter?"

"Never mind that," said Sushi. "It doesn't have a power module, for starters. But I just thought of something else—gambling is seriously illegal on this planet. This is some deep trouble. Let's get out of here before the boss lady sends somebody to check up on whether we're goofing off. Knowing Maxine, she's got some muscle boys around to keep people like us from screwing up her operation."

"Ahh, I ain't afraid of no farkin' muscle boys," said Do-Wop, brandishing the laser cutter.

Sushi rolled his eyes. "Come on, we're out of here—or would you rather hump some more boxes for free?"

"You got a point there, Soosh," said Do-Wop, pocketing the laser. "Let's blow this joint!"

Sushi cracked the door and peered out; the coast seemed to be clear. The two legionnaires crept into the hallway. "Don't forget, we've got to leave the note for the captain," whispered Sushi.

"Right," said Do-Wop. "Remind me—which way's his room?"

"Down one flight and to the left," said Sushi, starting off in the direction of the stairway.

The two legionnaires had just started down the stairs when a slim figure stepped onto the landing below them and started up. It took Sushi a second to recognize her, though he'd been looking for her ever since he'd left Omega Base. "Nightingale!" he said, stopping in his tracks.

Omega Company's truant medic looked up at him, surprise written plainly on her face. "You!" she said. "What are you two doing here?"

But before Sushi could answer, another voice came from the landing above them. "Oh, shit, it's Laverna. Security! Security!" shouted Maxine.

After that, Sushi and Do-Wop were far too busy making their getaway to notice which way Nightingale (aka Laverna) went, let alone say anything to her.

Phule sighed as he walked up through the gardens at La Retraite Rustique. The visit to the floral ballet had been a bust. Not only had he failed to spot Beeker, he'd been unable to leave the Pavilion until the end of the ballet's first act—a spectacle that was probably just fine if you liked that kind of thing. He could now say with not doubt whatsoever that he didn't like it. In fact, he *really* didn't like it.

Phule realized that something was wrong as soon as he entered the lobby. For one thing, nobody was at the desk. For another, several guests were milling about, arguing with hotel employees, who seemed every bit as confused as the guests. And behind the desk, he could see through an open door to an office that appeared to have been thoroughly ransacked.

"What's going on?" Phule asked the nearest person who seemed calm enough to have useful information, an elderly man with bristling white whiskers and a ghastly tweed jacket of a cut that only someone of long-established family could wear without being accused of trying out for a part in a bad period drama.

"Demmed 'f I know," said the bystander. "The management seem to have absconded without notice. Silly of them, what? Now we're all looking at cold supper, to say the least. Not quite fair play, say I. Not fair at all."

"When did this happen?" asked Phule. "Everything seemed fine just a little while ago, before I went into town."

"It happened all of a sudden," said another guest, a tall woman with startlingly red hair. "One moment, all was quiet—then, Madame came shrieking down the hall, saying that the Legion had come and all was lost. Her senior staff seemed to know what that meant, though I haven't a notion, myself."

"The Legion's nothing to be afraid of," said the bewhiskered man. "Stout fellows—they did my father a good turn, back on St. Elmo's. Must have been in '44 . . ."

"We haven't time for that old story," said the red-haired woman. "If these people can't provide the dinner I've paid for in advance, I need to find someplace that will."

"Unless things are corrected in short order, I shall have to write a letter to the *Forum*," said the man, firmly, turning to Phule. "I say . . . I say, where'd the fellow go?"

Phule had gone to inquire elsewhere. He pushed through the kitchen doors, looking for someone with more authority—and, he hoped, better information—than the busboys and dishwashers out front with the guests. Ahead of him, a group of cooks and waiters stood arguing with a woman dressed in a rumpled business suit—some sort of manager, Phule decided. She might actually know something.

"Excuse me, do you have a moment?" said Phule, stepping into the woman's line of sight.

Her eyes turned cold, and she all but snapped, "I'm afraid I'm pretty well occupied at the . . ." Then the woman's gaze fixed itself on the hundred-dollar bill Phule was rubbing between his fingers, and her mouth fell open. "Of course, sir. I'm Aster Igget, the personnel manager. What can I help you with?"

"If she can't help, I'll give it one helluva try," said a man in a white apron and chef's hat, ogling the hundred. The woman glared at him, and he backed off, grinning.

Phule lowered his voice. "Just before I left to go into town, the concierge told me that two suspicious-looking men had been asking about me. Did anybody else see these two men?"

"Well, I certainly didn't," said the woman. "But I do know that Madame came into the kitchen right as Robert, the concierge, was eating—she was ranting about someone trying to ruin her business. He went with her to her office, and apparently when they came out, they went straight to the door and left. It wasn't long before someone realized that they'd taken all the cash with them and wiped most of the office files."

"Interesting," said Phule. "Obviously they were trying to hide something—but what? And from whom?"

"The boss lady said the Legion had caught up with her," volunteered the man in the chef's hat. "That's your outfit, right? I recognize that uniform . . ."

"Funny, I've been here nearly a week and nobody seemed worried," said Phule, even more puzzled. "What I'd like to know . . . wait a minute. Did anybody see a *woman* in a Legion uniform?"

The employees looked at one another, then one of the waiters said, "*Somebody* in a black outfit ran through the kitchen and out the back door, right before the boss freaked out. I guess it could have been a woman."

"Aha," said Phule, putting two and two together. "Do you have any idea where the boss might have gone?"

"She didn't give her forwarding address to the kitchen help," said the man in the chef's hat. "But if she's in enough trouble to light out that fast, Hix's World's too small a place to hide. I'd bet she's on the way to Old Earth."

"Why Old Earth?" said Phule.

"There's a regular flight there three days a week," said

Aster Igget, apparently realizing how little she'd done to earn the hundred-dollar bill Phule was still dangling. "A lot of our guests go there after Hix's. Joyday, Floraday, Restday—that's today, at six P.M. It's the quickest way off-planet . . . and you can pick up a ship to anywhere from Old Earth. That's where I'd go if I were on the run."

"Something tells me that's where I'm headed, too," said Phule. He handed the hundred to Aster Igget and dug out two more for the other employees who'd offered information. Then he headed for his room to check what the Port-a-brain had to tell him.

Sure enough, it showed Beeker's computer exiting Hix's World on the way to Old Earth. He sighed and began packing for the next flight out.

14

Journal #842—

The mere fact of Old Earth's continued existence is something of a miracle—even if one does not entirely accept its claim of being the aboriginal cradle of the human species (a point on which the evidence remains murky). In any case, there are few worlds in which the incredible variety of humanity is on such constant display. Both folly and vice are represented in multiple forms, some perhaps even new.

In the short distance between the spaceport dock and the ground transportation ramp, I was accosted by no fewer than seven individuals offering to relieve me of my cash or credit in furtherance of some scheme or another, none remotely legal. I respectfully declined their offers, confident of finding an abundance of such opportunities should I wish at some future time to avail myself of them.

Phule sat and fiddled with his Port-a-Brain. He'd called up the data on Old Earth, the next stop in his search for Beeker and Laverna. It felt as if the search had been stretching out for months, now—although he knew it couldn't be that long. Travel by starship was always disorienting, of course, and strange things could happen to time when you ducked through the shortcuts between distant stars. It was widely rumored that a space traveler sometimes arrived at his destination after several hyperspace jumps, placed a call to the home office back on the planet he'd started from, and found himself answering his own call . . .

Phule had never heard of a documented case of someone arriving back home before he left, although old space hands were always ready to tell tales to groundlings. Phule didn't like to think about it. All he really wanted to do was to find his missing butler and get him to hand over the Port-a-Brain. He knew there was a chance he might lose the butler's trail, and the security chip would throw him into hibernation.

Phule leaned back and sighed, then punched a fist softly into his cupped hand. *Time to face reality.* Old Earth was going to be his last stop. He'd put all the time and money and energy at his command into the job.

A confident grin came to his face. He wasn't going to give up the game without putting on a good show. He had more resources on this world than anywhere else he'd been so far—in fact, Old Earth was one of the centers of the family munitions business. Normally, he tried not to take undue advantage of his family connections. But this wasn't a normal situation—not after he'd searched three planets without so much as a sight of his butler. First thing off the ship, he'd call the local offices of Phule-Pruf Munitions and see what they could do to shorten his search. Unless there'd been unusual friction between the branch office and the community, a request for help from a well-established local business ought to carry some weight with the authorities.

What else? He'd need to find somebody with the local

knowledge to expedite his search—looking back, he had to admit that the various "native guides" he'd picked up on the other worlds he'd visited hadn't been a whole lot of help. Here, at least, there was a family member in charge of the local branch office of Phule-Pruf Munitions. He hadn't seen his uncle in years, but Phule knew without asking that the fellow *had* to be more reliable than Buck Short or Perry Sodden . . .

He realized with a start that there had only been one really reliable person in his entire life—good old Beeker, who despite his ill-concealed disapproval of Phule's behavior on many occasions, had always been there with sound advice and an unfailing fund of practical know-how in the most surprisingly diverse areas. The real irony was that Phule was trying to find his one reliable servant—and falling on his face because he didn't have anyone reliable to help him in the search! If only he could call on *Beeker* to help him find Beeker . . .

In fact, there was a way—or at least in theory there was a way. Unfortunately, it depended entirely on Beeker's being willing to give up the mad pursuit and come back to his employer. Right here on the Port-a-Brain was a direct link to Beeker's corresponding machine, which Phule could punch up to send a near-instant message to his absent employee from halfway across the galaxy.

It had one significant shortcoming: There was no way to force Beeker to pay attention to messages he didn't want to read. In fact, Phule thought, even Beeker might be reluctant to take time on his vacation to read a message from his boss. So until Beeker decided he wanted to hear from his employer, paging him was going to be about as effective as attaching a paper note to a bird's wings and asking it to deliver it to someone on another planet.

Phule sighed. He'd promised himself he wasn't going to get sidetracked by pessimism. Not that it was all that easy—especially times like now, when it seemed like the only sane attitude to have . . .

• • •

"What's wrong with hi— er, *it*?" asked Gears, looking at the Andromatic robot simulacrum of Phule. In the absence of Sushi, the company's closest thing to a computer expert, Lieutenants Rembrandt and Armstrong had decided that Gears might be their best bet for a diagnosis of the robot's problem. At least, Gears was good with other kinds of machines . . .

"Hit on the forehead with a golf ball," said Armstrong. "There's no visible damage, but then it started acting strangely."

"And in this outfit, how'd you notice?" said Gears, with enough of a straight face that Armstrong nearly answered him. "Seriously, though, what's it acting like? Maybe that'll give me some kind of clue. Although it'd be nice to have a schematic of this baby's brain."

"If the captain ever had a schematic, it's probably back at the casino offices on Lorelei," said Rembrandt. "But to answer your question, the best way to describe the problem is, the robot's trying to do everything by the book, the way General Blitzkrieg wants the company run. It's acting just like that Major Botchup they sent to run the company the last time the captain was away."

"Whoa, that's scary," said Gears. His face turned serious, and he said, "I hate to tell you this, Lieutenant, but I'm afraid this robot's *broke*."

"You're kidding," said Armstrong.

"No, really, it's pretty messed up," said Gears.

"All right, I believe you, Gears," said Rembrandt. "Question is, can you fix it so the general can't tell?—and I mean really fast?"

Gears shrugged. "Robot repair's a real specialized field. I guess I know my way around the innards of a hoverjeep about as well as anybody in the Legion. I'm not going to tell nobody otherwise. If you want me to fix something else . . . well, no promises. Maybe Sushi could figure out what's wrong with it, if he was around. But if this was my robot, I wouldn't even open the cover. I'd send it right back to the factory. These Andromatic models are supposed to come with lifetime guarantees, I hear tell. You know Captain Jester always buys the best."

"Yeah, too bad the factory's a couple dozen parsecs away," said Armstrong, drumming his fingers on the arm of his chair. "How about a quick fix? It just has to keep working until the general goes away . . ."

"Which he isn't showing any signs of doing, thanks to all the golf matches," said Rembrandt. "You'd think he'd get tired of the game."

"He enjoys beating the captain," said Armstrong, shrugging. "The robot, really, but the general doesn't know that. Actually, I think the general's spent so long thinking of Captain Jester as the adversary that winning—and taking a bit of the captain's money, as well—is a special treat, even if it's only a game."

"Makes sense," admitted Rembrandt, frowning. "But wait a minute . . . what if the robot started *winning all the time*?"

"Well, the robot has been winning, every now and then," said Armstrong. "Just enough to keep the general from figuring out it's letting *him* win the matches." He gave the robot a long stare, then said, "I'm not sure just what it's likely to do now. Today it started playing like a world champion. The general's not going to appreciate that. So we've got to fix it . . ."

"Yeah," said Rembrandt. "The question is, can we?"

It took Major Sparrowhawk about three milliseconds to notice that General Blitzkrieg was boiling mad. It didn't take a lot of thought; he pretty much gave it away when he burst in the door, bellowed out a string of curses, and threw his golf bag halfway across the office they'd been assigned on Zenobia Base.

Sparrowhawk wasn't upset. She'd seen her boss in that condition plenty of times before. Some might even argue that it was the general's normal mood. Whether it was or not, he'd been in an abnormally pleasant state for nearly two weeks.

She gave a mental shrug and prepared to deal with the situation. That was really the essence of her job as Blitzkrieg's adjutant: figuring out what to do when the general was so pissed off at the universe that nobody else wanted anything to do with him. Not surprisingly, there weren't very many other junior Legion officers willing to take on the task. That gave her a fair measure of job security, as well as a quite decent lifestyle back at Rahnsome Base, where most of the Alliance military maintained their general staff and headquarters. Here at Zenobia Base, the lifestyle was another story—although she certainly couldn't complain about the food.

And, in fact, she'd had more than the usual amount of downtime, with the general concentrating so totally on his golf game. She felt a certain grudging admiration for Captain Jester, who'd had the foresight to build a golf course here, and to entice Blitzkrieg into an apparently endless series of matches. It had certainly kept the general out of her hair. She hadn't even felt the usual pressure to snoop around the base, compiling a list of the violations, screwups, and deficiencies every base commander tried to sweep under the rug when a staff officer came to visit. She had developed a knack for finding sore spots for the general to pounce on once he'd stopped having fun. Well, it looked as if the fun was over—for her as well as for the general. And as much as she'd come to like the people she'd been dealing with on Zenobia, she knew her job.

She reached for her digital notepad. "I think you'll want to look at this, General," she said, in a tone of voice carefully modulated to pique his interest rather than add to his annoyance.

"I'll be damned if I want to look at anything," roared Blitzkrieg, pretty much the response she'd expected. He plopped himself in the padded desk chair and bellowed, "Pour me a Scotch, damn it!"

"Yes, sir," said Sparrowhawk, already moving toward the portable bar discreetly installed on one side of the office. She quickly fixed a drink to the general's usual specifications and carried it over to him. As he took the drink, she set the notepad down on the desk slightly to one side of him and went back to her own desk. It wouldn't be long before curiosity got the better of him . . .

In fact, he succumbed to the temptation after his second sip, picking up the notepad and staring at it for a solid minute before growling, "What the hell is this about?"

"Oh, probably nothing important," said Sparrowhawk, brightly. She took out her laser trimmer and began evening up her fingernails, then said, "I believe it's some sort of apparatus the Zenobians are running here on the base. I'm not certain what it does, though."

Blitzkrieg snorted and looked at the notepad again. "Are they allowed to do that?"

"I think the treaty lets them, sir," said Sparrowhawk. She inspected her left hand. "Captain Jester would certainly know. I think he had a lot to do with the terms of the treaty," she added.

"Damn thing looks suspicious as hell to me," said Blitzkrieg. "Some kind of spy apparatus, I'd wager . . ."

Sparrowhawk looked up with an expression of feigned innocence. "Spy apparatus? Do you really think they'd be snooping on the Alliance?"

"I wouldn't put anything past the scaly little bastards," growled the general, peering at the image on Sparrowhawk's notepad. "Knew we couldn't trust 'em right from the first."

"Well, whatever this apparatus is, they've got it set up

right out by the perimeter," said Sparrowhawk. "They aren't even guarding it. You could probably just walk right up and inspect it."

Blitzkrieg sipped his drink in silence, nodding slowly. After a moment he said, "Walk right up. *Walk right up.* You know, Major, I think I'm going to do exactly that." He stood up and strode forcefully out the door.

Sparrowhawk waited until she'd heard the outside door close behind him, then let out a long sigh of relief. "Well, that ought to keep him out of my hair for a while longer."

In the view screen, Old Earth was now close enough to show detail from space. It looked much like any developed world: a garland of lights across the nightside, hazed by the no-longer-pristine planetary atmosphere. The shapes of the continents were familiar from hundreds of tri-vee dramas, the stock establishing shot for what usually turned out to be the inspiring tale of an idealistic youngster struggling against the ancient, rigidly stratified society where every tiny gesture was an irrevocable status marker, and where raw talent came in a distant third to graft and nepotism. Having come from a family where he was a lifelong bene-ficiary of graft and nepotism, Phule had never been able to take such stories very seriously.

So Phule looked at the panorama with jaded eyes; he'd set foot on too many different worlds in the last few weeks, each at first promising and each at last a disappointment. Just as on Cut 'N' Shoot, Rot'n'art, and Hix's World, he was best advised to put aside his preconceptions and take Old Earth for what it was.

On the other hand, maybe Old Earth *would* be different. If you could believe the tourist brochures and guidebooks, it was the original home world from which the human race had spread out into the galaxy. But even if that was true, Phule didn't see how it made any difference to his search.

All he wanted here was to catch up with Beeker, the right-hand man he'd taken for granted until events had proved just how indispensable he was. And when he'd found the butler, and gotten his Port-a-Brain, he'd gladly shake the dust of the home world of humanity from his shoes and return to Omega Company.

The speaker crackled, and a pleasant (if somewhat bored) female voice said, "All passengers for Old Earth please report to the shuttle boarding area. There will be three landing shuttles; the first will depart at eight-twenty-five, Galactic Standard Time, and will accept passengers from cabins eleven through forty-five . . ."

That would be the landing group he was in, Phule realized. He shouldered his duffel bag and headed toward the shuttle boarding area, which was just abaft the last row of first-class cabins.

He was three-quarters of the way to his destination when a stateroom door just to his left flew open just as he went past, and the occupant barged directly into him. They both went sprawling, and Phule looked up to see a pair of green eyes framed by bright red hair looking down at him. The eyes went wide with surprise, and a lush voice said, "Oh—I'm *so* sorry! I was on my way to the shuttles . . ."

"Well, so was I," said Phule, indulgently. The pretty green-eyed young woman who'd bumped into him was pleasantly padded, and her oversize suitcase had fallen clear of him. So he hadn't taken any damage, except perhaps to his dignity—which was not one of his particularly vulnerable areas. "Why don't we both just head on down to the boarding area while we're still on time. Could I help you with that bag?"

"Why, thank you, Captain," she said, smiling. "My name's Samantha Beliveau, by the way—but you can call me Sam. Everybody does."

"Nice to meet you, Sam," said Phule. "Now, we should

hurry up if we're going to make it to the shuttle. There'll be plenty of time on board to talk."

"Oh, I'd *like* that," said Sam. Phule smiled. At least the trip down to Old Earth promised not to be boring . . .

Just visible from the landing area were the port facilities of Old Earth. As on most advanced worlds, the traveler's first taste of the world was a meeting with humorless uniformed officials whose job was to intercept smugglers, terrorists, low-wage workers, and other interplanetary criminal types. Phule stood nonchalantly in line, waiting for the inspectors to begin processing passengers. He had been through customs on a hundred worlds and knew the routine by heart.

On nine out of ten worlds, the officials were unlikely to bother a Legion officer in uniform. Despite coming from the least prestigious branch of the Alliance armed services, Phule could usually count on being waved right through, or at the very most being asked to show his passport.

Today, he was glad to see, the line seemed to be moving steadily through the gates. The shipboard lunch menu hadn't appealed to him, and as a result he hadn't eaten since breakfast. Once through customs, he fully intended to find the best restaurant in the vicinity and enjoy a leisurely meal, with a glass or two of Old Earth's legendary vintages. His luggage could wait . . .

Finally, he came to the head of the line, waited a moment for one of the agents to become available, and stepped up to the desk. "Good afternoon," he said, smiling pleasantly. It never hurt to be polite when dealing with bureaucrats, he'd found.

The agent was a human male of average height, with dark hair and a bushy moustache. On the lapel of his decidedly dowdy uniform was a regulation plastic name tag that read AGT. G.C. FOX. To Phule's surprise, the agent snatched his passport as if he suspected it of being contraband. "State your reason for coming to Old Earth," he said, sharply. His tone suggested that describing the afternoon as "good" was the height of impertinence.

"I'm here on personal business," said Phule, keeping his face neutral.

Fox alternately stared at the passport and tapped a small keyboard attached to the computer screen on his desktop. After an uncomfortably long interval, he snapped his gaze back to Phule. "Planet of residence," he barked. "Zenobia," said Phule. "I'm stationed there with . . ."

"Just answer the questions I ask," said Fox. "Zenobia . . ." He tapped a key, looked at his screen, then glared at Phule. "There's no listing for a planet Zenobia in my database."

"They're independent allies," said Phule. "I'm stationed there with . . ."

"You already said that," Fox scolded. He looked back at his screen, taking his time. Abruptly he pointed at Phule and barked, "Are you importing any prohibited organic substances?"

"Of course not," said Phule, standing up straighter. "I am an officer of the Space Legion!"

Agent Fox snorted. Then Phule noticed, a short distance away, a stern-faced man in the same blue uniform as Fox, watching him. The man's name tag read SUPERVISOR L. HAWKRIDGE. Suddenly aware of Phule's gaze, the man gave a stiff nod toward Fox, then moved on to survey another part of the entry concourse.

"As if that made any difference," said Fox, visibly relaxing as the supervisor walked away. "With what the Legion pays, a little income on the side looks pretty good to most officers." The customs agent looked at Phule's passport again, then leaned forward on his desk and lowered his voice. "Sure you're not importing anything prohibited? There's people I know that might be interested."

"Yes, interested enough to throw me in the cooler for a

few years," said Phule. "If I were bringing in anything illegal, do you think I'd tell a customs officer?"

"Hey, ya never know," said Fox, shrugging. "In this business, a guy's gotta take whatever comes along. If a smuggler's dumb enough to tell me he's bringing something in, I'd be crazy not to take advantage." He slid Phule's passport back across the counter.

Phule noticed that Fox hadn't made it exactly clear whether "take advantage" meant arresting the smuggler or taking a cut of the proceeds in return for letting him through. It might be very useful to know which he meant—just in case, as Chocolate Harry might have put it. He turned a knowing smile on the agent, and said, "Well, how do you catch the smart ones?"

Fox stroked his moustache with a thumb and index finger. "Well, we've got our tricks, and I probably shouldn't give them away. To tell the truth, we probably don't catch the really smart ones, but not everybody's as smart as they think they are. You'd be surprised how many people think they can just give the agent a couple of bucks to turn a blind eye, right in front of everybody . . ."

Phule shrugged. "Some people never learn how to handle things discreetly." He tucked his passport back into his pocket, not bothering to look whether the hundred-credit note he'd folded inside it was still there. He had a pretty good idea, though. If he needed help with immigration matters in the future, he was pretty sure he could turn to Agent Fox.

As Phule went away, Fox quickly noted down the name and hotel address from the captain's passport. He was pretty sure he recognized the name from somewhere—he was the kind of person who kept track of such things. And if the captain was who Fox thought he was, certain people would be very interested in knowing he'd come to Old Earth. In any case, as Fox had learned, it never hurt to keep an eye open.

• • •

"I'll be damned," said General Blitzkrieg. "Right in the middle of an Alliance base . . ."

He was staring at a strange machine, tended by a group of the native Zenobians, all wearing what he assumed were local military uniforms. Just what the machine was, he couldn't quite make out. But he knew an infringement on Legion prerogatives when he saw one. And he was just mad enough to go ahead and call the damned lizards on it.

"See here, what's this all about?" he bellowed, striding forward in his most intimidating manner. Even dressed in his golf shorts and cap, he could summon up a galaxy-class bluster. "I demand an explanation!"

The lizards turned and looked at him, their expressions bright and curious. One of them—evidently the group leader—stepped forward. It was wearing a translator, which intoned, "Salutings, alien creature! Is it not that you are the General Flashbang? Flight Leftenant Qual has reported all to us."

Confused, the general reverted to his tried-and-true strategy: bellowing louder. "I'm General Blitzkrieg, and I want to know what the hell you're doing here on a Legion base!"

Another Zenobian answered him. "We faithfully regulate the *sklern*," it said, in a nasal monotone.

"Regulate?" stormed Blitzkrieg. "I'll show you regulate—and I mean Legion regulations! This entire base is three hundred sixty-five degrees out of regulations, and this infernal device is just the tip of the ice cube! I'll have every one of you in the brig for espionage!" Blitzkrieg paused for breath, but he was interrupted before he could crank his tirade into a higher gear.

"Evenin', General," came a drawling voice from behind him.

The general turned; there stood Rev, the preposterous chaplain of this preposterous company. "What the hell are

you doing here?" said Blitzkrieg. "Better scurry back to
your chapel before you find yourself in more trouble than
your King can get you out of!"

"With the King on my side, I can handle a heap of trouble," said Rev. "But there's no sense lookin' for trouble
where there ain't any. What's your problem with these
fellers?"

Blitzkrieg waved a hand. "Why, it's obvious! These
damned foreigners are using a Legion base to spy on the
Alliance! And Jester's letting them do it, without blinking
an eye!"

Rev scratched his head. "Beggin' your pardon, General—
it don't seem quite right to call these fellers foreigners.
They're the ones who live here, and they invited us in . . ."

"This is still a Legion base," countered Blitzkrieg, in a
full roar. "Not as if anybody here seems to act like it.
Look around—you'd think there wasn't any such thing as
regulations . . ."

"We regulate the *sklern*," chorused all three of the Zenobians, in slightly different mechanical voices.

"Who the hell asked you?" Blitzkrieg bellowed, loud
enough to rattle windows on the other side of the camp.

The three Zenobians stood there unperturbed, baring
their carnosaur grins at the general. After a moment, one
said, "We take self-regard that you inquire of our tasking,
oh mighty Flashbang." The others nodded and clapped
their miniature hands.

"There y'go, General," murmured Rev. "Little fellers
just love to work."

"They're spying!" shouted Blitzkrieg. "I don't know
what this machine does, but . . ."

"We shall gleefully elucidate, oh mighty one," said the
Zenobian with the nasal translator. "Engage the revealing
rings, my hearty fellows!" The others fell instantly to
work, throwing foot-long toggle switches and adjusting
knobs the size of dinner plates.

"What the hell are they doing?" said Blitzkrieg. "I don't like the looks of this . . ."

"All will be transparent in a small fraction of a time unit," said another Zenobian. Out in the desert beyond the edge of the camp, something purple hovered in the air. "Ho, Svip! Retreat the dexter node, lest it overwarm!"

"Dexter node withdrawn," said Svip. "Reification proceeding." The purple something became clearer, and perhaps a bit closer.

"Aw, this looks like one of their real good ones," said Rev, staring at the purple. "I don't understand jes' how this thing works, but it sure does beat anything else I've seen . . ."

Just as he'd said this, the purple shape coalesced into a life-size *gryff*, one of the large herbivores native to the fertile plains that covered much of the continent west of the desert in which the Legion camp lay. It appeared to be munching on a thick cud of greenery, staring complacently into space, perhaps a dozen yards beyond the base's perimeter.

"What the devil is that thing?" said Blitzkrieg.

"Some kind of critter," said Rev, looking at it with mild curiosity. "That might be the kind they call a *grip*—they claim it won't bother you if you keep your distance. The locals say they've kilt off all the dangerous ones. They didn't get all the ones that like to nibble on *people*, though."

"The *sklern* performs exemplarily!" said Svip, the monotone of the translator not entirely suppressing his enthusiasm.

"I don't like the way that damned thing's looking at me," muttered Blitzkrieg, drawing back a bit from the perimeter.

"Aw, it can't hurt nobody, General," said Rev. "It's jes' an . . ."

At this point the *gryff* let out a roar and tossed its head, its eyes—which were about the size of grapefruits—apparently fixed on Blitzkrieg. The general withdrew another step, and even Rev seemed startled by the sudden noise. The *gryff* raised one foreleg and began pawing at the ground—it would have taken a keen, cold-blooded observer to note that the claws of its pawing foot were disturbing neither the dirt nor the vegetation through which they passed.

Give Blitzkrieg some credit for courage, in any case. It wasn't until the *gryff* let out another snort, tossed its head, and broke into a full charge in the general's direction that he broke and ran.

It wasn't until he was nearly back to the base module that he stopped to determine that it hadn't followed him; indeed, it was nowhere to be seen.

15

Journal #846—

On most planets, the customs officials perform a cursory examination of one's papers and wave through all but the most blatantly irregular. Naturally there are local quirks and quibbles—only a nitwit would attempt to smuggle raw Lupretian pastries onto Nostilla II, for example. And if there has been some recent smuggling scandal, or some outrageous crime blamed on an off-worlder, inspections understandably become more stringent. But otherwise, little short of an automatic weapon strapped across one's shoulders seems to catch the agents' attention.

Things are arranged otherwise on Old Earth. There, the agents inquire closely into one's origins and business on the planet. Considering that the planet claims to be the home world of the entire human species, one would think the doors would be open to those scattered human descendents seeking to visit the world of their ancestors. Not so—a Syn-

thian goes through Old Earth immigration with fewer questions asked than a human bearing an off-world passport.

And so, upon my arrival on the planet, I found myself dealing with a customs official whose interest in my background would have been more appropriate in a bank officer deciding whether to advance me a substantial loan than in a government functionary on whose world I intended to spend a large fraction of my disposable income. My efforts to point out this discrepancy met, I am sorry to report, with utter incomprehension.

After a considerable delay, the two legionnaires had worked their way to the front of the spaceport line leading to the Old Earth customs inspectors. An incredibly archaic-looking electric sign lit up with the word NEXT in three languages that Sushi recognized and a couple more that he didn't. He and his partner picked up their duffel bags and moved forward.

The official in the booth was a bored-looking Terran with dark hair and a bushy moustache. He raised an eyebrow, and asked, "You two are traveling together?"

"Yeah, we're on assignment together," said Sushi, putting his passport on the agent's desk. He and Do-Wop had worn their Legion uniforms on the assumption that customs might go easier on servicemen. The ploy had worked on enough planets that it couldn't hurt to try it here.

"Really," said the customs man, dryly. His plastic badge read AGT. G. C. FOX. "I wasn't aware there were any Legion bases on-world. Exactly what assignment do you have on Old Earth?"

"Military secret," said Do-Wop, before Sushi could get his mouth open. "You shouldn't wanna know, y'know?"

"Personally, I really couldn't give a fleener," said Fox, leaning forward on the desk. His hand rested lightly on Sushi's passport. "Mind my own business, that's my policy. But my bosses want to know why people are coming to our planet—they have the idea that's a good way to prevent trouble. Since they're the ones paying my salary, I always ask. So I'll ask you again—secret or not, what kind of assignment do two Space Legion men have here on Old Earth?"

This time Sushi got the first word in edgewise, largely by the expedient of tromping down hard on Do-Wop's toe. "That's a great policy, Agent Fox," he said, while Do-Wop groaned out a series of muffled curses. "As it happens, my friend was a bit hesitant about telling you what we're here for, because it's a special training mission for the intelligence branch of the Legion, and of course one of the things they've been emphasizing is that we should always keep our real mission secret. But of course, that hardly applies to somebody who's pretty much in the same kind of business, you know?"

Fox frowned. "Intelligence branch of the Legion? This is the first I've ever heard of it."

"Well, that just goes to show how top secret it is," said Sushi, with a wink. "I'm sure we can trust you to keep it under your hat, Agent Fox."

"Oh, I'm very discreet," said Fox, nodding. "And I certainly understand how an intelligence operation needs to be kept quiet." He paused, looking first at Do-Wop, then at Sushi. "The only thing is, I've been doing this job so long that I have a pretty good nose for a scam. And if this isn't the biggest scam I've seen this month, I'm going to put in for early retirement. Not that that's a bad idea anyhow. So—one more time: What's your business here? And if I don't like your answer this time, I'll introduce you to the fellows in the back room. They've got suspicious minds and disgustingly long fingers."

"Hey, we ain't done noth . . . OW!" said Do-Wop. He began hopping around, holding his injured foot in both hands.

"Well, Agent Fox, the truth is . . ." Sushi began. Then he caught a glimpse of the customs agent's face and did an instant revision of his comment. "The truth is, we're trying to find our commanding officer. He's needed back at the base, and our last report had him on the way to Old Earth. His name is . . ."

"That's enough—I don't need his name," said Fox. "The question is, even if I believed you, why should I tell you anything?"

Sushi's eyes lit up. "Not only do you believe me, you know just who we're looking for, don't you? He must have come through here . . ."

"Now, don't be hasty," said Fox, wagging his finger. "I may or may not have seen a Legion officer come through—they're not common hereabouts, you know."

"That means that if you did see our captain, you'd probably remember him," said Sushi. He reached in his pocket and extracted a ten-dollar piece. He put it on the counter near his passport. "Does this help your memory?"

"Maybe . . ." Fox looked at the passport for a moment, then looked back at the coin, before adding, "Two of 'em might make my memory even better."

Sushi sighed, then turned to Do-Wop, who had recovered his balance and stood glaring at the two of them. "OK, buddy, your turn to chip in. Let's see what the man knows."

"How come I gotta chip in?" said Do-Wop.

"You want to chip in, or you want to see the guys with long fingers?" said Sushi.

Do-Wop dug into his pocket. A moment later, Agent Fox was filling them in on a few—but by no means all—of the things he'd learned from Phule upon his arrival on Old Earth. They didn't notice that, at the same time, he was skillfully getting them to tell him far more than he was telling them. "Give a little, get a lot," was Fox's motto. He was really very good at it.

• • •

Do-Wop gaped at the Roman cityscape, amazement written plainly on his face. "Jeez!" he said, after a moment. "Here I am in Italy—I never thought I'd see the place!"

"Yeah, it's pretty quaint," said Sushi, eyeing the odd juxtaposition of hypermodern tourist traps and ruins dating to an age before space travel. "Could use a bit of maintenance, if you want my opinion."

"Ahh, you wouldn't understand class if it bit you in the ass," said Do-Wop, scoffing.

"Y'know, I don't think anybody with real class would be interested in that," said Sushi. "Don't go quoting me, though—I don't want people to think I'm provincial or anything."

It would have been hard for either of the two legionnaires to look much more provincial than the tourists thronging the streets around them. The dress code appeared to require some sort of garish locally purchased T-shirt. They were visible everywhere, with cryptic slogans ranging from VINI, VIDI, VICI, and ILLEGITIMATI NON CARBORUNDUM, to straight advertisements, one of the most popular being SINGH'S PIZZA—YOU'VE TRIED THE REST, NOW TRY THE BEST! In contrast, the two black-uniformed legionnaires were practically the definition of class.

On the other hand, to judge from the looks some of the passersby shot at them, the class they represented was not in particular favor locally. Even Do-Wop sensed the undercurrent as they walked through the Forum. When the stares continued, he eventually turned to Sushi, and said, "What's up, Soosh? Some of these civvies are lookin' at us like we're farting in their lifeboat."

"I feel it, too," said Sushi. "And I heard one of them muttering about spies. I don't know what it means, but I think we need to find out before we get in some kind of trouble."

"Hey, I ain't gonna run away from—OW!" said Do-Wop, as Sushi grabbed him by the ear and hustled him away from the open Forum. A short distance away, the crowd thinned out and the two legionnaires found themselves in the shadow of a dilapidated building. Do-Wop glared at Sushi. "What the hell was that for?"

"Something fishy's going on here, and I don't mean anchovy pizza," said Sushi, in a voice just above a whisper. "Those people are mad at the Legion for some reason. I think we need to get some civilian outfits before we get in real trouble. For now, a couple of T-shirts will probably do the job."

They found a tourist trap, not half a block away, with a full display of garish overpriced T-shirts. If the sophont behind the counter had anything against their Legion uniforms, he kept it to himself and pocketed their money with a smile and a very credible *"Grazie, signori!"* His Italian was good enough that he could have passed for a native Roman, if he hadn't been seven and a half feet tall with bluish green skin, bright pink hair, and eyes on stalks. As they left the shop, Sushi wondered briefly whether the salesbeing was a genetically altered human or a member of some nonhuman species he hadn't met before.

Back on the street, the two of them passed almost unnoticed in the crowd. "I guess that just goes to show the value of camouflage," said Sushi, in an exasperated tone. After a moment he added, "I think it's the locals, not the tourists, who're staring at us—which is weird. If that customs agent is right, they don't see very many legionnaires on Old Earth. There's no reason they'd be mad . . ."

Do-Wop stopped in his tracks. "Y' know what I think? Somebody's been goin' around bad-mouthin' the Legion. That's the only thing makes sense. Question is, who? And why?"

"Partner, you just asked the gigabuck question," said

Sushi. "I don't know the answer—but I bet when we find it out, it'll have something to do with the captain."

"I don't think I'm gonna take that bet," said Do-Wop.

Late that night, behind closed doors, the leaders of Omega Company assembled. In the wake of the Andromatic robot's golf accident, Rembrandt had called the command cadre to an emergency meeting. Ironically, nobody was quite sure what the emergency was, although they all agreed it had to be tackled at once.

"The robot's damaged, that's the main problem," said Armstrong, who'd been on hand to witness the event. "A hard shot smack in the middle of the forehead—I don't know what kinds of circuits are up there, but they must be important."

"Well, I'm sure not a roboticist," said Rembrandt. "But from what you tell me, the main problem was that the robot captain started to play much better than before. I wouldn't take that as automatic evidence of damage."

"How much do you know about golf?" said Armstrong. "What if I told you the robot shot a twenty-four on the back nine?"

"That's pretty good, isn't it?" Rembrandt asked.

Chocolate Harry answered her. "Shee-it, that ain't just good, it's *scary*. Machine that can do that can do *anything*. I don't even want t'think about it." There was genuine awe in the Supply sergeant's voice.

"I think the general's in total shock," said Armstrong. "It's the only explanation for why he didn't instantly smell a rat when the robot started driving the ball four hundred yards and knocking in putts as if the green was a big funnel."

"But he's going to figure out something's wrong," said Brandy. "That man's not so dumb he won't notice a complete SNAFU, and that's what this sounds like to me."

Armstrong nodded. "That's the problem. Maybe we can pass today off as an aberration, but if the robot starts playing killer golf again tomorrow, the general's going to have us all on the carpet."

Escrima was not impressed. "Ahh, what's he gonna do, send us to Omega Company? I'm not afraid of him."

"There are now a lot of things worse than Omega Company," said Rembrandt. "Captain Jester's done right by us, you know. Do you want to find out what a Legion detention barracks is like?"

Nobody said anything for a moment. Then Chocolate Harry broke the silence. "OK, here's an idea," he said. "We lock the 'bot up someplace, tell the general the captain's had a delayed reaction to bein' hit on the head. Somebody else can show the general around, maybe Armstrong can play golf with him, and meanwhile maybe Gears can try to fix the problem."

"Yeah, that might work for a couple of days," said Brandy. "But do you think Gears can fix the robot? It's a whole lot more complicated than a hoverjeep . . ."

"If we had Sushi here, I'd be a lot happier," said Rembrandt. "He might not be a roboticist, but he could probably figure something out just on general knowledge. As it is, we'll have to let Gears give it his best shot."

"I don't know," said Armstrong. He took a couple of paces, then spun around to face the group. "The thing is, the general really did come here looking for trouble. When he got into the golf matches with the robot, that distracted him from looking at everything else that's going on around here. I'm afraid that if he isn't playing the captain, and winning just often enough to give him the satisfaction of beating a hated rival, he's going to go looking for trouble again. And I guarantee you, he's going to find it. None of us are going to like that."

"I don't like the situation we've got now," said Rembrandt, frowning. "We've got to have something ready to go tomorrow morning, though." She mused a moment, then turned to Armstrong. "All right, you've spent as much time with the general as anybody, this time around. Do you think you can jolly him along for at least one day if the official explanation is that the captain's recovering from a concussion?"

"I can try," said Armstrong. "As long as he's willing to stick to golf and doesn't want to start poking his nose into other stuff . . ."

"Good," said Rembrandt. "Harry, you'll get Gears and anybody else with mechanical know-how to work on the robot—maybe put a call in to the Andromatic factory—and see if we can get it back in shape by the next day. And meanwhile, everybody try to think of alternative plans in case things don't work out."

"Got it, Remmie," said Chocolate Harry. "I'll have Gears get to work on the 'bot—say, where is it, anyway?"

Rembrandt and Armstrong looked at each other, their eyes growing wider.

"Did you . . . ?"

"I thought *you* were going to—"

"No, didn't you—?"

"Well, where the . . ."

"Oh, *damn!*" they both cried together, leaping to their feet. The room emptied in something like ten seconds as the entire command cadre of Omega Company rushed out into the night to find the missing Andromatic robot.

The crowd on the streets of Rome, one of the major cities of Old Earth, seemed to be made up of two elements: off-worlders gaping at the wonders of the oldest of all human worlds and natives seeking to separate them from their money.

Phule had more urgent business than either group. He'd spent far too much time in his search for Beeker and Nightingale. He had no idea how Omega Company was doing in his absence, although surely he'd have heard before now if any real crisis had arisen. The Omega Mob was an ongoing crisis in and of itself, but that was a different story.

Today he was on his way to visit a local branch of his family, one with access to various unorthodox sources of information. The address he had seemed plain enough, although the streets of Rome were filled with rubble and the house number he had was nowhere to be seen. He stopped half a dozen times to ask directions, but everyone he asked either glared at him, then replied with a rapid-fire burst of Italian, or smiled and said, "Sorry, I'm a tourist, too."

At last he approached a hulking fellow who leaned against the corner of a building, hands stuffed in his pockets and a fearsome scowl on his face. "Excuse me," he said. "I'm looking for 45 Via Poco Lente—I thought it was near here, but I can't seem to find it."

"Aha!" The man's voice was a basso rumble, but unlike most of the street Italians in the area, he spoke Standard almost without an accent. "You looking for Pitti da Phule, no?"

"That's right, how'd you know?"

"He gave you that address, he wants to see you," said the man, with a shrug. "Good thing you find Hugo, I know just where to take you. Most people around here—they don't want nothing to do with da Phule."

"Well then, Hugo, I'm glad I met you," said Phule. "How do I get to Via Poco Lente?"

"You don't," said Hugo. "Most people don't want nothing to do with da Phule, and he don't want nothing to do with them, either. That's a password, not an address. You ask the right guy—which today happens to be me—and I take you to da Phule."

"I guess I've already found out what happens if you ask the wrong guy," said Phule. "What if you don't find the right guy?"

"Then you don't want to see Pitti da Phule bad enough,"

said Hugo, spreading his arms wide, with palms upward. "Come on, I take you there."

Phule followed his guide down a series of narrow, winding streets, turning seemingly at random; indeed, at least twice he thought they'd passed a house he'd seen a few turns previously. But after perhaps twenty minutes, they came to a graffiti-covered stretch of stone wall, nine or ten feet high, at one end of which was a wooden gate with peeling green paint. Hugo pushed it open and waved Phule forward. "This is the place," he said, grinning broadly. "You go in, I wait for you here."

The circuitous route and his guide's mysterious behavior had put Phule on his guard. "Why don't you go first?" he said, taking the other man firmly by the elbow. He added, as Hugo showed signs of balking, "Really, I insist."

"Smart of you," said a smooth baritone voice from just inside the door. A slim middle-aged man stepped forward, holding a wineglass in one hand. Around his neck were several thick gold chains. "Smart, but not necessary this time around. Hugo's a *condottieri* at heart, but he knows not to fool with anybody who has my password. You must be Cousin Victor's boy—last I heard, you were the only family member in any kind of uniform."

"Uncle Pitti?" said Phule, stepping forward to shake the older man's hand. "I remember meeting you years ago, at somebody's wedding . . ."

"That must have been Stella Phule," said Pitti da Phule, nodding. "She married Juan Feryou, out on Tau Ceti Four. A really big affair. I think they're still talking about the Phule-Feryou wedding out there . . ."

Phule grinned. "Right, I spent the afternoon hanging out with the groom's younger brother . . ."

"Right, Nomarr Feryou," said Pitti. "He was a little hell-raiser, back then. So were you, if memory serves me right. That doesn't look as if it's held you back, *Captain*." Pitti punched Phule in the arm, playfully, then raised a finger to his lips. "But I'm not being much of a host, am I? We'll get you a glass of *vino* and something to eat with it, and then we can talk business."

Pitti da Phule took his nephew through a side door into a garden, where a marble fountain bubbled musically. An ancient-looking wall served as the backdrop for a row of fruit trees, and the walk was lined with flowers. Small birds darted between the branches, watched by a lazy orange cat. Pitti gestured to a pair of benches, with a small marble table in between. The top of the table, Phule noted, had an inlaid chessboard.

They talked for a few minutes, until Pitti's robutler brought them a plate of anchovies, peppers, cheese, and olives, a crusty loaf of bread, and a bottle of a full-bodied Tuscan red. After they'd put a satisfactory dent in the hors d'ouvres, Pitti steepled his fingers and said, "Now, it can't be just coincidence that you've come looking for me. In fact, there's talk going around about the Space Legion. Is there anything to the rumor that your outfit is doing a job for the IRS?"

Phule practically burst out laughing. "That's about the last governmental organization I'd do a job for," he said. "I guess it would explain the funny looks I've gotten on the street. But you may not know about some of my troubles with them . . ." He described his previous run-in with the tax agency, and finally Pitti nodded.

"It didn't sound like anything one of our family would be involved in, but you can't ignore something everybody's talking about. I wonder who started that rumor?" Pitti studied his nephew for a moment, then said, "But you came here to ask something. What can Uncle Pitti do for you?"

Phule outlined his situation, for what felt like the hundredth time since he'd left Zenobia in search of his errant butler and Nightingale. This time, at least, he could tell about the Port-a-Brain—although he decided to leave out the hibernation problem. No reason to spread that information any farther than strictly necessary, even within the family. Pitti da Phule listened in silence for a while, taking an occasional sip of wine. At last he held up a hand. "Good enough," he said. "I see what the problem is. Let me find out what I can do for you. I'll get in touch—where are you staying?"

Phule gave him the address of his hotel. "Not a bad place, for what you're probably paying," said Pitti. "Try Trattoria Alfonso, on the next block, for lunch. I think you'll like it—tell the waiter I sent you. Now, go do some sightseeing, relax, eat—and let me handle things for a while. *Ciao!*"

And with that, he pushed Phule out the door onto the streets. A moment later, he beckoned to a servant. "Get the prints and DNA on this analyzed," he said in Italian, pointing to Phule's wineglass. "The kid looks and talks like Willard, but it's been a long time since I've seen him. And call his old man, too—yes, I know how much it costs to call intersystem. But this kid's claiming to be family, and with all the rumors going around, I'd like to be sure that's really who I'm dealing with."

Brandy found the robot in the gym. It wasn't all that hard to find, actually. She could hear it all the way down the hall. She opened the door to discover that it had a squad of frightened legionnaires lined up for a roasting that many old-time drill sergeants might have gotten pointers from. Several veteran smart-mouths and goof-offs were among the roastees, and their shocked expressions were all the evidence Brandy needed that the robot had caught them completely off guard.

She stepped forward, trying her best not to draw attention, but the robot picked her up in its peripheral vision, and barked, "Sergeant! Come forward."

"Yes, Captain Jester," she said, putting on her best military manner. She marched briskly to the front of the formation, stood at attention, and snapped off her best salute. "What are your orders, sir?" she barked.

"Well, at least one person here knows how to show proper respect for an officer," the robot drawled. "What I don't understand is why none of these so-called legionnaires seem to have learned it. This *is* the squad you've supposedly been training, isn't it, Sergeant?"

"Yes, sir, no excuse, sir," she said, keeping the surprise out of her voice as best she could. Clearly, the errant golf ball had done even more damage than they'd realized. Not only was the robot playing superhuman golf, it had turned into a by-the-books officer of the worst sort. Unless they could get the damage fixed—and quickly!—Omega Company was in for a shock of tectonic proportions.

Meanwhile, her mind was racing at top speed. How was she going to defuse the immediate confrontation? The question was more delicate than it first appeared. After all, the robot nominally outranked everyone on the base except for General Blitzkrieg and his adjutant, neither of whom was likely to intervene. Just telling the legionnaires to ignore the robot was the most obvious method; the robot had no way to enforce its orders, after all. But the rank and file had no idea this Captain Jester was a robot. Only the command cadre were in on the secret, and she wasn't going to change that without orders from the real captain. Besides, what if some future crisis required the real Captain Jester to issue unpopular orders? She didn't want to do something now that would give some wise guy an excuse, no matter how phony, to claim he didn't believe it was the real captain giving the orders . . .

The robot captain rubbed its chin, as the real Phule would have while thinking about some point. Brandy was impressed by how well the robot's manufacturers had captured Phule's body language and casual gestures, in addition to giving it a near-perfect physical resemblance to its protoplasmic prototype. Then it spoke again. "Sergeant, I am appalled by these legionnaires' discipline—or nearly total lack of discipline, I should say. It's past time that somebody got them to shape up—and I'm beginning to wonder whether you're the woman for the job or not."

"Yes, sir," said Brandy. "Permission to ask a question, sir." It was uncanny how much it resembled Captain Jester, even though it was acting in a way that threatened to undercut everything he'd accomplished so far.

"Permission granted, Sergeant," said the robot.

Out of the corner of her eye, Brandy could see Mahatma's eyes bulging out in anticipation. He would undoubtedly be taking mental notes on her performance—and giving postmortem analysis to his fellow legionnaires. In spite of having been his target so many times, Brandy felt a rush of inspiration. *I can't disappoint the little guy,* she thought. Carefully, she summoned up her long-dormant memories of how she'd dealt with rulebook officers in the past.

"Sir, any failures of discipline in this training squad are my responsibility," she began, making it up as she went along. "But may I remind the captain that I was given orders to train this group to pass as civilians in enemy territory. Their apparent lack of military polish is designed to lull the enemy into overlooking their specialized skills, which meet and surpass Legion standard, sir. May I give the captain a demonstration?"

The robot looked at her for a long moment, then said, "Very well, Sergeant—I can hardly deny you the opportunity to let your troops show me their capabilities. For your sake, I hope the demonstration is convincing."

"Yes, Captain! Thank you, Captain," said Brandy, still thinking fast. She turned to face the puzzled-looking group of legionnaires. "Mahatma! Step forward." Perhaps the little legionnaire's habit of asking impossible questions would hold the robot's attention long enough for her to discover a way out of the situation.

"Yes, Sergeant Brandy," said Mahatma, striding briskly out of the formation. As usual, his face betrayed nothing of his inner thoughts. *I hope he catches on quick,* thought Brandy.

But before she could say anything, another voice broke the silence. "Well, well, Captain—what the devil's going on here?"

Brandy turned her head to see none other than General Blitzkrieg, with an expression that might have made a full-grown *gryff* turn and run for its life.

16

Journal #852—

Many humans, when first encountering Zenobians, think of them as a backward and slow-witted species. I believe there are two reasons for this: their reptilian appearance and their short stature. Their appearance leads humans to think of them as more primitive than they are; the small size conveys, to many of us, the suggestion of immaturity. Those impressions ignore the fact that the first Zenobians our race encountered were aboard a spacegoing survey vessel, a considerable distance from the Zenobian home world.

I do believe that the Zenobians have fostered these mistaken assumptions about their species. It can be a considerable advantage if the other party in a business transaction consistently underestimates one's intelligence and sophistication.

I have sometimes wondered if my employer is familiar with this strategy. It would explain a great deal . . .

• • •

Phule's trip back to his hotel was somewhat more of an adventure than he'd planned on. He'd been warned about Old Earth's ubiquitous pickpockets, con artists, and identity thieves, as well as Pitti's news about rumors connecting the Space Legion with the IRS—guaranteed to make the black uniform unpopular. Still, nothing he'd heard matched the experience of walking through the streets of Rome. In fact, the only thing that came close was spending an equivalent amount of time with some of the enlisted legionnaires of the Omega Mob.

Phule knew enough not to carry anything valuable when he went out on the streets. He knew more than enough not to fall for the myriad sob stories and come-ons that someone on every street corner seemed ready to offer to prosperous-looking passersby. And his personal information had been specially encrypted in the experimental Zenobian-based code that Sushi was developing. Sushi had assured him that only a native speaker of Zenobian was going to have any chance to crack the code. Earth's hackers and crackers might be the best in the galaxy, but Agent Fox's ignorance about Zenobia was a pretty good indication that nobody on Old Earth was likely to have the necessary knowledge to make use of his information, even if they did manage to steal it.

Meanwhile, he was enjoying the energy and the color of the bustling Roman streets, which had become far safer for pedestrians with the arrival of hovercars, which the Romans drove with the same recklessness they'd driven ground cars—but well above street level, and with better automatic safety devices. It might be fun to walk around the city with Samantha Beliveau, the pretty redhead he'd met going to the landing shuttle. He'd been meaning to call her and make a lunch date, possibly at the restaurant Uncle Pitti had mentioned—Trattoria something or another. They'd probably know at the hotel . . .

He was still trying to remember the name of the restaurant when he heard a woman scream. The sound came from an alley he'd just walked past. He turned and looked carefully down the narrow passageway—no sense sticking his neck out unless he knew what he was getting into.

Just as he looked, a weasel-faced man in a shiny dark suit struck a young woman across the face with a backhanded slap. The woman was nearly knocked off her feet by the blow. Only the man's rough grip on her arm with his other hand prevented her from falling outright.

"What's going on here?" shouted Phule. At the sound of Phule's voice, the man turned and looked at him—indignant at being interrupted, to judge from his expression. But at the same time, the woman broke the grip and stumbled toward Phule, who stepped forward to shelter her. He quickly pulled her out of the alleyway and onto the crowded street.

"What's the matter?" said Phule. The woman looked to be in her early twenties, and wore something that Phule mentally classified as a "peasant dress"—not that he had any knowledge of what peasants wore these days, let alone whether any peasants were still around to wear it.

The woman cast her gaze back over her shoulder. There was a bruise starting to form under her left eye. "That man—he tried to kill me!" she gasped, turning to look up into Phule's eyes. Her eyes were dark and pleading as she held onto his arm, obviously frightened.

"You get in my way, I kill you too!" said the man, waving a fist. He took a threatening step forward.

That made up Phule's mind. "Come on!" He grabbed her hand and set off at a pace he hoped she would be able to keep up with. A block away, he looked back at the alleyway; Weasel-face was standing there, hands on hips, staring angrily at them. But he had made no effort to follow.

"I think we're safe," he said. "Do you have anywhere safe to go?"

"I do, but I am afraid of him," she said. "What if he follows up?"

"Well, come along with me," said Phule. "We'll go someplace he can't follow us, and then we'll figure out how you can get away from him. I can't really do much else for you—I'm just here for a short time, and have important business of my own." He made a mental note to himself to stay alert for any funny business on the woman's part; it wouldn't be unheard of for an attractive "victim" to lure an off-world tourist into following her someplace where Weasel-face, who would of course turn out to be her accomplice, could rob him.

"Yes, I will come with you," said the woman, darting another glance backward. "But hurry, please—I am afraid of him."

"He doesn't look very frightening to me," said Phule. "Just stay close to me and I'll make sure he doesn't bother you." He led her in the direction of his hotel, glancing over his shoulder to see if Weasel-face was following. Apparently not; so far, so good, he thought. He wondered if there was some way to give the woman any long-term security. She did seem to be genuinely afraid. Pitti da Phule might have some suggestions on that score . . .

Suddenly he realized that it seemed to be taking a long time to get to the hotel. It should be just a block or so ahead, on the right-hand corner . . . but no, it was nowhere to be seen. *I ought to stop and get my bearings,* Phule thought to himself. "Hold on a second, miss," he said to the woman. To his surprise, she just kept walking—and he kept walking with her. His feet didn't seem to want to stop . . .

"What's happening?" he said. For some reason, he couldn't raise his voice above a husky whisper. Then, he remembered: When she'd taken his arm after coming out of the alleyway, her nails had dug into his skin. A glance down showed a small red mark on his wrist. Putting two and two together at last, he blurted out, "You've drugged me! Where are you taking me?"

"Not to worry, *signore*," she said. "Nobody wants to hurt you. I'm sure you are worth very much more un-harmed, and I don't think you would enjoy it, either. Just come along quietly with me. Don't fight the 'zombie' shot, and my friend Carmelo doesn't have to do anything. He is so much happier when he doesn't have to do anything, *capisce*?"

Phule looked behind him, and saw Weasel-face—undoubtedly Carmelo—walking a short distance behind, a sardonic smile on his face. But whatever drugs the woman had given him, they seemed to work just fine. He followed her without question along the Roman streets, his feet moving steadily despite his urgent desire to turn and run away.

General Blitzkrieg let out a deep breath. The charging Zenobian monster hadn't breached the base perimeter. And he felt good that he'd managed to sprint a solid thirty meters—or at least, as close to a sprint as was consonant with the dignity of a senior officer. His heart had stopped pounding after no more than five minutes, and he'd man-aged to avoid being seen by any low-ranking legionnaires. Only that phony chaplain, Rev, had seen him flee in panic, and Rev had looked genuinely scared himself when the beast put on its charge. So the story wasn't likely to leak out from that quarter.

He still hadn't figured out what the damned Zenobians' spy apparatus was all about. With their impenetrable jar-gon, the little lizards had managed to keep him from learn-ing anything about it. And then that monster had shown up . . . just in time to keep him from asking the pertinent questions he'd had right on the tip of his tongue. Maybe the monster would attack the lizards. Or maybe they'd called it somehow—with the machine? Could they be training it to attack the base at their command?

Well, there was one person on this godforsaken base who'd better know what it was all about: Jester. The fellow was supposed to be in command here, not that Blitzkrieg had seen any sign of it. Had to admire the way the fellow hit a golf ball, though—that was quite an exhibition he'd put on today. The rap he'd taken on the noggin must've gotten him riled up. He'd made some spectacular shots, and with a few lucky breaks, he'd put together a round of golf a lot of pros would have envied. Of course, tomorrow was another day—and Blitzkrieg knew that, except for today, he'd more than held his own against the local talent. Luck had a way of evening out.

But he had other business with Jester, now. Serious Legion business. Time to take the gloves off and show Captain Smart-ass Jester who was in charge. And if the little rich brat didn't have some damned good answers, the general was going to make him wish he'd never heard of the Space Legion. There were a lot of Legion posts that could make this planet, even with its desert climate and alien monsters, look like a playpen. And Blitzkrieg was just itching to find an excuse to send Jester to one of them . . .

Blitzkrieg walked to the nearest door and entered the base module. He still hadn't learned exactly how the thing was laid out—Jester had set the thing up according to some half-baked plan of his own rather than following the approved plans for Legion installations. Here was the enlisted men's barbershop, closed for the evening now, and over there was a bank of vending machines—a small but lucrative profit center that no Legion base could afford to do without. If he turned left here, it ought to take him to Comm Central, and from there, Jester's office was in easy reach. Assuming the fellow ever spent any time at all in the office—it was beginning to look as if he was a full-time golfer, with Legion responsibilities a distant second. Probably just as well, considering that Jester was a lead-pipe cinch to screw up any Legion work that came his way . . .

Halfway down the hall to Comm Central, General Blitzkrieg stopped as a familiar sound caught his ear. He'd been hearing it for his entire Legion career, on bases spanning half the galaxy. It was such an inevitable part of the usual background noise of a Legion base that he'd almost failed to notice it—except that *here*, here on rich-boy Jester's custom-built base, it seemed out of place. It was the sound of a squad being chewed out by a superior. And to his utter astonishment, the voice doing the chewing out was none other than Jester's!

The sound came from a side corridor leading to a set of double doors. A small printed sign above the doors identified the room as the gym. His curiosity running rampant, Blitzkrieg pushed open the doors and stepped inside. There stood Jester, bracing a motley collection of Omega Company legionnaires with their first sergeant—the fat woman who'd taken a Legion name after some kind of liquor, exactly in character for this sorry outfit. And for once, Jester was the perfect image of an officer—his uniform immaculate, his posture exemplary, and fire in his eye. And for all their shoddy appearance, the grunts were showing something resembling respect, as well. It was so completely out of character for Omega Company that General Blitzkrieg was speechless for a moment.

He watched in shocked silence as the sergeant called forward one of the recruits—a little, round-faced fellow with eyeglasses. Then, unable to contain his curiosity any longer, he blurted out, "Well, well, Captain—what the devil's going on here?"

Cool as a comet at the farthest reaches of its orbit, Jester turned to face him and snapped off a crisp salute. "General Blitzkrieg!" Behind him, the sergeant barked "Ten-hut!" and the legionnaires straightened up—about as well as he'd expect from their sort. The open fear on their faces was a sight the general had never tired of seeing. Involuntarily, he felt an evil grin spread across his face. He'd come all the way from Rahnsome to Zenobia to strike fear and awe into these third-rate legionnaires. Up to now, he'd frittered away his stay playing golf with Jester—not that he hadn't enjoyed it.

Now he was really going to have some fun. "On second thought, don't mind me, Captain. The sergeant was about to give some kind of demonstration. By all means, carry on. I'm just as eager to see it as you are."

And when it collapsed into an utter fiasco, as it was bound to do now that he'd scared the crap out of these lowlifes, he'd show them what a *real* chewing-out was like. He could barely keep himself from laughing out loud with anticipation . . .

"Very well, Sergeant," said the robot, raising an eyebrow. "You heard General Blitzkrieg. Proceed with your demonstration."

Brandy struggled to keep from showing her chagrin. She'd meant to lead Mahatma through just enough of a show to support her pretense that she'd been training her legionnaires in espionage skills, then dismiss the squad and cut short the robot's attempt to enforce Legion discipline. Mahatma was enough of a natural actor to bring it off without the rest of the squad figuring out what had happened—in fact, they'd probably just be grateful to go back to their bunks. And if she played her hand right, she could shepherd the robot off so Gears could begin work on repairing it.

But the general's arrival changed everything. Now she had to make the demonstration convincing enough that the general wouldn't smell a rat, while maintaining the pretense that the gung ho robot really was Captain Jester. She also wanted to keep her legionnaires from taking any more flak than they absolutely had to. This meant fooling not only the malfunctioning robot but the general, who despite his recent good mood was infamously hostile to Omega

Company and Captain Jester. And she was the only one here who knew what was really going on, not that there was anybody who could help her if the general decided to fly off the handle.

I've just got to tough it out, she thought, turning to face Mahatma again. The little legionnaire was actually standing at a pretty fair semblance of attention; that might prevent the general from losing his temper prematurely. He *was* going to lose his temper; that much Brandy took for granted. Especially since the robot had picked today to hand him a beating on the golf course . . .

"Legionnaire Mahatma!" she barked, in her best parade-ground voice. "You heard the captain. We are going to demonstrate your infiltration and intelligence-gathering training for the general."

"Yes, Brandy," said Mahatma. "May I ask a question?"

All right, Mahatma! Brandy thought. *I hope you make it a good one, this time.* "Permission granted," she said, crisply. Out of the corner of her eye, she could see the general's jaw drop. If this didn't work, she could forget the remainder of her Legion career. So she might as well have as much fun as she could, while it lasted.

"Thank you, Brandy," said Mahatma, still maintaining an almost acceptable military stance. He shifted his eyes toward the general, who was still wearing his golf togs, and asked, "Why is the commanding general so fat and out of uniform?"

General Blitzkrieg's face turned crimson. He took two steps forward and began to bellow, "Why, you impertinent—"

The robot stepped ahead of him and cut him off, barking out, "Sergeant! I have never seen such flagrant insubordination! How do you explain this?"

"Sir!" said Brandy, keeping a straight face. "Nobody who saw this legionnaire's disrespect for authority could possibly believe that he has any military training. That is

Omega Company's secret weapon. Because the enemy underestimates this man—and most of our legionnaires—they
can exercise their military skills in conditions where they
have the element of surprise completely on their side."

"Military skills!" This time it was Blitzkrieg who
spoke. "Military skills, my blinking arse! What possible
military skills could this grinning imbecile have?"

"With the general's permission, Legionnaire Mahatma
will now demonstrate his military skills," said Brandy.

The robot looked at the general, who clenched his teeth
and nodded, turning a beady-eyed stare toward Mahatma.
"Carry on, Sergeant," said the robot, crossing its arms over
its chest.

Brandy suddenly realized that the robot had an expression that she had never seen on the real Captain Jester's
face. It took her a moment to figure it out, doing her best
not to stare, which the general was sure to consider insub-
ordinate, whether the robot noticed it or not.

The robot didn't have real emotions, as far as she could
understand. (Roboticists apparently had long, ongoing ar-
guments on the subject.) Apparently, all the robot could do
was display the external appearance of the human emotions
it was programmed to simulate. Brandy had no idea
whether these were installed from some standard menu at
the factory or customized for each model. Given the amount
of money the captain had spent, the latter was a good bet.
But whatever the case, the robot shouldn't be showing any
emotion it wasn't already programmed to show.

So why did she get the distinct impression it was doing
its best to hide utter irrational fear?

Phule came to his senses in a small room with a south-facing
window. Actually, he'd never really lost consciousness—
he'd just been unable to exert his own will power, following the woman who'd somehow managed to drug him. But
he'd sat in a kind of stupor for an unknown time in this

little room—wherever it was. Still somewhere in central Rome, he figured—he couldn't have walked any real distance, and he had no memory of entering any kind of vehicle. On the other hand, he had only the vaguest memory of the last . . . how long was it, anyway? And he didn't have to try the door to have a very good idea he was for all practical purposes a prisoner.

He got up and tried the door anyway, careful not to make any noise in the process. Whatever had happened to him, it had no obvious aftereffects; his head was clear, and his balance and coordination seemed to be fine now.

At least, his muscles seemed to be under his own control again. On the downside, the door was very definitely locked. So was the window, he quickly learned—locked and fortified on the outside with bars that looked quite sufficient to hold in one lone Space Legion captain. And it looked onto the blank wall of another building about five meters away, so there was no easy way to signal anyone.

Signaling . . . he quickly looked at his wrist. Sure enough, his communicator was gone. His pockets had been emptied, too. That gave him a brief moment's panic. Then he remembered that he'd left his Dilithium Express card and other items of value in the hotel safe; at most his captors would have a couple of hundred euros and his Legion ID card. Nothing he couldn't get replaced quickly enough. So—what now?

He did a quick search of the room, looking for anything he might be able to turn to his advantage. A makeshift weapon, an alternative way out, even some clue as to his kidnappers' identity. He turned up nothing besides the furniture he'd already seen—a bed, a chair, a side table. In a real pinch, he supposed he could club someone with the chair, or tie them up in the bedsheets. But those were desperate plays, to be saved for a desperate situation. The easiest way out of the room looked as if it started with getting the door opened. He went over and knocked.

After a moment he heard footsteps on the far side. "All right, stand-a back from-a the door," said a raspy voice with a thick Italian accent. *Weasel-face*, thought Phule, moving back as requested. He heard keys rattle in the lock, and then the door swung partway open; Weasel-face looked inside, squinting suspiciously. "What do you want?" he said, in an accent several degrees more educated than Phule expected. Behind him was another man, large and frowning—presumably the one who'd answered first.

"Giving my property back would be a good start," said Phule, in as even a voice as he could manage. "Then you really ought to let me go—I have important business that can't wait."

"Funny man," said Weasel-face, sourly. "What, do you think we locked you up for our own entertainment?"

"Well, I'm sure you didn't do it for mine," said Phule. "Just what do you think you've got to gain by holding me prisoner?"

"You should be able to figure that out by yourself," said Weasel-face. "But I'll save you the time, because I want you to know where things stand. You're a rich off-world snot, and we're underprivileged locals. Your people pay us, and we let you go. If they don't pay us quickly enough, maybe Vinnie and I get annoyed. Vinnie can be nasty when he's annoyed, and then you'd have something to worry about besides being late for your important business. *Capisce?*" Vinnie continued to frown, deploying what looked to be the preferred weapon in his arsenal of facial expressions.

Phule shrugged. "If I were you, I wouldn't count on collecting any ransom money. There'll be people coming to look for me, and they aren't amateurs. Or haven't you figured out who I was visiting earlier today?"

"Pitti da Phule doesn't frighten us," said Weasel-face, with a quiet smile. "If he tries to interfere in our business, we can call on people who'll make him think again."

"Well, it's not so much a question of interfering in your

business," said Phule. "I believe Pitti's approach is more likely to be total cancellation of your business plan."

"My friend, you aren't in a position to be issuing threats," growled Weasel-face. Phule remembered now that the woman who'd tricked him had called the man "Carmelo," although there was no guarantee that was the man's right name. He'd remember it, anyhow—just in case.

"Two points," said Phule. "First, I am not your friend. And second, what I just said wasn't a threat."

"Oh yeah?" said Weasel-face. "What do you call it, then?"

Phule smiled, and said softly, "In my line of business, we call that an ultimatum."

"Carmelo" just snorted and walked out, locking the door behind him.

Agent G. C. Fox drummed his fingers, waiting. The number he'd called rang for the fifth time, then a voice came through Fox's earplug: "The party you are calling is not available. Please leave a message and your call will be returned." A cacophonous beep followed, but Fox had already started the disconnect process. This was his fourth attempt to reach Captain Jester, and the message he'd left the first time had not been returned. Considering the message, it should have been.

So what did that mean? Fox took a sip of shandygaff, wiped the foam from his moustache with the back of his sleeve, and thought. The more Fox thought about it, the more convinced he was that the captain was already in trouble—and that he was going to need help getting out of it.

Helping off-worlders get out of trouble wasn't really Fox's job at all. He wasn't any kind of cop or a detective—just a customs inspector. But he made it a point to keep track of interesting visitors to Old Earth. Sometimes, he could steer them to a business or service they could benefit from. His friends who ran those businesses benefited from it, too—and so did Fox, thanks to the finders fees and commissions his friends passed along to him. They helped stretch the customs agent's not-so-grand salary enough to bring in a few of the better things of life.

He'd made it a point to look up Willard Phule on the newsnets, after he'd seen him come through customs. He'd learned a fair amount about the captain's background, and his career on the various worlds Omega Company had been posted to. It might or might not turn out to be profitable—but it never hurt to do the research. Fox had learned that knowing something always paid better than not knowing it.

He'd liked the Legion captain when they'd talked. And right after Phule's passage through customs, he'd read over a list of recent immigrants to Old Earth—all agents got the lists, and some of them—like Fox—made it a point to read them. Later, when he did his research on Phule, one name had jumped out at him. He had an excellent memory for names. A particular person had arrived on Old Earth two days before Phule. Her presence here might be a coincidence, of course. On the other hand, this was somebody Phule had bumped heads with in the past. That, Fox figured, was exactly the kind of information that a prudent man like Willard Phule would want to have. He might even find it in his heart to reward the person who'd brought it to him. Why shouldn't Fox be the one to reap the reward?

The only problem was, he couldn't get in touch with Phule . . .

There was someone else he could call, though. Someone who might be very grateful for advance warning of possible trouble for the young Space Legion captain. Fox picked up his vidphone, entered a number, and in a moment a face appeared on the screen. For a moment the other party frowned, reacting to Fox's uniform. Then the man relaxed, recognizing his caller. "Ah, *Signore Volpone*, what can I do for you today?"

Fox smiled. "Actually, it's the other way around this time," he said. "I've learned something I think you'll want to know . . ."

After Fox told his story, and added the fact that Phule hadn't been answering his phone, the other party nodded. "This does not smell good," he said. "*Grazie, signore*—if this is what it seems to be, I am in your debt."

"Think nothing of it," said Fox. "I don't like to see somebody get in trouble when I could have prevented it."

"*Grazie* again, then," said Pitti da Phule. "I will remember this." He broke the connection.

Thumper and the other members of his training squad were well into an evening of creative goofing off when the captain walked into the Enlisted Legionnaires' Lounge. By this time of day, they were usually free to follow their own routines—which, in the Omega Mob, included drinking, swapping stories, playing bar games, dancing to Roadkill's band, or joking around. Unless there was a real emergency, sergeants and officers tended to leave them alone.

So nobody was expecting Captain Jester to order them to report to the gym, on the double. If he had been a mere sergeant, they might have complained. But the captain was a different story; not only was he the top authority on the planet—at least, when generals weren't visiting—he also knew when to give his people a little slack. So Roadkill and his buddies shut off their instruments, and Omega Training Squad obediently trooped down to the gym. They lined up in a formation that would've made even Brandy proud. Or so Thumper thought, as he took his place at one end of the front rank, next to his buddy Mahatma.

Surprise! For the first time since he'd joined Omega Company, Thumper found himself being yelled at by his company commander. Not by a sergeant, which wouldn't have been any surprise—yelling at the troops was what sergeants were supposed to do. Not even one of the lieutenants, who were usually too busy to bother. Nope, this was the CO himself, hollering and cussing worse than Sergeant Brandy.

"You look like a bunch of Fungolian weevils! Who taught you how to stand at attention? Do you call that a regulation haircut? Wipe that smirk off your face, legionnaire!" The entire squad seemed stunned—they'd never seen the captain like this.

But after a little while, Brandy showed up, and things started looking normal again. Thumper wondered if this was some kind of training exercise; that was the best explanation he could think of for the way Brandy and the captain acted. After all, he'd seen a good bit of Captain Jester while he was caddying for Flight Leftenant Qual in the golf matches. He hadn't expected the captain to act like this, not at all.

Then—surprise number three!—General Blitzkrieg walked into the gym! Thumper hoped the general didn't remember that unfortunate incident with a bucket full of stinky stuff back in basic training. It hadn't really been Thumper's fault, but it sure looked like it when somebody handed him the bucket after emptying it over the general's head while the lights were out. The general seemed to be the kind of human who remembered things like that. Or maybe he didn't; at least he hadn't said anything out on the golf course, while Thumper caddied for Flight Leftenant Qual. Still, the general might not pay attention to his golf opponent's caddy; but here he was on Legion business. In spite of himself, Thumper shivered.

Sergeant Brandy called Mahatma forward, and told the general about the squad's special mission. This was the first time Thumper had heard anything about it, but as he listened to her, he thought it would explain a lot of things that hadn't made sense before. Even when Mahatma asked the general one of his pain-in-the-ass questions, Brandy explained it so the general seemed to understand it.

The only thing that didn't fit was the captain's reaction. Thumper thought he looked surprised. Was the secret mission supposed to be a secret from the captain? He certainly didn't look as if he'd ever heard of it. Or was he worried that Mahatma wouldn't be enough of a pain?

Thumper was still trying to figure it out when Brandy said, "Legionnaire Mahatma will now demonstrate his military skills." That caught Thumper's attention, all right. Mahatma was the only member of the training squad close to Thumper's size, so the two of them often ended up as sparring partners in hand-to-hand combat drills. Thumper had a lot of respect for Mahatma's skills. The little human was fast, and sneaky, and a lot stronger than he looked.

So it was only natural when Sergeant Brandy pointed to Thumper, and said, "Legionnaire Thumper, front and center to spar with Mahatma."

Thumper had taken two steps forward when the general barked, "Wait a minute! If you're going to demonstrate this man's military skills, I want to see a real opponent out here. You're not going to match him with some fluffy bunny, Sergeant."

Thumper thought he was a pretty decent opponent, but he could sort of see the general's point. Even Brandy made sure each of them sparred against everybody in the squad. She always said, "You don't get to pick out an opponent your own size in a real fight." So he stepped back into the formation as Brandy asked, oh so politely, "Perhaps the general would like to select an opponent for Legionnaire Mahatma?" Only someone who'd watched her for weeks under the hot sun would have noticed a faint smile.

General Blitzkrieg scanned the training squad, a scowl on his face. After a moment, he pointed, and said, "That one looks fit enough. You, legionnaire. Front and center!"

"Yes, sir!" said a mechanical voice, and Thumper involuntarily turned to make sure he'd heard correctly. Sure enough, stepping forward came Rube, one of the three Gambolts assigned to Omega Company.

"Hello, Rube," said Mahatma, waving. The Gambolt wasn't a bad choice, if you were looking for the strongest possible opponent for Mahatma. Never mind Rube's genial attitude; like most of his species, he was powerfully built, tachyon-fast, and loved nothing more than a good fight. He was more dangerous unarmed than most other sophonts would be with a full kit of advanced weaponry.

But Mahatma wasn't about to let his opponent make the first move. Even as Rube opened his mouth to reply to the little human's greeting, Mahatma was in action. It happened so fast that Thumper wasn't quite sure what he saw, but it seemed as if Mahatma simply launched himself at the Gambolt's head. Rube dodged, reacting instinctively, but Mahatma's toe snaked out and caught the Gambolt under the chin, snapping his head back. As Rube fell backward, Mahatma's arm came whipping down to strike a blow flat on the side of his head. Rube fell to the floor and landed on his back.

The Gambolt recovered almost instantly, but Mahatma was faster. He landed on his feet and, before Rube could get his feet under him, put a hand atop his opponent's head and poised another at his throat to signal that he could strike a crippling blow.

Brandy clapped her hands once. "Halt!" she said. The two opponents relaxed, and Rube leapt to his feet, evidently unhurt by his fall. Then Brandy turned to the general. "Would you like another demonstration, sir, or is that sufficient?"

In the gaping silence that followed, it was easy to hear Mahatma's cheerful voice, "Perhaps the general would like to demonstrate his own combat skills?"

17

Journal #866—

There are few experiences more flattering than learning that one has been missed. Being sought after may be among them; but it depends heavily on just who is doing the seeking, and why. Consider the different impressions one would have from learning one was being sought by an attractive person of the opposite sex, and by an armed band of revenue officers . . .

Sparrowhawk heard the office door open and quickly blanked her screen. Not for security—unless you included job security in that category. She did know Legion security officers who would argue that anything a general's adjutant did had the potential to give an enemy valuable intelligence—even the games she played while she waited for the general to give her some actual work—but she didn't buy that argument. No, she just had every office worker's instinctive aversion to letting the boss look over her shoulder. And sure enough when she turned around, there he stood—looking somewhat dazed, she thought.

"Good evening, sir," she said, automatically forcing herself to perk up. "Did you find out what the natives are up to?"

General Blitzkrieg shook his head. "I'll be damned if I've ever seen the like," he said. He shuffled over to the large easy chair at one end of Zenobia Base's VIP quarters, turned around, and plopped into it.

Worried in spite of herself, Sparrowhawk broke the growing silence by asking, "The likes of what?"

"Excuse me, Major?" The general looked up in bemusement.

"You said you'd never seen the like of . . . *something*," said Sparrowhawk. "I was asking what."

"Oh, Jester, of course," said the general. He still looked a bit dazed. Sparrowhawk looked at him closely and made a decision. She quickly splashed two fingers of Scotch into a glass and handed it to the general. He took it in his hand and sat swirling the glass, so far without taking a sip.

"Jester's got a squad training for infiltration work," said Blitzkrieg, in a flat tone of voice. "Who'd have thought it? But after seeing them, I'm almost ready to believe it. Why, there's one little devil who could make you think he's a store clerk, or maybe a waiter—almost anything but a legionnaire . . ."

"Very interesting," said Sparrowhawk, trying to figure out where the general was going.

"You'd think so, wouldn't you?" said Blitzkrieg, still swirling the glass. "But I'm beginning to wonder . . . What do you know about bugs, Sparrowhawk?"

"Bugs?" Sparrowhawk frowned. "I guess I know as much as anybody who's not a scientist. What were you thinking about?"

"Way back when, on Old Earth, there was a time when

bugs were the main cause of lots of diseases. So they invented chemicals to kill 'em."

"Yes, I've heard about that," said Sparrowhawk. "Some of the chemicals were apparently worse than the bugs."

Blitzkrieg went on as if he hadn't noticed her comment. "Thing is, some of the bugs were immune to the chemicals, so they invented more chemicals. And some of the bugs were immune to the new chemicals, too . . ."

"I think I've heard that story," said Sparrowhawk. "Instead of getting rid of the bugs, they ended up breeding a new kind of superbug that was worse than the ones they'd started with."

"That's right," said Blitzkrieg. "My point is . . . This legionnaire Mahatma—believe me, I'm going to remember that name—is damn near the biggest pain in the ass I've ever had to deal with—and that's saying a mouthful. Perfect fit for Omega Company, if you know what I mean."

"Yes, sir," said Sparrowhawk. "That's pretty much the whole purpose of Omega, isn't it? A place to send the problems, get them off everyone else's back."

"Of course, of course," said the general. "But I'm beginning to wonder if we haven't created a monster, here."

"A monster, sir?" said Sparrowhawk, frowning. "Surely one smart-mouth legionnaire can't amount to that much of a problem."

"Oh, it's more than just one," said Blitzkrieg. He finally seemed to notice the glass he held, and took a long sip. "The sergeant was doing her best to cover up just how widespread insubordination has become in Omega, but I haven't spent this much time in the Legion without figuring out how these noncoms think. I'll guarantee you, she picked out that Mahatma rascal because he's one of the best recruits in her squad!"

"I suppose that makes sense, General," said Sparrowhawk. She wasn't convinced, but she had long ago learned that contradicting Blitzkrieg was pointless.

"But do you see what that means?" the general continued. "By concentrating all the bad eggs in Omega, we've created a breeding ground for even worse eggs—this Mahatma may be the first of a new breed of super-pain-in-the-ass legionnaires! My God, I tremble to think what could happen if this spread to the rest of the Legion!"

"Well, there's only one answer to that," said Sparrowhawk. "It's a good thing you've already anticipated the answer."

"Excuse me, Major? I'm not sure I follow you," said the general. It was some measure of how disoriented he was that he actually admitted his confusion to her.

It gave her considerable satisfaction to explain the whole thing to him. The best part about it was that it would get her exactly what she wanted, without requiring her to do anything beyond convincing the general that the problem was already solved. Which, as far as she was concerned, it was.

"This is stupid," said Do-Wop. He looked around the little moonlit plaza, empty except for the two legionnaires. "Somebody tells us to come here for some important news, then don't bother to show. I ain't got the time for this kinda . . ."

"Then go on home," came a voice from just behind him.

"What the . . ." Do-Wop whirled to face the speaker, as did Sushi. Both legionnaires assumed defensive stances as a figure emerged from the shadows. "Who you think you are, scarin' us like that?" said Do-Wop.

"I know exactly who I am," said the newcomer, a middle-aged man in an expensive suit. He spoke excellent English, with just a trace of an Earth Italian accent. "So do quite a few people here in Rome. And I suspect if you knew what some of them know, you'd be even more scared. But that's not why I asked you to meet me here. There are two other people you need to talk to." He gestured, and another pair of figures came into the light. A man and a woman . . . Beeker and Nightingale!

"Wow, you two picked a great time to finally show up," said Sushi. "You wouldn't believe how many planets we've chased you across . . ."

"I expect I would believe it, providing the number is no greater than four," said Beeker, dryly. "I will say I was surprised to learn of your pursuit—which came to my attention back on Hix's World—and, thanks to this gentleman, here on Old Earth." He indicated the older man standing next to him.

"And who is this guy, anyway?" asked Sushi.

"Pitti da Phule," said the newcomer, in a soft growl.

Do-Wop bristled. "Who you callin'—" he began . . .

Beeker cut him off. "Mr. da Phule is one of your captain's relatives living in this city. What he has told me has brought us all here tonight."

Do-Wop snorted, still not quite mollified. "It must be pretty hot stuff, to make you change your mind after you up and run away from the captain . . ."

"I'd hardly call it running away," said Beeker, raising an eyebrow. "In fact, I have done nothing but take my accumulated vacation time, as the young master himself had encouraged me to do. It had been nearly three years since I had more than a weekend away from my duties. Nightingale was entitled to leave after finishing her training, as well, and she decided to take it with me. She'd been planning our vacation for some time, in fact. Unfortunately, my gentleman was away from his office when Nightingale and I learned that the Lorelei space liner schedules had changed. We had to leave Zenobia immediately on the outgoing Supply shuttle if we were to make connections to Cut 'N' Shoot in time for the roundup festival."

"Roundup festival?" Do-Wop was incredulous.

"I read about that as a little girl, and I always wanted to see it," said Nightingale, enthusiastically.

"But we can talk about that at some more appropriate time," said Beeker. "As this gentleman has informed me, your captain is in trouble. In fact, he has been kidnapped, and we need to act quickly—and in close cooperation—to set things right."

"Sure, who we gotta kill?" said Do-Wop, striking a belligerent stance.

"We won't need that," said Pitti da Phule, calmly. "If we did, I could arrange it with local contractors—I think it's always better to deal with people you know. No, what I need you to do is a bit trickier. But from what my nephew's butler tells me, it should be right up your alley . . ."

Beeker, Nightingale, and the two legionnaires listened carefully while Pitti da Phule outlined his plan, with Sushi and Nightingale occasionally asking questions. Finally, everyone knew their part in the operation. With a final handshake, the group split up—Beeker and Nightingale headed in one direction, Pitti da Phule in another, and Sushi and Do-Wop headed back toward their hotel. They'd have to get some supplies in the morning, but there was plenty they could do before then. And if they were lucky, they just might get some sleep before the whole thing was over.

Then again, they might not.

About the only good thing Phule could say about being kidnapped was that somebody in the neighborhood made really good take-out pasta. Dinner last night had been an excellent lasagna with mushrooms and spicy sausage, and the thugs made sure he had plenty of *vino* to wash it down. Good robust Tuscan red—they left him the bottle. Wanting to keep his wits about him, he made it a point to pour a good bit down the sink when nobody was watching. If he could get the kidnappers to underestimate how alert he was, that was an advantage he might be able to use.

On the other hand, that was about the only advantage he could see them giving him. The door stayed locked; so did the window, and the bars on the outside looked plenty strong enough. Breaking the glass was the only way to test them, and if the bars really were immovable, breaking the glass was just a good way to annoy Weasel-face and Vinnie, neither of whom seemed to sympathize with his desire to escape.

Judging from the sky, it was still early morning. The kidnappers had taken his watch, so he had no way to be certain. But the fact that breakfast had yet to appear seemed to confirm his guess—not that he had any reason to expect them to coddle him. They didn't seem interested in providing entertainment, either. He had nothing to read except an Italian-language advertising flyer of some sort that came in the bag with the wine last night. He'd been desperate enough to try reading it, though his Italian was so rudimentary he couldn't really make out what it was trying to sell.

If I ever kidnap somebody, I'll make it a point to provide plenty of entertainment, he thought to himself. *If these people had given me a good action game to play or some exciting vids to watch, I might not be working on an escape plan.* At that point he sat up straight and shook his head. *And here I am, instead, trying to figure out how they might have done a better job of keeping me from escaping.*

He stood and went to look out the window—probably for the twentieth time since getting up. Judging by the building across the way, he was on about the third floor, so even if he could somehow get past the bars, he'd have a dangerous drop to ground level—which, as far as he could tell by looking out the window, was a narrow back alley. So while there were no passersby to signal for help, there were also no watchers if he did somehow manage to escape out this window. A possible advantage, though not one he could see any way to exploit just now.

That was the real problem; he had any number of intangible advantages over his kidnappers—he was younger, probably smarter, certainly richer, trained in several military combat disciplines, and much more alert than either of them seemed to be. But, totally unfairly, they were the ones who had him locked up, and he had yet to find a way out of this place.

He supposed he could always try to offer them ransom, but he'd learned at a young age—almost as soon as he'd been allowed outdoors by himself—that paying ransom was never an option. Let anyone know that they could grab you and get payment for your release, and there was no end to it. The only answer was to make it clear that there'd be no ransom payment, ever. Few people would bother kidnapping someone if there was no possibility of a payoff for his return. Of course, that didn't seem to have deterred the people who'd captured him. Were they too stupid to have figured it out? Or were they taking the chance because they didn't know his real identity? For the first time, he began to think there was a downside to the Legion practice of assumed names.

His best bet, at the moment, seemed to be Pitti da Phule. If his uncle had made an attempt to contact him at his hotel, he should already have realized that Phule was missing. On the other hand, Pitti had advised him to spend some time sightseeing and playing tourist—so even if he'd tried to get in touch and found Phule away, Pitti might just assume that his nephew had taken him at his word and gone on a side trip to Venice, or Pompeii, or some other tourist attraction. On the third hand . . . Phule grimaced at the metaphor. But while his captors might be anxious to find someone to ask for ransom, he doubted they'd have Pitti on their list.

Who else might he call on? Beeker would be more than willing to come to the rescue, of course. Unfortunately, the butler probably had no idea that Phule was on Old Earth—and Phule had no idea where Beeker was, even if he had some way to contact him. Worse yet, he had no way to keep the butler from leaving the planet—which would shortly thereafter cause the hibernation chip to take effect. That would effectively bring the kidnapping to an abrupt end. Not that he was looking forward to an indefinite period of enforced hibernation, but there didn't seem to be much he could do to prevent it, under his present circumstances.

Phule was trying to figure out whether there was anything concrete he could do, when motion in the alleyway below caught his attention. He leaned close to the glass, trying to see better. But before he could make out what was happening, a loud explosion shook the building. As he ducked back from the window, he could hear voices shouting . . .

The explosions triggered Phule's Legion training. Within seconds of the first sound, he'd knocked over his table, dumping last night's dinner dishes on the floor. He turned the top to face the window and shielded himself behind it. The inch-thick wood wasn't going to protect him from major ordnance, but it would stop flying glass—and possibly keep a sniper in the opposite building from spotting him. At the moment, he had no idea whether the explosions had anything to do with him. The smart way to handle the situation was to get under cover and stay there until he had better information.

Of course, Phule didn't always handle things the smart way. Quietly, he hitched the table in the direction of the door, keeping it between him and the window. Even if they hadn't heard him knock over the table, his captors would eventually look in on him, if only to make sure their hostage was still there; when they did, he wanted to have a surprise waiting for them.

From beyond the door, Phule could hear muffled voices arguing in Italian—at least, the volume and tone sounded like arguing to someone who couldn't understand any of the words. He waited, listening. Footsteps approached the door, then stopped. The voices resumed, louder this time, then he heard a key turn in the lock.

As the door swung open, he rushed forward with the tabletop in front of him like a bulldozer blade, bowling over the person who'd stepped into his room. Not waiting to see the results of his attack, he leapt over the table and burst into the outer room, ready for action. His best guess was that the person who'd come through the door was Vinnie, and Weasel-face had stayed behind to guard the exit.

He was partly right. Weasel-face was there, all right. But two uniformed figures were also standing there, one with a gun trained on Weasel-face, who stood ashen-faced, his hands over his head. Phule did a double take as he recognized the newcomers: Customs Agent G. C. Fox, and holding the gun, someone he'd been chasing halfway across the galaxy.

Phule blurted out the first thing that came into his mind. "Nightingale! Where have you been?"

It wasn't General Blitzkrieg's style to sneak off-planet after a setback. He wasn't particularly likely to admit that he'd had any setbacks, to begin with. Even with egg all over his face, and his uniform and boots as well, he didn't believe in letting anyone see that he knew he'd lost a round. But his departure from Zenobia Base was as close as he could contrive to being a triumph. He'd conveniently forgotten that the original idea came from his long-suffering adjutant, Major Sparrowhawk.

It helped that Captain Jester seemed completely willing to uphold the illusion. Blitzkrieg was sufficiently relieved not to be reminded of the actual circumstances of his departure that he even forgave the captain for having somehow run out of golf balls just as they were getting ready for the general's revenge match. Then again, considering the way Jester had played the last time out, Blitzkrieg wasn't entirely sure he'd be getting much revenge.

Other times, Blitzkrieg might have let his loss in the final golf match eat at him. But after stumbling upon the late-night demonstration of just how hopeless Omega Company was, the general was more than willing to postpone the chance to win back a few bucks. After all, he was well ahead of Jester and his officers if you looked at the whole series of games. A profit was a profit. And it was an even greater pleasure to know that Jester had the insuperable task of trying to bring his pack of misfits up to snuff. If he didn't despise the pup so much, Blitzkrieg might even have felt sorry for him.

It was a bit gratifying that Jester had his whole company turned out for the farewell ceremony. OK, it was Omega Company, but it was hard not to appreciate that they'd made some effort to do things right. Especially now that Blitzkrieg could see what kind of insubordination, incompetence, and downright idiocy Jester had to deal with, day in and day out. No wonder the fellow spent so much of his time on the golf course . . .

"General, I'm glad you got the chance to see what we're doing here on Zenobia," said Jester, dressed for once in his Legion dress blacks. "It's a very unusual opportunity, and I only hope we're giving the natives a good impression of the Alliance."

"I hope you'll make the most of the opportunity, Captain," growled Blitzkrieg. He leaned forward and lowered his voice. "And keep an eye on that infernal machine they've got out by your perimeter, will you? The damned thing worries me."

"We've got it under surveillance, sir," said Jester, in the same lowered voice. He put a hand up, shielding his mouth, and added, "Fact is, we've got a pretty good idea what the lizards are trying to do—and the joke's on them. It'll never work!"

Blitzkrieg considered for a moment, then said, "Send me a report on it, Jester. I expect you're right, but I want the intelligence boys to give it the eyeball before I make up my mind." He somehow resisted adding, *And I hope the damned natives' intelligence boys can't tell how screwed up Omega Company is. If they get the idea the whole Alliance is like this outfit, they'll be making plans to take us over.*

Ordinarily, that might not be an entirely bad thing. For a moment, Blitzkrieg had a fantasy of the little lizards wiping out Jester and his pack of incompetents—thereby eliminating the Legion's biggest headache. But with Jester's uncanny luck, not to forget his ability to convince politicos and newspapers that he was actually a competent officer, the pup was likely to come out of it covered with undeserved glory. On balance, it was probably better for the Legion—and particularly for Blitzkrieg—if Zenobia stayed peaceful.

On the whole, as Sparrowhawk had pointed out, the mission to Zenobia had been a success. Blitzkrieg had come here planning to cashier Jester, then break up Omega Company and disperse its members throughout the Legion. But after seeing the company with his own eyes, he realized that the only safe thing was for Omega Company and its commander to stay right here—permanently, if possible. He couldn't risk the possibility that Legionnaire Mahatma and his ilk might spread to other companies. No, let them stay here; let poor Jester try to whip them into shape—for all the good that was doing them, or Jester, either. It was beginning to look like a classic case of the punishment fitting the crime! Almost involuntarily, Blitzkrieg chuckled.

If Jester had been the kind of lazybones Blitzkrieg had always thought he was, Omega Company would have been a dream assignment. But now that Blitzkrieg had seen that the poor deluded nincompoop actually thought he could make these misfits into a crack unit, he knew that Jester would be miserable for the rest of his days in the Legion. A failure even by his own lights! Nobody could shape up this pack of total losers. Now Blitzkrieg could cherish the memory of Jester's hopeless midnight exercise. He chuckled again, relishing the irony.

"Did you say something, sir?" Jester asked.

"Yes, Jester," said the general, gruffly. "This base is a disaster." He paused a beat, then said, "Next time I come out here, I'll want to see a full nine-hole course, you understand?" He punched Jester in the biceps—a little too hard to be entirely friendly, but of course there was no way for Jester to take offense.

"Consider it done, sir!" said Jester, grinning idiotically.

Blitzkrieg smiled. Then he added, in a harder voice, "And as for the discipline—you've got to keep at it, Captain! A hard job, but time well spent, say I! Don't let it slide an inch, do you hear me?"

"Yes, sir," said Jester, grinning just as enthusiastically as before. "It'll be my top priority."

"Good, we'll expect to see your reports, then," said the general. He grinned again, and ducked his head to get into the shuttle; Major Sparrowhawk was already strapped in, waiting.

"That ought to hold them," said the general, sliding in next to his adjutant.

"Yes, sir," said Sparrowhawk. "One question, if you don't mind?" The general nodded, and she continued, "It seems to me you let them off pretty easily. What am I missing, sir?"

"The good old double bind," said Blitzkrieg. "The poor idiot will work his tail off trying to get that golf course in shape, and at the same time try to whip some discipline into those oafs. He may get the golf course playable, but the discipline's a lost cause. It'll drive him crazy. Heh-heh. Just what I want."

"Very good, sir, very good," said Sparrowhawk. Then the shuttle's engines began warming up, putting an end to any semblance of casual talk.

Meanwhile, outside, just as soon as the shuttle door closed, Lieutenant Rembrandt reached to a special point at the back of the robot's neck, activating a switch, and spoke a code word, quietly. Without changing its posture or expression, the robot went instantly into standby mode. It would take no more independent action until it was reactivated—after a long and painstaking overhaul.

And for the first time since the shuttle's arrival, everyone on Zenobia took a deep breath and relaxed.

"So that's who's behind it!" said Phule. "I'd never have thought she had any power beyond Lorelei . . ."

It was barely an hour after the rescue, and Phule's head was still spinning with all that he had learned. At least, he'd gotten Nightingale to promise that she'd tell Beeker to give him the Port-a-Brain. Then he could relax—and let the two lovebirds make their way back to Zenobia at their own rate.

"Maxine's plan was very nasty," said Pitti da Phule, filling his nephew in on the kidnap plot. "She spread a rumor that the Space Legion—the boys in black, she called them—were spying on tax evaders and smugglers. If she'd had a little longer to work on it, half the population of the planet would have been ready to stuff you into the nearest garbage disintegrator. You're lucky I found out about it before it got that far."

"I'm glad you found out about it," said Phule, raising a glass in Pitti's direction. "But how did you find me in that place they had me hidden? That's a pretty impressive piece of detective work."

Pitti smiled. "Not so hard to do, with what you told me about your computer. Your father told me about that security program it has. It doesn't just send out a signal when the stasis field is working. If you know what to look for, the signal's there all the time, *capisce*? Your father told me . . ."

"Say no more," said Phule, suddenly realizing that his

father had put a permanent tracer on him. The old rascal
had always worried whether Phule could handle himself in
a tricky situation, but this was taking it a bit too far. Still, it
had saved his bacon, this time. Best to accept it for what it
was worth.

"And I really appreciate your, uh, unofficial help." Phule
nodded to Agent Fox, who'd joined them in the little cafe
that Pitti had brought them to, just down the street from
where Phule had been held prisoner. The owners had
brought out an enormous antipasto and a bottle of wine.
Phule, who hadn't yet had breakfast, had ordered coffee
instead—and was rewarded with the best espresso he'd
tasted on Old Earth. The headwaiter was watching their
table discreetly to make sure no need went unfulfilled.

Pitti waved an expressive hand. "The *agente* and I have
worked together before," he said. "Keeping lines of com-
munication open, that's good for business. *Capisce?*
Where we both have an interest, there should be profit for
both. And his news that Maxine Pruett—your old enemy—
had come to Old Earth was what convinced me to trace
your whereabouts instead of just assuming you'd gone to
see the sights."

"What's going to happen to Maxine?" said Phule.

Fox shrugged. "Depends on whether we can scare the
hoodlums who kidnapped you into naming her as the mas-
termind," he said. "I wouldn't bet the house on it. Her connections on Old Earth aren't exactly nobodies. She'll
probably have to pay a fair amount to keep from being sent
back to Hix's World, where they're really mad at her. But if
she's smart, she's already gotten off-world and left the
lawyers to clean up the mess."

"She's that smart, she wouldn't stick her nose in my
family's business," said Pitti, dryly. "I'll make her and her
lawyers both sorry."

"Hold on a minute," said Phule, sitting up straight. The

coffee had finally kicked in. "What was Maxine doing on Hix's World?"

"What, you didn't figure that out yet?" Fox chuckled. "She'd gone to Hix's World to set up a casino at that hotel of hers. She'd been lobbying for a change in the laws, throwing bribes around as if they were birdseed. It probably would have passed if she hadn't jumped the gun and brought in a shipment of quantum slots while they were still illegal. When you caught her with them, she figured you were going to inform on her, and left the planet in a hurry. That's why when she found out you were here on Earth, she persuaded some local goons to kidnap you, figuring she'd get her revenge that way."

"Inform on her? I never even knew she was on Hix's World," said Phule, scratching his head. "It must have been Beeker and Nightingale who found out about her. I wonder if that's why they went there to begin with . . ." But Nightingale had disappeared again almost immediately after setting Phule free, and wasn't here to confirm or deny his guess. At least, she had promised to bring Beeker to his hotel—and Phule could hardly wait to see the butler.

"Maybe," said Fox. "The lady did sound as if she enjoyed the Floribunda Fete. Can't say that I'm all that much a flower fanatic, myself."

"I can sum it up in one word," said Phule. "*Bo-ring*. And you can quote me on that."

"Oh, I agree—but don't say that to *her*," said Fox, with an amused smile. "A woman like that, you want to keep her on your side. Even if she and the butler fall out . . ."

"Yes, I've thought about that," said Phule. "I really have to talk to them both before we get back to Zenobia, though. I owe them my freedom, obviously. That's a big one. But I need to get Beeker to enter a certain code in his computer. I wonder why he never read the mail I sent him?"

"I tell you, there's gonna be a good reason," said Pitti da

Phule. "That Beeker, he's old-school—solid like a rock. He does something you don't understand, it's because *you* don't understand it. Take my word for it."

Phule shrugged. "Yeah, that's what I figure. But I'm still curious to find out why he never responded."

"You worry later about that," said Pitti. "For now, we got good food, good *vino*—you listen to your uncle and enjoy while you got it!"

"And that's the best advice you're going to get today—or any other day," said Fox, raising his glass.

18

"Well, sir, it'll be good to get back to Rahnsome Base," said Major Sparrowhawk, looking out the window of the shuttle at the disk of Zenobia gradually shrinking behind them. They'd left in a hurry, but it was none too soon for her.

"Good to get off that damned hellhole world," growled General Blitzkrieg. "At first I was beginning to think Jester had drawn an ace in the hole, what with his private golf course, friendly natives, and all that. I tell you, Major, I had a good mind to pull Omega Company out and put somebody more deserving in there. No point in giving the screwups such a plum assignment."

"No, sir," agreed Sparrowhawk. "There are lots of regular companies that deserve good assignments."

"Well, that's just what I was thinking," said Blitzkrieg. "But then—did you see some of those monsters that live in the desert outside that camp? I'm surprised half the complement hasn't been eaten alive."

"No, sir," said Sparrowhawk. She'd heard the general's

description of the—what had he called it?—the *gryff*. "From what you tell me, I don't want to."

"I tell you, it's enough to change my whole opinion of the place," said Blitzkrieg. He swirled his drink, took a sip, and continued. "Ironically, that constant danger might just be the thing to turn Jester into a competent officer, after all. Much as I'd hate to admit it, there's a hint of iron in his backbone. I don't think he meant me to see it, but I caught him chewing out a squad after a surprise inspection. Most commanders want the top brass to think their units are perfect, of course. So they try not to ream 'em out where I can see it."

"Yes, sir," said Sparrowhawk. She knew it well. Most of the time, she was the one who did the snooping to uncover the problem areas on bases the general went to inspect. The local officers might manage to hide things from the general, but very few of them could hide anything from her. She'd been ready to do it on Zenobia, but the general had been so involved in his golf match that he'd never asked her for her findings.

"I don't have much use for Jester, but I give him credit for how he handled it," said the general, staring out the window. "Clever dog called his troops out late at night, right when they'd least expect him, and gave 'em the royal roasting, as hot as I could've done it myself. Did my heart good to see it. I think the boy's beginning to understand how to treat those scum. If he'll keep it up a few more years, Omega might actually start to look like a Legion company." *And shrimps might learn to whistle, too,* he added silently. "Then, I might just remember where I filed Jester's promotion papers."

Blitzkrieg chuckled and took another sip of his drink. Then he leaned back, and said, "Or did I just pitch them? I suppose I'll have to look into it . . . someday."

"Yes, sir," said Sparrowhawk, who knew exactly where those promotion papers were. Mailing them to the captain was one of several things—not the first, but high up—on her private list of actions to be taken if the general ever stepped over certain lines she had defined in her own mind. Being a powerful man's confidential assistant brought with it a certain amount of power over one's superior. She knew that exercising that power might be the last thing she did in her capacity as a Legion officer. But she knew that General Blitzkrieg's subsequent career would also be quite short—and thoroughly unpleasant.

The general, who was naturally unaware of her thoughts, rubbed his chin. "Anyway, it'll be good to get back to the office. I didn't expect this visit to end up as a golfing vacation, but in a way I'm glad it did. My game's as sharp as it's been in ages—why, I whipped that young upstart five or six different ways, even though he did try bringing in that little lizard as a ringer. I must say, he got lucky the last day we played. And then, to run completely out of balls! You'd think that's something any golf course would make sure to have plenty of."

"Yes, it does seem odd," said Sparrowhawk, smugly.

"Just as well in the long run," mused the general. "I need to get back to Rahnsome Base. I expect the boys've missed me—and I've got some damn good stories for them, now. Some of those fellows never get out in the field, see the troops, at all. Good way to go soft, if you ask me."

"Yes, sir," said Sparrowhawk. "As much as I enjoy getting out of the office, there's going to be plenty of work waiting when we're back."

"It'll be a little longer, yet," said Blitzkrieg. "We stop over at Lorelei, you know. I have a lucky feeling, and I'm going to put it to the test in those casinos. You need to play that kind of hunch when you have it."

"Very good, sir," said Sparrowhawk. "I hope you'll forgive me if I catch up with some work, instead. I'm afraid I've never been very good at gambling." *Why gamble when you've got a sure thing in the market?* was her unspoken thought.

"All work, no play, eh? You'll wear yourself out at a young age," said the general. "One reason I can keep going is that I've learned to pace myself, take time to smell the roses and pick a few, too. Why, I remember . . ." And the general was off on one of his rambling, self-congratulatory reminiscences.

Sparrowhawk smiled quietly. She'd heard it all a thousand times before. An occasional nod or "Yes, sir," would suffice to convince Blitzkrieg that she was listening. And when they got to Lorelei, she'd take the opportunity to revamp her stock portfolio. All of a sudden, Phule-Pruf Munitons was looking like a must-have commodity . . .

"Back again!" said Phule, as he stepped off the shuttle onto Zenobian soil. "Funny, this place is starting to feel like home."

"I wouldn't get too used to it, sir," said Beeker. The butler followed close behind Phule, arm in arm with Nightingale. They'd decided, after some discussion, to end their vacation in Rome and travel back to Zenobia with Phule. He continued, "The Space Legion does have a policy of rotating its personnel from one assignment to another. In the normal course of things, another company will eventually get the Zenobia assignment. Now that General Blitzkrieg's had a chance to see the place, he may realize that Zenobia is hardly the hardship duty he thought he was doling out when he agreed to let Omega Company come here."

"Don't bet on it, Captain," said Lieutenant Armstrong, who'd accompanied Gears out to meet the shuttle. He chuckled, and added, "After some of what happened to him here, the general's likely to think Zenobia's the worst hellhole in the galaxy."

"Really?" said Phule, raising an eyebrow. "I hope the company didn't go out of its way to give the general trouble . . ."

"Oh, no," said Armstrong. "In fact, we went out of our

way to make him feel at home. Built a golf course for him and everything . . ."

"A golf course?" Phule's eyebrow went up another notch. "That's definitely bending over backward. I didn't know anyone here even played. I mean, it's been years since I even had a set of clubs, but I daresay I hit the ball pretty well back when I was in practice."

"I—and a few other people on base—will be glad to give you the chance to prove that," said Armstrong, grinning. "Just one warning—we've had a lot of practice since you were gone."

"Practice?" Phule was even more puzzled. "I thought the general was here . . . How in the galaxy did you ever get a chance to practice golf while he was stalking around and growling at everything on the base?"

"Well, it's a long story," said Armstrong. "Why don't we get you back to your office, and you can listen to it in comfort, with a cold drink in your hand."

"Excellent advice," said Beeker. "I suggest we follow it, sir. There are tales to tell on all sides."

"So it appears," said Phule, shaking his head in bewilderment. "Gears, pop open that luggage compartment and we'll stow our gear for the ride back."

"Sure thing, Captain," said Gears, pushing the button to open the hatch. Phule lifted his duffel bag, and Gears stepped out to help stow the luggage.

Suddenly a voice came from the intercom speaker on the hoverjeep's dash: Mother, from Comm Central. "Welcome back, darlin'—you too, Beeky. Suggest you all duck inside the jeep for a sec—we got another incoming shuttle, and you might want to get out of the backwash when it lands."

"Another shuttle?" Phule was genuinely astounded now. "Who in the world could be landing so soon after us? Why didn't the shuttle service put them on the same ship as us?"

"I dunno, but I reckon we're about to find out," said

Gears, tossing in Phule's bag and returning to the driver's seat. "Hop in and close the doors, unless y'all want dust in your drawers."

"I'll take a pass on that," said Nightingale, climbing into the jeep's back seat. Phule, Beeker, and Armstrong followed suit. After a moment, they could make out a moving object high above the desert, somewhat to the east of the landing site. Gradually it came west and descended until they could see that it was, in fact, another shuttle like the one Phule's group had arrived in. In due time it slowed and touched down in a cloud of dust, not far from the first shuttle, which was still waiting for its passengers to clear the area before taking off again.

After a couple of minutes the dust settled. To Phule's surprise, two familiar figures, both in Legion uniform, emerged. "Sushi!" he exclaimed. "Do-Wop! What were you two doing off-world?"

"Chasin' our tails in a circle," said Do-Wop, sourly. "If it hadn't been for the last bit, I'd say it was all a waste of time."

"Waste of time? How can you say that?" said Sushi, although he had a weary look on his face. "You've had a first-class tour of the triffest vacation spots of the galaxy, at company expense. And in the end, we did our job—see, the captain's home, all in one piece. And so are Beeker and Nightingale."

"Yeah, yeah," said Do-Wop. "Except we're back on a freakin' Legion base, too. Back to the same lousy routine, sergeants and marchin' and orders and drills . . . You tellin' me that's good?"

"It could be worse, young man," said Beeker, with a barely raised eyebrow.

Do-Wop stared at the butler, scowling. "OK, I'll bite," he said at last. "What's worse than the same lousy routine?"

"Why, no routine at all," said Beeker. "I would find it intolerable to arise each morning with no clear idea what to expect that day."

"I can vouch for that," said Nightingale, smiling at the butler. "I had to hide the power module for his Port-a-Brain to stop him from trying to work on the captain's portfolio. He was so antsy for his routine that he couldn't just take it easy, even on vacation."

"That sounds just like good old Beeker," said Phule, grinning. "I guess I know why you never saw my emails, too."

"As much as I enjoyed the vacation, I have to say I was disappointed not to be able to use the computer, sir," said the butler, holding his head high. "After all, if I'd been able to work on your portfolio, I'd have had a perfect excuse to skip the Floribunda Fete."

"You jerk!" said Nightingale, punching him on the arm—but grinning, at the same time. "Just see if I take you along on my next vacation!"

"That's all right," said Lieutenant Rembrandt. "Next time you go on vacation, I think there'll be plenty of volunteers to go with you. In fact, you can put me first on the list. How about you, Armstrong?"

Armstrong raised a quizzical eyebrow. "What, and miss golfing with the general?" he said.

Phule knew he'd eventually figure out why everyone found Armstrong's remark so hilarious. For now, he was just glad to be back with Omega Company.

The few. The proud. The stupid. The inept.
They do more damage before 9 a.m.
than most people do all day...
And they're mankind's last hope.

ROBERT ASPRIN
PHULE'S COMPANY
SERIES

Phule's Company   0-441-66251-X

Phule's Paradise   0-441-66253-6

by Robert Asprin and Peter J. Heck

A Phule and His Money   0-441-00658-2

Phule Me Twice   0-441-00791-0

No Phule Like an Old Phule   0-441-01152-7

Available wherever books are sold or at
penguin.com

From the *New York Times*
bestselling author of the
Phule's Company series

ROBERT ASPRIN

Follow apprentice magician Skeeve, his scaly
mentor Aahz, and beautiful ex-assassin Tanda in
their high *myth*-adventures.

Check out these 2-in-1 Omnibuses

Available wherever books are sold or at
penguin.com

THE ULTIMATE IN
SCIENCE FICTION AND FANTASY!

From magical tales of distant worlds to stories of
technological advances beyond the grasp of man, Penguin has
everything you need to stretch your imagination to its limits.

penguin.com

ACE
Get the latest information on favorites like
William Gibson, T.A. Barron, Brian Jacques,
Ursula Le Guin, Sharon Shinn, and Charlaine Harris,
as well as updates on the best new authors.

ROC
Escape with Harry Turtledove, Anne Bishop,
S.M. Stirling, Simon Green, Chris Bunch, Jim Butcher,
E.E. Knight, and many others—plus news on the
latest and hottest in science fiction and fantasy.

DAW
Mercedes Lackey, Kristen Britain, Tanya Huff,
Tad Williams, C.J. Cherryh, and many more—
DAW has something to satisfy the cravings of any
science fiction and fantasy lover.
Also visit dawbooks.com.

*Get the best of science fiction and fantasy
at your fingertips!*